For Once in My Life

For Once in My Life

A Novel

Marianne Kavanagh

EMILY BESTLER BOOKS

ATRIA

New York London Toronto Sydney New Delhi

A Division of Simon & Schuster, Inc.
1230 Avenue of the Americas
New York, NY 10020

This book is a work of fiction. Any references to historical events, real people, or real places are used fictitiously. Other names, characters, places, and events are products of the author's imagination, and any resemblance to actual events or places or persons, living or dead, is entirely coincidental.

First Emily Bestler Books/Atria Paperback edition June 2014

EMILY BESTLER BOOKS / ATRIA PAPERBACK and colophons are trademarks of Simon & Schuster, Inc.

For information about special discounts for bulk purchases, please contact Simon & Schuster Special Sales at 1-866-506-1949 or business@simonandschuster.com.

The Simon & Schuster Speakers Bureau can bring authors to your live event. For more information or to book an event, contact the Simon & Schuster Speakers Bureau at 1-866-248-3049 or visit our website at www.simonspeakers.com.

Interior design by Dana Sloan
Cover design by Laywan Kwan
Cover art © Shutterstock

Manufactured in the United States of America

10 9 8 7 6 5 4 3 2 1

Library of Congress Cataloging-in-Publication Data has been applied for.

ISBN 978-1-4767-5527-4
ISBN 978-1-4767-5531-1 (ebook)

For Matt

2002

Oxford Street hadn't woken up. It was still lying in bed with a hangover wearing last night's makeup. All the shops were shut. There was a pigeon pecking at a paper bag, a man carrying a yellow bucket full of soapy water, and a few office workers with headphones. It was half past eight on a Friday morning and very cold. The sun had got stuck in Soho.

Then the body hit her. It hit her with such force that she wondered, for a moment, if she'd walked into a wall. At the same time, she knew this sudden lunging body belonged to the woman with red lipstick and earrings who, seconds before, had been walking towards her, heels clacking on the pavement. She staggered backwards, taking the weight, and someone shouted, "Hey!" and the woman's wiry hair was in her mouth and there was a sharp pain in her ribs. Then the woman shouted, "My bag!" and Tess, being a Londoner, felt her heart sink and focused—even though her arms were full of black polyester and the smell of hairspray—on the small, skinny man racing away down the street, ducking into a side road. Behind him, in hot pursuit, was a second man—youngish, average height, wearing a brown leather jacket—just disappearing from view, swallowed up by the same blind corner. Then there was nothing—just a half-empty street with passersby giving them quick furtive glances and just as quickly looking away.

She tightened her grip on the woman in a sort of despairing hug. The woman made a kitten-sized mewl of misery and said, "He took my bag."

Tess, releasing her, said, "I think there was someone chasing him," but they both knew, standing there on the shadowy street in the early morning of the grubby West End, that the bag had gone forever.

Tess said, "Are you all right?"

The woman nodded. But her red lipstick was smudged and her eyes, spiky with black mascara, were full of tears. She had fine lines round her mouth as if she smoked, or used to.

"Shall I call the police?"

The woman shook her head. "I'd only had it two minutes. It was a present. For my birthday."

"You've had a terrible shock. Let me buy you a cup of tea."

But the woman said, "No, you're all right. I've got to get to work. I'm late already."

Tess felt almost as desperate as if she'd been pushed, humiliated, and robbed herself. "I'm so sorry."

"It's the time it takes. Stopping all your cards, getting new keys, buying new makeup. I just wish he'd asked me for money. I would have given it him. It's only the money they want."

"I still think you should report it," said Tess. "Just in case that man catches him and gets it back."

The woman looked down the street in a vague sort of way as if she half-expected to see them still—the small, thin mugger and the man in the brown leather jacket.

"He won't catch him," she said bitterly. "Not unless he's Linford bloody Christie."

The sun, outwitting the concrete, flashed round the buildings and shone on the dirty plate glass of the shop windows. Oxford Street was waking up.

. . .

Somewhere round Wardour Street, George admitted defeat. He stood there, his ears deaf with pressure, filling his lungs with huge gulps of air. He felt a peculiar mixture of shame, rage, and exhilaration. He also felt very hot. He hadn't run that fast, or that far, for a long time. It had been the impulse of the moment to chase after the thief—a reaction to the fury that rushed through him as he saw the woman fall, pushed to the ground.

George wondered, as he waited for his heartbeat to return to normal, whether he should go back to Oxford Street and tell the woman what had happened. "I'm sorry. I ran after him for a long time but he got away. He dodged behind a delivery van and I lost him." But would she still be standing there? He had no idea how much time had passed. Surely she would have gone by now.

Maybe he should have stayed at the scene. He could

have been a witness. "About five feet five inches, very thin, dark hair, fourteen maybe, fifteen, white, no distinguishing features." Would that have helped? "Would you recognize him again, sir?" For one bright moment, George was 100 percent certain that he would. Then, just as quickly, he knew for a fact that he wouldn't.

Standing there, smelling vanilla sugar, coffee, and hot milk from the Italian café behind him, George felt a familiar sense of gloom. It was something that settled on him, like a heavy overcoat, whenever he was surprised from his thoughts (a permanent soundtrack) and made to face reality. It often hit him at this time of day. It wasn't just muggers, or the random violence of a city full of strangers. It wasn't even the bewildering chaos that followed him round wherever he went—lost keys, odd socks, off milk, red bills, bank cards that wouldn't work and passwords he couldn't remember, a seething, scuttling mass like cockroaches in a dark basement that you only see, for one horrified moment, when you turn on the light.

No, this was something much worse. This was the growing conviction that he'd made a complete mess of his life, that he was a failure, that somewhere along the way he'd taken the wrong path, or made the wrong choice, and he was now facing a brick wall, a dead end. This was the gloom that filled his head whenever he stood in the middle of Soho and realized it was 2002, he'd been out of university for nearly five years, and he was still doing the same stopgap temporary job that he'd been doing since he left Manchester—a job he'd only taken on to pay the bills until the band took off.

But the band hadn't taken off. And the temporary job suddenly looked very permanent.

George stood there, puzzled. But what was the answer? His father always said, "I had the choice between music and medicine." Well, thought George, I had the choice between music and music. As his hero Thelonious Monk once said, that's all I ever wanted to do. Recently it had got even worse. Now, thought George, I have the choice between carrying on and giving up. Giving up seems attractive. You just listen to all the thoughts you've been trying to push away—I'm never going to make it, it's too competitive, there's no point. But if I'm not playing, there's no point anyway. So where does that leave me?

Soho's bikes and delivery vans and taxis skidded and revved and braked around him.

After a while, because this line of thinking never got him anywhere, George took a deep breath, moved his head from side to side to ease the tension in his neck, and headed off for work.

He arrived at the shop early. He didn't, after all, normally run half the way from Oxford Circus. Rajesh came down to let him in. Inside it was dark because no one had opened the security shutters. Rajesh said, "All right?" and George nodded, even though his legs still felt unreliable, like baggy elastic. He said, "Who's in today?" Rajesh said, "Freya, Vince, and Carmel." George, hanging up his coat, felt his spirits lift. The day was going to be good after all. Freya only knew about violins. But Vince played keyboard like Art Tatum.

He turned on the nearest light, and suddenly all the guitars strung up on the back wall gleamed gold like cymbals.

. . .

"You'd like him," said Kirsty.

She was sitting in a yoga position, each long leg wrapped in an opposite direction round her body.

"Who?" said Tess.

"George," said Kirsty.

It was Saturday morning. They were drinking coffee in their ramshackle living room, Kirsty on the floor, Tess curled up on the sagging sofa. Faint, unwilling light glanced through the big bay window, as if apologizing for showing up quite so much dust. There were stray belongings strewn everywhere—hoodies, bags, books, earphones, inflatable pillows, oversize pink socks. People were always staying at the flat—old friends from Manchester, pub mates who'd missed the last tube home. On bad days, when Tess came home to an empty fridge and a ring round the bath, she wondered if their hospitality had gone too far.

This morning they had the flat to themselves. Kirsty had just got in. She didn't look like someone who'd been clubbing all night. Her long black hair was smooth and shiny. Her eyes were still perfectly made up, Cleopatra-style.

Tess said, "You're doing it again."

"What?"

"You don't like Dominic," said Tess, "so you keep trying to introduce me to other people."

Kirsty looked hurt. "When have I ever said I didn't like Dominic?"

"Ever since I met him?"

Manchester University. The first term of the first year. Three girls in one flat and a shared bathroom from which Dominic had emerged wearing nothing but a small white towel. Kirsty, looking past him to Tess, had raised one beautifully arched eyebrow. But Tess could explain nothing. Why had a man who looked like an underwear model spent the night in her bed?

"Dominic," said Kirsty, "is extraordinary."

Tess, suspicious, said nothing.

"But George," said Kirsty, "is your soul mate."

"My soul mate."

"You'd love him. He's a musician. He likes arty stuff."

"So do lots of people," said Tess.

"And he's old-fashioned."

"I'm not old-fashioned."

"Says the girl obsessed with vintage fashion."

Tess, who had spent all morning reading a 1944 copy of *Woman* magazine ("5 Spring Tonics for Your Clothes!"), was silenced.

"I promise you," said Kirsty, "he's your type."

"What's my type?"

Kirsty looked up at her from under lowered lids, like a small girl about to say a rude word. "Anyone who isn't Dominic."

Tess opened her mouth to protest and quickly shut

it again. This was a running joke. Whenever Kirsty saw Dominic—once or twice during the week, and almost every weekend—she looked at Tess with an expression of slight surprise, as if Tess had started wearing blue eye shadow or taken to eating raw kidneys. Tess had decided some time ago that there was no law that said your best friend had to like your boyfriend. Both had claims on you, and each probably resented the time you spent with the other. So you just had to carry on as if the rivalry didn't exist.

Dominic found Kirsty incomprehensible. He said he had no idea how someone who never got to bed until four in the morning could possibly hold down a job. To Dominic, Tess said, yes, isn't it amazing, she's got so much energy. To Kirsty, she said, don't you think it would be a good idea to take work a bit more seriously so you don't get fired all the time? To which Kirsty replied, I can always get another job.

This was true. Model good looks and a maths degree—what did a few holes in the CV matter? You can't waste time worrying about work, Kirsty said. Work is what you have to do to pay the rent. Life is what happens when your shift is over.

Tess said, "So where were you last night?"

"Watching Rhys's band."

Tess frowned, trying to remember. "Who's Rhys?"

"Gareth's older brother."

"So was Gareth there?"

Kirsty looked at her as if she was insane. "Hardly."

"He still hasn't forgiven you?"

"Rhys says he cries himself to sleep."

Tess was shocked. "But that's terrible!"

"It's just Rhys talking," said Kirsty, "making a crisis out of a drama. It's the Dylan Thomas in him."

Tess thought about Gareth, lying alone in the dark, his heart breaking. It made her sad. Of all the men Kirsty had been out with—and most of them, like her jobs, only lasted a fortnight—Gareth was the one Tess had liked the best. He had red hair and freckles across his nose and looked like someone who spent his life outdoors building dry stone walls and splitting logs with an axe. None of that was true, of course. Gareth worked in a call center selling insurance. Tess hated thinking of him cramped behind a fake wood desk with earphones and a mouthpiece.

"So where did you go?"

"A club," said Kirsty. "Near Smithfield." She stopped, remembering. "It's a bit weird walking through Smithfield in the early hours. You keep bumping into pig carcasses." Tess had a sudden mental picture of Kirsty surrounded by racks of ribs. "And George was playing keyboard and he was really, really good. Everyone kept standing up and yelling and clapping. And then we went back to Rhys's house in Hackney, and had some tea, and we were sitting there, talking, and I thought, Tess would really like him. Tess would really like George."

Tess was trying hard not to look interested. Kirsty had a good instinct for people. If she got chatting to someone at a bus stop at three AM, they'd turn out to be an actor from the Old Vic or someone who worked with Vivienne Westwood. So she said, casually, "Everyone says that."

Kirsty put down her coffee cup and unwound herself to sitting cross-legged. "Everyone says what?"

"That I'd like George."

"Who, exactly?"

"Ellie and Lauren. They knew him at Manchester."

"How come?" said Kirsty. "He left before we started."

"I don't know," said Tess. "Through friends of Lauren. You know what she's like. The networking queen."

"Well, there you are, then," said Kirsty. "All the prerequisites of a perfect relationship. You went to the same university, have the same friends, and you're both free and single."

Tess straightened her back. "You're forgetting about Dominic."

Kirsty got up in one easy movement. She stood there, graceful, poised. "Easily done," she said.

• • •

That night, Saturday night, Tess didn't think about George. She thought about Dominic, because he was there in her room, lying on her bed, propped up on one elbow like a sculpture in a stately home. Whenever she saw Dominic naked, Tess felt breathless. She couldn't believe that a man so perfect had ended up on her duvet. Dominic had long limbs, broad shoulders, and taut muscles that defined his waist and buttocks. His skin was uniformly honey colored, as if he sunbathed nude. He had straight blond hair, which he kept quite long; very blue eyes; and just the right amount of stubble. Each time she met him after work midweek, when he wore his dark gray suit, blue shirt, and navy tie, Tess was stunned all over again by his beauty. They would sit silently side by side, eating dough balls and pizza, and she would wonder how many women in the restaurant were watching her, ripped to shreds inside by raw, bleeding envy.

It was completely new to her, this feeling of being with the best-looking man in the room. At parties as a teenager, hiding her suddenly curvaceous body under baggy T-shirts, she cringed against the walls. No one noticed her, and she kept her eyes firmly fixed on the floor. At school on Monday mornings, she had nothing to offer—no tales of kissing or cheating or flirting. And then, suddenly, in her first week at Manchester, there was Dominic, appearing in all his magnificence like an angel sent from heaven. He picked her out. He chose her. He made her feel desirable.

Still, even now, she couldn't quite believe it. On top of his breathtaking physical perfection, Dominic had a steady, even temperament. She knew he wouldn't play games, lead her on, dump her. He was loyal. He was dependable. He was so in control of his emotions that everything he said was thoughtful and considered. He said that everyone should talk less—that you should contribute to a discussion only to correct misunderstandings or to make a point that others had overlooked.

Because of this, phone conversations with Dominic were never much fun.

But Tess, who worried sometimes that whole sentences slipped out of her mouth before she'd even worked out what she thought, found this reserve admirable.

"Does he talk to you when you're alone?" Kirsty said once as they halfheartedly cleared up the flat.

"Of course he does," said Tess. "Why?"

"I was counting how many words he said in the pub last night," said Kirsty. "I made it to forty-three."

"Well perhaps if everyone else had talked a bit less," said Tess, "he might have had a bit more of a chance."

"Really?"

"Yes," said Tess, firmly.

In fact, Dominic didn't talk to her much. But, as she often thought to herself in a haze of astonishment as they lay entwined, skin slippery with sweat, heartbeats returning to normal, there are other ways to communicate.

So Tess didn't think about George until Monday morning when she was sitting on the Victoria line on her way to work. She had a relatively easy commute—six stops from Brixton to the West End—and usually spent it daydreaming. She was looking, lost in admiration, at the peplum waist of the dark green dress worn by the woman straphanging in front of her when the tube rushed into Oxford Circus. Startled, she scrambled to her feet and was shoved by the crowd onto the platform, where she found herself, for one strangely still second, in front of a poster for *The Piano Man*.

It was, according to the *Daily Mail,* "a rip-roaring success of a musical."

And now she thought about George. She knew he played keyboard. But what kind of music? she wondered, as the crush of bodies moved her towards the escalator. Because it was still early and her brain hadn't quite woken up, she started imagining George—a man she had never met—sitting at a grand piano playing Rachmaninoff, until she remembered he was part of a band and so probably didn't perform symphonies. By the time she reached the ticket barrier, and had been hit in the head twice by someone's rucksack, she had also remembered what Kirsty said about his being old-fashioned. What did that mean, she thought, as she made her way towards the Argyll Street exit. Covering old Beatles songs?

On Great Marlborough Street, at the junction with Poland Street, a man crossed in front of her with a tall black canvas bag—the kind that contains a digital keyboard—sticking up from one shoulder. There are so many musicians, she thought, in this part of London. They flock here, like pigeons to Trafalgar Square.

At the Italian coffee shop, Tess picked up two cappuccinos as usual and arrived at Daisy Greenleaf Designs ten minutes early. In the doorway of the office block next door, hunched in his black coat, his collar turned up against the cold, Colin seemed to be dozing. Tess crouched down, trying not to breathe in too deeply. He smelt of old, damp rottenness, like compost.

"Colin?" she said.

He opened his eyes, winced, and coughed. You could hear the London traffic in his lungs.

"I've brought you your coffee," said Tess.

"What day is it?"

"Monday," said Tess.

Colin sighed. His beard was gray. His skin was gray. Sometimes Tess thought he must be seventy, at least. But she wasn't sure. Sleeping rough made even the young look old.

"Bad night?" she said.

"Can't complain."

When Tess got to the top of the stairs, Glenda was already in the office, picking away at the keyboard with her shell-pink nails. Glenda was never still. Even when sitting apparently motionless, she quivered—flesh, curls, silver hooped earrings—like a soapy bubble on the point of explosion. She had an uncanny ability to type and talk at the same time, often doing both while checking her frosty pink lipstick—which glistened like glacé icing—in the mirror attached to the desk lamp. By midafternoon she had built up an atmosphere of such a multitasking frenzy that Tess sometimes had to take herself outside into the gray London air and walk round the block until her heartbeat returned to normal.

"I'm just dealing with some of the liars," said Glenda, without looking up. "I've left you the moaners."

They sat opposite each other every day, separated by

two screens, Glenda's large makeup bag, and thirty years of experience. Glenda had spent her life soothing the public. On Tess's very first day, she explained that people who complained could be divided into four groups—moaners, shouters, liars, and genuines.

"There's not many genuines," she said.

"Really?" said Tess, polite but confused.

"Well, it's like life, really, isn't it?" said Glenda.

Daisy Greenleaf Designs was ten years old. It was an online company selling specialist stationery, including handmade paper, tiny notebooks decorated with beads and mirrors, and envelopes sealed with ethically sourced glue. Glenda and Tess formed a department loosely called "customer services" but more accurately described as "complaints." The trouble with arts and crafts carefully sourced from the global village was that the products often fell apart. Added to this, prices were ridiculously high. It took all of Glenda's tactical genius and Tess's gentle, persuasive kindness to get customers to reorder at all.

Daisy Greenleaf herself didn't exist. She was the brainchild of Oliver Bankes, who had already flirted with online haberdashery supplies, online picnic hampers, and online party games. He was now pinning his hopes, and the rest of his inheritance, on baby-pink notepaper in which you could still trace the woodchip.

"Did you have a nice weekend?" said Tess, taking off her jacket and squeezing behind her desk. Space, given West End prices, was at a premium. Sometimes she had to pretend very hard that she couldn't hear Oliver shouting into his mobile or see him, through the open door of his office, rearranging the contents of his trousers.

"I drove down to Swanage," said Glenda. She sighed. "I'm thinking very seriously of retiring there, you know. You can get a bungalow right on the sea."

"My grandmother lives near there," said Tess, "in Poole."

"Almost as many days of sunshine as Cornwall," said Glenda. She stared into the middle distance. "Who was it who said that when you tire of London you tire of life?"

"Dr. Johnson?"

"Well, he was wrong," said Glenda. "The point is, when you get to my age, you want a bit more. I mean, I still love the theater. Musicals. Nothing like a West End show. Sitting in red velvet seats. But I'm tired of all the mess, you know, and the concrete, and the crowds. And the grime. And the smell of burning plastic. Everywhere you go. It must be the roads. The number of times they dig them up I'm amazed they've got any tarmac left. Daisy Greenleaf Designs?" she said, picking up the phone without pausing for breath.

At one o'clock, Tess took her sandwich to the patch of grass in the middle of Hanover Square. There she waited for Ellie, who, as she was working unpaid as a fashion intern for a glossy magazine, couldn't afford to go anywhere for lunch but a wooden bench. Ellie looked like a boy. Tess was never sure whether this was a public statement, a fashion choice, or a sensible way of capitalizing on a body with no recognizable female characteristics. Whatever the reason, the way she looked turned heads, which wasn't easy to do in the middle of London. Today she was wearing a white cotton shirt, men's trousers, suspenders, and flat brown lace-ups. Her dark brown hair was cut short and she wore no makeup. She looked as if she should be carrying a cricket bat, or a model Spitfire, with a homemade catapult stuck in her waistband.

Tess waved and Ellie, hands in pockets, strolled across the square. There were little shiny slants of sunlight coming through the leaves of the trees. Ellie's pale skin was so clear it looked almost translucent.

"So how's the world of ethical stationery?" she said, sitting down on the bench.

"Very purple this morning," said Tess. "Our French suppliers have misdyed a whole batch of notebooks and there have been a lot of complaints."

"Stressful?" said Ellie, frowning.

"Only when I'm sitting there. Out here, it all seems a little bit hysterical."

"You've got to keep your customers happy."

"I know," said Tess. "And it's a job. Dominic's always telling me how lucky I am."

They sat, watching the sunshine play on the grass.

Ellie said, "I always thought you'd do something in fashion."

"Did you?"

"Yes," said Ellie, making a face as if stating the obvious. "You're the only person I know who went to lectures dressed as if she had a ration book."

Tess blushed. "Did it look stupid?"

"No. It was great."

"It was that vintage shop. It had so much 1940s stuff. And I love it. The tailoring. The shoulder pads, and neat waists, and hems just over the knee."

"It suits you," said Ellie.

Tess smoothed the skirt of her pale green dress (Irish linen, Fred Howard, circa 1943). "Because I'm small and what is euphemistically known as curvy."

"Don't knock it," said Ellie. "I wouldn't even know where to put a belt if it weren't for the loops on my trousers."

"I've got old pictures of my grandma wearing the same kind of clothes," said Tess. "My mum says I look like her. She was small and round, too."

"You're not round," said Ellie.

"I wish she'd kept some of them. But she says they all wore out. She cut them up into dusters."

They sat watching a peg-legged pigeon hop between the empty crisps packets. Tess thought of the way they had to make do in World War II, and the ingenuity involved in scrubbing up for a local dance. Beetroot juice to stain your lips red. Lines drawn down the backs of your legs to look like seams. They would have played Glenn Miller. "A String of Pearls." "That was the best moment," her grandmother used to say, "before the dancing started, when the hall was empty and the band was playing and people were just starting to arrive. You felt the excitement all down your spine."

The pigeon cocked its head and looked at her. Tess gave

herself a little shake, and the 1940s disappeared. She said quickly, in case Ellie realized her mind had wandered off elsewhere, "So what are you up to this week?"

"More of the same," said Ellie sadly. "Photocopying, filing, running errands."

"It's what you've got to do, though, isn't it?" said Tess. "You've got to get it all on your CV."

"I'd rather be working. Like you."

"I don't know," said Tess. "I like the money. But sometimes I think, What am I doing? Does it really matter?"

"Well, stop then," said Ellie. "Get out and do something else. Grab hold of it before it's too late."

Tess, frightened that it had all become too serious, rubbed her hands together, getting rid of the crumbs. "Oh, maybe," she said. "Let's talk about something nice. I've only got half an hour."

"We're thinking of having a party," said Ellie.

"Oh," said Tess, brightening. "When?"

"For Lauren's birthday. May twenty-fifth."

"Who's coming?"

"Everyone, I hope."

"Can I bring Dominic?"

Ellie looked at her. "You need to ask?"

"I'm being polite," said Tess.

"You two have been joined at the hip ever since you brought him back to the flat. What was it? The second day?"

"It wasn't that soon," said Tess, mumbling.

"Yes, it was," said Ellie. "I was shocked."

"You weren't. And anyway, it wasn't like that."

"You may look all demure and conventional on the outside," said Ellie, "but inside you're a seething mass of animal passion."

"But it wasn't like that," said Tess again, looking up, her cheeks hot. "I just knew, right from the beginning, that I was going to be with him forever."

"Forever?"

"Yes," said Tess.

"If you say so," said Ellie.

• • •

On Tuesday night after work, when Dominic was studying—he was training to be an accountant, working for a large City firm that had taken him into their graduate entry scheme—Tess went to Central Saint Martins college of art to see Toby's degree show. Toby was an old friend from primary school in rural Kent who now lived in a squat in Camden. He didn't look like an artist. He had neat black spectacles and usually wore a fawn Fair Isle vest that had shrunk in the wash. He carried a satchel and always forgot about the bicycle clips on his trousers. But he had big ideas. He designed installations. The first one Tess ever saw—a giant bra, made entirely from chicken bones, suspended from the ceiling—had made her laugh. She wasn't sure if that was the right reaction. But it made her want to see more.

Tess had asked Kirsty to come with her to Saint Martins, but Kirsty was working—a new job in a cocktail bar in Covent Garden. So Tess queued up alone, surrounded by people she didn't know, entranced by the hats, the shaved heads, the facial jewelry, and the thick theatrical makeup.

Inside it was very crowded. It was hard to see anything at all. Sometimes Tess found herself face-to-face with a gargoyle-like mask, or a dog-sized papier-mâché bee with gauzy wings, but most of the time, being only five feet two inches, she found herself staring into the middle of someone's back.

The noise was incredible. Some of the installations used sound—squeaky whining like high-tensile wires being scraped with a violin bow, or drum and bass vibrating from black speakers. There were people shouting to be heard over recordings of massed choirs. There was the level of conversation you get at a cocktail party when everyone's drunk too many margaritas. Added to this, it was hot. She tried to take deep breaths, but the air was chalky, as if full of paint particles, and smelt slightly chemical, like the disinfectant you use in toilets. By the time she'd climbed two sets of stairs, propelled by other people's knees, Tess felt sick. Her shoes, which were vintage brown alligator—to die for—pinched. She longed for a glass of water.

And then, quite suddenly, she found herself in front of a small white cardboard notice that said, "TOBY WALTERS *Anywhere Else Than Here Today*," and, without making any conscious decision, she was standing in line waiting to go through a small doorway. When the crowd moved, she was jostled next to the arm of someone wearing a brown leather jacket, and for a moment she wanted to look up for reassurance, to say, "Do you know what this is?" But there was no time, because now she was in the room, and she heard the door shut behind her and, without warning, the lights went out.

They were standing in total blackness. It felt for a moment, beneath her feet, as if the ground had changed and become soft and mossy. Was she standing on grass? She breathed in, and she could swear she smelt sweet clover and the dampness of leaves—new green leaves covered in dew. The air was cool and fresh, as if someone had opened the window onto a summer morning in the country. She could still hear every sound from the degree show—the choirs, and the shouting, the squeaky wires and the drum and bass—but now it was muted and distant, a long way off, as if it didn't really matter. And the darkness, the cool black darkness, became almost tactile, like that moment when you know the night is ending and the day will begin, and beneath the blank nothingness the shapes of real objects slowly start to appear. The air was expectant. No one moved. No one spoke. And Tess, for the first time that day, felt happy.

Then, gradually, as the minutes passed, she became aware of the crowd shifting because there was a sliver of light on the opposite side of the room and a door was slowly opening. Now she could hear the sounds of the exhibition quite loudly and she was back in the heat and noise of the degree show as the darkness disappeared and the lights came on, brightening to intense white. She looked down at her shiny, bump-toe shoes, and there beneath her was gray lino, not grass. She could smell nothing but stale air and, perhaps, old sweat. She smiled. Clever, Toby, she thought. How did you do that? And as she followed the man in the brown leather jacket out of the room, she swelled with pride. I know the artist, she thought. I have known the artist since he was seven years old and we made rubber balls out of the elastic bands the postman dropped on the pavement.

. . .

"I'm worried about her. After all, she's getting on. She'll be eighty in July."

"But she's fit and well," said Tess.

"I know," said her mother. "But you only need one bad fall at that age, and it all gets very complicated."

Tess shut her eyes. From the clatter at the other end of the phone, she knew exactly what her mother was doing. She was wandering round her kitchen in Kent, starting lots of jobs and abandoning them halfway through. That's what she always did, even when she wasn't on the phone. Her mother never finished anything. She would half-empty the dishwasher, half-fold the washing, half-make a cup of tea. Bags of carrots lay about half-peeled. Letters lay half-read. Drawers and cupboards were permanently wide open as if someone had shouted "Fire!" in the middle of Sunday lunch and everyone had rushed out in a panic. When she was much younger, Tess had followed on her mother's heels, trying to restore order. These days, recognizing an impossible task, she did nothing and tried to see the chaos as charming.

"Has she always been like that?" said Dominic after Tess had taken him home for the first time.

She thought back. "I think so."

"That must have been hard," he said, "growing up."

"Neatness isn't everything," said Tess.

But part of her thought it probably was. Her parents had always been kind and gregarious, happy to drop everything for a surprise party with cheese wotsits and a bottle of Liebfraumilch. But by the time she was about ten, Tess realized that any kind of forward planning was beyond them. They couldn't organize anything. Pipes burst and boilers broke down. Clothes hung around in various states of disrepair. Trains were missed and passports lost. The turkey was always frozen on Christmas Day. Money, especially, was beyond them. They never opened bank statements. When Tess's father died of a heart attack just before her sixteenth birthday, her mother had found all the final demands in Tesco carrier bags under the bed.

Tess, burned by the memory of her mother's hopeless crying, now thought of money as risky and unreliable—something that disappeared, without warning, into thin air. Fear of money wiggled through her life like a vein of thin blue mold in Stilton.

"Spend it while you can," her mother always said. She thought Tess was far too cautious. She herself was always optimistic. Her favorite phrase was Scarlett O'Hara's "Tomorrow is another day."

Dominic, thank goodness, knew about money. He liked money. He found accountancy interesting.

"It's logical," he said.

He was generous with his knowledge. He helped Tess find the best bank account, the cheapest insurance, the most attractive ISA. He checked her records were up-to-date. He balanced her checkbook.

"He'd breathe for you," said Kirsty, "if you let him."

"Everyone's got their weaknesses," said Tess. "I hate money. It terrifies me. I'd much rather he dealt with it all."

Dominic kept her safe.

"I've tried to persuade her to move a bit closer," said her mother.

Tess, whose mind had drifted off, struggled to concentrate.

"But she says she's happy where she is," said her mother, who now, by the sound of it, was rummaging around in a drawer full of bottle openers and tent pegs. "She's lived in Dorset all her life. She says she can't imagine not living by the sea."

"I can see why you wouldn't want to move in your eighties," said Tess. There was a loud whoosh as the kitchen tap was turned on full blast. "Mum?"

"Yes?"

"What are you doing?"

"I can't remember," said her mother. "Did I want a cup of tea?" The tap was turned off. "What were we talking about?"

"Gran."

"Oh, yes," said her mother. "You see, the problem is, it's such a long way from here. It takes me a good four hours to drive down there."

Tess shuddered. She hated thinking of her mother driving anywhere. The car was covered in dents from minor collisions at traffic lights and sudden lane changes on motorways. "What's wrong with everyone today?" she'd say, as she swerved in front of white delivery vans, causing them to brake violently. "Everyone's driving so badly."

"I could go and see her," said Tess.

"She'd love it if you did. Could you find the time?"

"It's quite quick by train," said Tess. "Two hours from Waterloo."

"What I'm most worried about," said her mother, "is that she'll get in a muddle and lose something. It's what happens when you get older, I think. You just can't keep things organized anymore."

• • •

The flat in Brixton was the top half of a narrow Victorian semi. The year before, when Tess had first seen the house—when she and Kirsty had just left uni and were looking for somewhere to live in London—she was enchanted. There was a pale pink rose just coming into flower on the trellis and a heavy brass knocker on the door. But all charm ended there. It was a bad conversion, done on the cheap. The sash windows had to be wedged open to stop them crashing down. There was damp in the bathroom and none of the bedroom radiators worked.

But, worst of all, Tess and Kirsty had to walk right into the middle of someone else's family life before climbing the stairs to their own front door. Every time she came home, Tess felt like an intruder. One of the children from the downstairs flat had a red plastic tricycle with brittle yellow wheels that he scooted up and down the narrow hall, scraping the tessellated tiles. Whenever he saw Tess, he stopped and stared at her with big, terrified eyes.

Tess's room was a converted attic at the top of the house. From the window she could look down onto the backyard and the washing line permanently festooned with small T-shirts. Because of the sloping ceiling, Dominic was only ever able to stand upright just inside the door. The rest of the time, he had to bend double, like a soldier running through enemy lines.

In the tiny box room next door to her own Tess had set up a black metal clothes rail. Here was where she kept her collection of vintage dresses, blouses, coats, and suits, with shoes and boots neatly paired beneath. Handbags sat on a wooden shoe rack beneath the window. Tess never bought anything that wasn't strong enough to wear. She had become adept at checking for seams that couldn't be repaired, underarms where the fabric was stained, and the seats of skirts where the material had worn thin. But she knew enough about basic sewing to replace ripped linings and edgings, and could stitch back missing buttons, loose facings, and broken zips. If, sometimes, she bought a jacket that had lost its belt, or a hat without a hatband or a bow, she turned the pages of her old fashion magazines until she could guess at what the original might have looked like. Then she hunted through all the bargain buckets in charity shops until she found what she needed.

The real excitement, as she explained to Kirsty, was finding a Utility Clothing label in the seam, with those two distinctive circles, each missing a wedge. "CC41. It means Controlled Commodity 1941. It's what the government brought in as part of rationing to limit what materials could be used. So dresses could only have two pockets and five buttons. Only six seams in a skirt. Men weren't allowed turn-ups in their trousers. But some of the young ones got round it by pretending their legs were longer than they were, and then going home and turning up the hems."

Kirsty gave her a long, hard look. "You're like one of those men with a model railway in the spare room."

"They're clothes," said Tess. "I wear them."

"Most people go to Topshop," said Kirsty.

You don't understand, thought Tess. They made the best of what they had. Good design within severe limitations.

"We hated those labels," said her grandmother, who'd been seventeen when the war broke out. "We always cut them out."

From time to time, Tess tried to persuade Dominic to try on a vintage suit. She got nowhere. He didn't like the idea of dead men's clothes. Luckily for him, being just over six foot, he was too tall for most of them anyway. Men used to be smaller when food was in short supply.

Sometimes, tempted beyond common sense, Tess would buy a man's black fedora, or a silk tie, or a wartime bib-fronted dress shirt, and hang it up in her room just for the pleasure of looking at it.

"But what's it for?" Dominic would say.

"I like the workmanship, I suppose. Or maybe imagining the person who used to wear it."

Dominic would look at her with his clear blue eyes, and she could see that he didn't understand at all.

It's the attraction of opposites, she said to herself firmly. You see it all the time. You look for the person who supplies what you lack. It's yin and yang, logic and feeling, head and heart. You come together as one complete whole.

"Someone told me once," she said to Kirsty as they walked down Brixton Road to the tube on Saturday afternoon, constantly separated by people shouting on mobiles and pushing buggies and pulling tartan shopping trolleys on wheels, "that every soul is divided at birth and you have to search and search until you find the other half. It's an old Indian legend."

"Are you lost?" said a thin man in a striped woolly hat. She was about to say, no, I'm fine, thank you, I live round here, when she realized he was holding a notice on a wooden stick saying "Jesus Saves" and the question was entirely spiritual.

"But do you think it's true?" said Tess, running to catch up with Kirsty.

"Is what true?"

"That there's just one person in the world who can make

you happy, and you have to keep looking until you find them?"

"No," said Kirsty. "Lots of people can make you happy."

Tess looked at her, crestfallen.

"Besides which," said Kirsty, "there are seven billion people in the world. You haven't got enough years in your life to search through them all."

"You're forgetting about fate," said Tess.

"Fate?"

"Fate brings people together."

"Like two people applying to the same university."

"Well, yes," said Tess. It seemed a bit trite when you reduced searching the Sahara, the Himalayas, and the North Pole to bumping into each other in a café in Manchester.

"I think that just proves," said Kirsty, "that people make conservative choices. You fall in love with the person standing in front of you."

"What about your parents?" said Tess. "What were the chances of them meeting?"

Kirsty's mother was Irish and grew up in Cork. Her father had arrived in Birmingham from Somalia at the age of three. They met at a bar mitzvah in Finchley.

"Most people," said Kirsty, "aren't like my parents. Most people end up with partners born in a thirty-mile radius. That doesn't sound like fate. That sounds like apathy."

Tess opened her mouth to disagree. But then she remembered that Dominic had been born in Croydon and she'd been born near Tonbridge, which sounded like the correct distance, roughly speaking. So she said nothing and changed the subject.

. . .

Dominic was waiting for her outside the huge multiplex on Leicester Square. He was leaning against the wall, hands in pockets, effortlessly cool. When she saw him, her heart beat fast, as it always did, as if offering a round of applause.

"Am I late?" she said, breathlessly.

"Only a minute," he said.

As they queued for tickets, Tess wondered, as she often did, when they'd move in together. Dominic had gone back to live with his parents after they graduated—partly to save money but partly to help out with a complicated set of circumstances involving his sister and a husband from Catalonia with mental health problems. The family crisis appeared to be over, but Dominic stayed on in the room he'd had as a child, his accountancy books on the desk in front of the window.

Tess couldn't imagine Dominic living with her in the Brixton flat. Weekends were fine, because Kirsty was usually out, but she suspected Kirsty would blow a fuse if she thought she had to have Dominic around full-time. So, if she and Dominic wanted to be together, they'd have to find a place of their own. As the lights went down and the adverts started, Tess started imagining a modern flat with wooden floors and clean white furniture—the kind of thing you see in the room sets at IKEA. *I could buy a storage solution for all my vintage clothes*, she thought.

After the film, which had a lot of people being shot, and a complicated plot about double-crossings that Tess couldn't quite follow, they went to Chinatown and wandered about until the light started fading and hunger drove them into a cheapish-looking restaurant. They sat at a table right in the window with their backs to a large group of men shouting at each other. Tess thought, as they looked through the menu, It's so lovely that Dominic and I don't need to talk all the time. We can sit here, in silence, and it's comfortable and relaxed. I read somewhere that whenever they ate out in public Wallis Simpson was so determined to be seen animatedly chatting to the duke that sometimes, if she really had nothing to say, she would recite the letters of the alphabet. Tess smiled to herself. I am so lucky that we can just be ourselves.

She felt herself being jostled from behind. A brown leather jacket flopped to the floor.

"I'll get that," said a very Welsh voice, and the jacket was picked up and hung back round the chair. "It's my friend, you see. He got up and knocked it off."

"Oh, that's fine," said Tess, only half looking round.

"It's not in your way, is it?"

"No," said Tess.

"Not a lot of room, is there really?"

Tess didn't answer, just edged her chair forwards to give the shouting men more space. "What are you going to have?" she said to Dominic.

"The usual," he said, closing the menu.

"Beer?" she said.

"Just water."

Dominic was careful about stimulants. He was always under twenty-one units a week and never drank coffee after nine PM. His one vice was fun-sized packs of Maltesers.

"What you're talking about," said the loud Welsh voice behind her, "is charisma."

And I really admire that, thought Tess, as the soup arrived and Dominic bent over his bowl, I really admire his self-discipline. I could do with a bit more of it myself. There are times when Kirsty and I stay up drinking red wine till the birds start singing and we realize we've gone all the way through the night and hit the dawn chorus. When that happens, I never dare tell Dominic. I put extra concealer under my eyes and hope he doesn't ask.

Behind her, the shouting grew louder.

And he doesn't ask because he finds the whole idea of excessive drinking illogical. It makes you feel sick. It gives you a headache. So why would anyone do it?

"And I'm not answering that," roared the Welsh voice, "until someone brings me a beer."

Sometimes, thought Tess, looking at Dominic, whose blond hair had flopped forwards, obscuring his face as he leant over his wontons, I feel like a child compared to you. You know what you're doing. You know where you're going. But I'm not really sure what's happening at all. When I'm with you, I don't worry. We lie in bed at the weekends, skin to skin, damply satisfied, and my mind drifts off like a feather. Sex is sweet and heavy, like double cream or liquid toffee. It coats your anxieties. But at some point you have to get up and go outside and walk on your own to the tube, and then you start thinking, as the sugar wears off, So what am I doing exactly? Where am I going? Is this the right direction or should I be heading somewhere else?

"I'm ready for Paris," shouted the Welsh voice, "but is Paris ready for me?" and the whole table behind her cheered.

Tess looked out through the window. It was dark now. The people outside were talking and laughing, their faces lit by the streetlamps. I wouldn't mind having a bit more conversation while we eat, she thought. Just a tiny bit more. He could tell me about something. He likes bringing me up-to-date with things I don't know. Like world events. Elections. Wars I might have missed. He has all the facts and figures. He remembers them. I'm not good at facts and figures. Maybe that's why I surround myself with people who can add up. I know, she thought, that when the bill arrives Dominic will be able to check it and add 15 percent service without even stopping to think. He's just brilliant at maths.

He's brilliant at a lot of things.

And now the waitress arrived with plates of noodles and vegetables, squeezing herself into the little gap between the table and the window because it was easier, probably, than negotiating her way past that huge table of shouting men behind them, and Tess found herself remembering the first time she'd met Dominic, in the café by the library, on the second day of the first term at Manchester. He couldn't get past my table. There were so many bodies he was pinned to the edge by the crush. So I sat there getting hotter and hotter, staring at his bottom in his tight blue jeans. He wore a checked shirt, like a cowboy on a prairie. When I looked at him that first afternoon, I saw light and blue skies and wide open spaces.

I still do, she thought, uncertainly.

But now, even though there was seaweed, which she liked, and oyster mushrooms, which she also liked, and she was sitting in a red and gold Chinese restaurant on a Saturday night with the most good-looking man in London or even, possibly, in the whole of the UK, she found, to her surprise, as the laughter behind her gathered into a kind of roar, that her eyes had filled with tears.

. . .

Sorting out extension leads in the music shop near Wardour Street, George was listening in his head to a 1946 recording of Gershwin's "Oh, Lady Be Good!" There was Lester Young playing tenor sax, Willie Smith and Charlie Parker playing alto, and Arnold Ross on the piano. George had memorized the piano solo the day before when it was quiet in the shop and he'd sat in the office, earphones on, ostensibly checking invoices. Now, in his mind, he was hearing another kind of rhythm running underneath it all and wondering whether this was a different take, a different way of playing, or something that was technically impossible, which no one who was thinking straight would ever even try.

He jumped. There in front of him, looming up like a lamppost in a mist, was a tall, stooped woman. Next to her was a boy of about ten. Customers, he thought to himself fiercely. Customers, customers. Concentrate. He forced the piano solo to the back of his mind.

"Can I help you?"

"We want a keyboard," she said.

"OK," said George. "Have you thought about the kind of features you need?"

"Black notes," she said. "And white ones."

George laughed. She stared at him, unsmiling. Hastily, he cleared his throat. "Anything else?"

She looked at the boy. The boy looked back at her.

"Well," said George, lost, desperate, trying to focus, "why don't we look at a few of the models we've got on display and see what you think."

"Are they the ones over there?" said the woman.

"Yes," said George.

"We've looked at those."

There was a small silence.

"And you didn't like them?"

"No," said the woman.

She looked at him expectantly.

George felt increasingly hot. He said, "We could look through some catalogs." But then he realized he had no idea where the catalogs were. So he took a deep breath and said, "Is it for someone who's just starting out or for an experienced player?"

"I couldn't see," she said, "how you could fold them. They'd never fit in a rucksack. And he's already got his PE kit and his lunchbox."

George stared at her in bewilderment.

"We want a pedal," said the boy.

"A pedal?" said George.

"Yes," said the boy. "For your feet."

George, who had been thrown a rope, hung on. "So is it for you, this keyboard?"

"No," said the boy. "I want a recorder."

• • •

"Why me?" said Tess.

Glenda frowned. "Don't you want to go?"

Her hooped earrings, swinging, caught the light. It was Friday morning. Outside was a percussion of metal, like someone delivering scaffolding poles.

"Yes," said Tess. "I do. Of course I do."

"Is it the boyfriend? Doesn't he like you going away?"

Tess blinked. "No, it's nothing to do with him."

"I don't know," said Glenda, quivering. "It seems perfect to me."

Tess said, desperately, "I want to go. Really."

"Paris, as well," said Glenda.

"Well, exactly," said Tess. "It's so lovely."

"So what is it?"

"I'm not sure I'm the right person. What about you? Why isn't he sending you?"

Glenda looked at her as if she'd said something extraordinarily stupid. "Well, I don't speak French, do I?"

"I don't, much," said Tess.

"If I were you," said Glenda, leaning forwards and lowering her voice to a theatrical whisper, "I wouldn't go on about it. I'd just grab it with both hands."

"But what am I supposed to do," said Tess, whispering back, "when I get there?"

"Build bridges."

Tess stared at her.

"It's the notepaper," said Glenda.

Tess waited, eyes wide.

"It's not up to standard."

"Really?" said Tess.

"I'm not supposed to say this," said Glenda, making huge mouth movements but producing very little sound, as if Tess were hard of hearing and had to lip-read, "but we've had a record number of complaints. Shouters, moaners, and genuines. And it's the second time. First it was the purple. And now it's the pink."

"Oh," breathed Tess.

"And now he won't pay," said Glenda. She leant forwards so far she was practically horizontal on the desk. "And they're threatening legal action. They say handmade means natural variation. Oliver says, within limits. So now it's a standoff. Stalemate."

"But what can I do about that?" said Tess, panicked.

"Be charming," said Glenda, almost hissing in her urgency. "Explain we're a small company. We can't afford to lose customers. People in the UK know about handmade. They don't expect uniform. But they do expect reasonable parameters."

"And I have to do all that in French?" said Tess.

"As much of it as you can," said Glenda.

Merde, thought Tess.

"So you'll be an ambassador," said Glenda, straightening up, her voice suddenly loud again, "representing the firm. Anglo-French relations. *Entente cordiale.*"

"Well," said Tess, "I'd better find out about tickets."

"No need. Nadine will do all that."

"Really?"

"Oh, yes," said Glenda, bleached blond curls bobbing. "Accommodation, travel—all arranged. It's official business."

"And when do I go?"

"Straight after the weekend," said Glenda. "First thing Monday morning."

. . .

"I just washed them down the sink," said Tess.

"So what are you going to do?" said Ellie.

"Wear my glasses, I suppose," said Tess, miserably.

"I didn't even know you had glasses. I've never seen you wearing them."

"They're about five years old," said Tess, "and really, really ugly. They're round and shiny and make my face look fat. I look like a doughnut with headlamps. My mum made me get them when I started A-levels. She said she didn't want me wearing contact lenses all the time. In case my eyes dried out."

"So where are they?"

"What?" said Tess.

"Your glasses."

"I don't know. In my room somewhere."

"So what can you see?" said Ellie. "Can you see this?" She held up a hand. "How many fingers?"

"I'm not blind," said Tess. "I'm just shortsighted."

"Can you see the fence?"

It was Lauren's party. They were sitting on the stone wall by the kitchen door in the tiny back garden. Tess looked up. She saw the pink cistus in the earthenware pot and the lilac bush next to it. But after that it was a blur.

"Not really," said Tess.

"Can you see Lauren?"

Tess screwed up her eyes. "No."

"You can't see Lauren?"

"No."

"You know what?" said Ellie. "I'd say that was blind."

"But I'm meant to be charming them," wailed Tess. "I'm meant to be going to Paris to charm them."

"You can be charming in glasses."

"Not my glasses," said Tess, gloomily.

"Can't you get new contact lenses?"

"Not by Monday morning."

"And you haven't got any spares?"

"I've never needed them," said Tess. "I've worn lenses since I was sixteen and I've never lost one. Ever."

Ellie—so beautiful in her boyishness that she might, if the whim took her, put on a pair of tortoiseshell spectacles with plain glass just because she fancied a change—studied her sympathetically. "I think you're worrying too much. Wear one of your wartime suits with a hat and gloves, and they'll just think it's part of the look."

"They're French," said Tess, imagining an office full of haute couture.

"Exactly," said Ellie. "They'll think it's English eccentricity."

Tess still sat there, a picture of misery.

"You need a drink," said Ellie. "Wait here."

Tess looked after her hazy figure and wondered, as a sea of bright colors washed round her, whether she should have come. On the way, she'd stuck to Kirsty like cling film. Now, sitting alone, she felt horribly vulnerable.

"Hello," said Lauren, sitting down next to her on the wall. "Ellie said you needed cheering up."

Lauren, who had bleached blond hair cut into a bob with a long asymmetrical fringe, had chalk-white skin and very dark eyebrows. She looked, Tess often thought, like a surprised doll. She had a strong Liverpudlian accent and a sharp mind—she was on the graduate fast track of one of London's largest multinational consultancy firms. She earned far more than any of the rest of them, which was how she could afford to rent a house in Clapham and support Ellie, who was still stuck in nonpaying jobs. But because of the way she looked, many people didn't realize how clever she was until it was way too late. Lauren's put-downs burned like the tail of a whip.

Today, on her birthday, Lauren was wearing a tight black dress. She was the kind of person who could wear a tight black dress. She had the discipline to go to the gym every day.

"Oh, ignore me," said Tess. "I threw my contact lenses down the sink. So I can't see anything."

"Why?" said Lauren.

"Because I'm shortsighted."

"No, I meant why did you throw your lenses down the sink?"

"I didn't mean to," said Tess in anguish.

"Where's Dominic?"

Tess looked sad. "He had to go home. His sister's falling to pieces."

"Is she the one married to the wife-beating Spaniard?"

Tess nodded. "She's found out he's having an affair."

Lauren shook her head. "That's men for you."

"They're not all like that."

"Aren't they?" said Lauren. "I don't think men are capable of fidelity."

"Women are unfaithful, too," said Tess.

"Not when they're with each other." Lauren looked up and smiled, and there was Ellie, carrying two glasses of white wine. Seeing the glance dance between them, love floating in the air, Tess felt bereft. She swallowed such a huge gulp of wine that she started coughing and had to be thumped on the back.

Lauren's party—because it was Lauren who had organized it—went extremely well. There were more women than men, perhaps, but this didn't seem to make much difference, except that most of the beer was untouched and the air was filled with soft, exotic scents like a well-stocked flower shop. News of Tess's temporary disability spread and people kept appearing beside her on the wall. So this is how to enjoy parties, Tess thought. You turn up without your boyfriend and sit in one place, and people come and tell you their secrets.

After an hour or so, her head was so full of one-night stands, stolen cocaine, backstabbing work colleagues, and a cousin with cancer that she began to feel quite dizzy. The wine didn't help. People kept filling her glass and she realized, very slowly, that she was getting quite drunk.

"Enjoying yourself?" said Lauren.

"Yes, I am," said Tess. "You know, it's quite good if you can't see people's expressions. You react to what they're saying rather than what you think they might be thinking, which makes the whole thing a lot easier."

"There, you see," said Lauren, "you were right to throw away your lenses."

"What did Ellie get you for your birthday?"

Lauren laughed. "It was homemade," she said.

Something about the way she said it made Tess knock

back the last of her wine in a rush of embarrassment. "Oh, how lovely," she said politely, trying to push away the big colorful pictures that had suddenly appeared in her head like porn on a plasma TV.

"She knows me very well," said Lauren.

Yes, thought Tess. "You're soul mates."

"Soul mates?"

"I was telling Kirsty," said Tess, in a slightly befuddled way, the wine having suddenly caught up with her and made her tongue large and floppy, "about soul mates. You spend your life looking for your other half. And then when you find them you feel complete."

"Your one true love."

"Yes," said Tess. "The one person who makes you whole."

Lauren put her head on one side. "I'm not sure about that. I think you could fall in love with any number of people."

Tess was almost shocked into sobriety. "But what about you and Ellie?"

"I love Ellie," said Lauren, "and I hope we'll be together for a long time. But I don't think it's happened because of some mystical connection."

"Don't you?"

"Why, do you?" said Lauren. "Is that why you think you and Dominic are together?"

"Yes," said Tess, wondering, as she said it, whether she did.

"I think the whole thing is a lot more pragmatic," said Lauren. "You meet someone and you like them enough to get to know them. You respect each other. You make each other laugh. And then you meet each other's friends, and go out, and get invited to weddings and festivals and funerals, and then you have all these memories, and you know who you are because you're with the person who's always been there by your side, doing it all with you. You stay together in the end because of all the stuff you share."

"But it has to be the right person," said Tess.

"One of the right people," said Lauren. "If I'd never met Ellie, if I'd met someone else a few years ago, and we'd got on and liked each other and built up a relationship together, I'd be with her now and not Ellie. A lot of it is chance. Who you happen to meet."

"I can't believe you think that."

"Why? I love Ellie. But I'm just saying that if she didn't exist, or if she'd been born in China and not Liverpool, and if she'd chosen to go to Cardiff instead of Manchester, I would have met someone else. And I'd be sitting here now talking about—this other person instead of her."

"But that's so cold," said Tess.

"No," said Lauren, "it's just realistic. Look at it this way. What would be much, much worse is that you're right, and everyone has just one true love. But the problem is that you live here and she or he lives in Moscow or Sydney or Hong Kong and you never, ever meet. So you spend your days feeling lonely and miserable and die alone with a broken heart."

"But don't you see?" said Tess. "Fate brings you together."

"Maybe you're right," said Lauren in a kind voice, as if

Tess was overtired and needed tucking up with her teddy bear.

"Tess," said Kirsty, looming up out of the blur, "come and meet George."

"Can't he come here?" said Tess, who had become, in her mind, glued to the wall.

"What are you?" said Kirsty. "The queen?"

So Tess stood up, swaying. She said, "I might have to hold on to you."

But Kirsty ignored her and turned away. Tess followed her up the shallow steps to the small uneven lawn of the raised garden and narrowly missed falling into the lilac bush.

"There he is," said Kirsty, as Tess righted herself, "talking to Rhys. What do you think? Do you like the look of him?"

The heels of Tess's dear little vintage shoes buried themselves in the turf.

"Which one's Rhys?" said Tess, but she was only saving face, really, because she couldn't see anyone at all.

"He's waving at us. The tall thin Welshman with the black hair and white shirt. George is the one with his back to us. Next to George is Walter, the big black guy. And next to him is Mo."

"Kirsty," said Tess.

"What?"

"How long are we staying?"

"Why?"

"I think I need to go home," said Tess. "I feel really, really sick."

• • •

Sunday is a hangover sort of day. You get up late, eat toast, drink coffee (and wish you hadn't, because it makes you feel worse), and take the sheets down to the launderette. When you've thoroughly depressed yourself with the Sunday papers, which are full of ambitious, thrusting people being bitchy about other ambitious, thrusting people, you come back home, make up the bed, have a cup of tea, change back into your pajamas, and curl up on the sofa with a KitKat to watch a rubbish film.

Everybody knows this, thought Tess. Everybody in the world knows this except Dominic. Sunday for Dominic is a day when you get up early and go for a run. Sunday for Dominic is a long complicated roast with purslane and salsify washed down with lemonade made with fresh lemons. And mint. She felt exhausted at the thought.

It was a relief that he'd decided to spend the weekend at his parents' in Croydon. She felt free. But in her greasy, paranoid, post-party state, this relief made her feel incredibly guilty. I should be missing him, she thought. And I'm not. I'm enjoying the solitude. I feel as if I've taken off some tight shoes and the muscles in my feet are shouting for joy. But it's probably because I'm preoccupied. I need to be alone to think about Paris. It's a huge responsibility. Glenda says I'm an ambassador for the company. (Me! An ambassador!) I've laid out everything I'm going to wear on the bed (with its clean sheets). I've got my bag ready with my passport, my euros, and my tickets. A midafternoon flight (why? was it cheaper?) and a hotel near the French headquarters. Everything's arranged. But still my heart keeps skipping in panic.

"You worry too much," said Kirsty when she finally appeared at four PM. "It's just a job."

"But I'm representing Daisy Greenleaf Designs," said Tess, peering at her anxiously through her round black glasses.

"You'll be fine. Enjoy yourself. Do some sightseeing."

"Dominic says this shows Oliver has got confidence in me. He says I might be promoted when Glenda retires."

"Is that what you want?" said Kirsty, curiously.

"Of course," said Tess. "It's important to have a good career."

"I think it's more important to find someone who makes you happy," said Kirsty.

"You don't really believe that."

"Yes, I do."

"Love is more important than a career?"

"It applies equally to men," said Kirsty. "Find someone who makes you feel good, and everything else falls into place."

"You know," said Tess, "I never know what you're going to say next."

"That's what makes me so interesting," said Kirsty. She wandered over to the mantelpiece. "What's this?"

"It came yesterday. It's an invitation to Lily and Tim's wedding. To both of us."

"Oh good," said Kirsty. "Rhys was talking about this last night. It's down in Dorset. The band is playing." She turned to Tess with a slightly mocking air. "If you wear your lenses and don't drink too much, you'll meet George."

"Maybe I don't want to meet George," said Tess.

"Of course you do," said Kirsty. "He's your soul mate."

. . .

When the engines rumbled like dragons and the plane took off, racing down the runway and throwing her back into her seat, Tess was so excited she had to shut her eyes. Was she really on her way to Paris, on business, with an overnight bag in the locker above? She'd rung her mother the night before, trying to sound cool and casual.

"I can have room service in the hotel," she said. "It's all on expenses."

"I'd go down for dinner if I were you," said her mother. "You might meet a lovely Frenchman."

"I've already got a lovely Englishman," said Tess tersely. What was wrong with everyone?

"Oh, I know," said her mother. "But it never hurts to broaden your horizons."

The trouble is, thought Tess, looking out at Toytown Heathrow below, I never really believe I'm flying. I think, Can a heavy metal bus full of people take off into the sky? And the answer is clearly no. So I just assume it's some kind of magic trick, with someone running a permanent loop of cloud pictures outside my window. She remembered going to see Father Christmas when she was little, in the local department store. All the children had to get into a tiny cabin. Through the windows they could see white snowy scenery and green pine trees, and someone locked the doors and jiggled the cabin around, and then opened the doors at the other end, and you were supposed to believe you'd traveled to the North Pole. But it didn't really work, because when you got out it looked like exactly the same room, except that Father Christmas was sitting there on a stool with a huge white beard and shiny black boots.

Tess felt she ought to open her bag and read through her notes. But she couldn't concentrate. She tried instead to run through some French in her mind. Oh, she thought in panic, I know the word for pink is *rose*. But I have no idea how to say purple.

They were getting near Paris when it happened. There was a sudden barking noise like a dog. Everyone looked up, surreptitiously, pretending they weren't. Then someone shouted, "Look out!" and three rows ahead a woman stood up. You could hear everyone thinking *hijackgunsterrorists*. Tess swallowed. There was a huge hole in the pit of her stomach. Now she could see a steward running towards them from the front of the plane. She said to the man next to her in the aisle seat, "What's happening?"

He said, "Someone's been sick."

Oh, thought Tess, breathing again.

A woman with black hair was being helped up by the steward. How horrible to be identified as someone who has just thrown up, thought Tess. She watched as the woman made her unsteady way past Tess to the toilets at the back of the plane. Now, quite suddenly, the smell engulfed them all. The steward was fussing round with paper towels and a black plastic sack, and all the passengers were trying to look serene and mature and understanding, which was impossible, given they were all disgusted. A middle-aged woman across the aisle was quietly retching into a sick bag. This is one of the perils of cramming people into a small metal cigar case, thought Tess. It works all right if everyone behaves like a shop dummy. But living, breathing humans act in unpredictable ways.

In the aisle just behind the steward, standing up, was a man hidden inside a large blue hoodie. He was struggling to take it off. And then she realized what had happened. Oh no, she thought. Oh no. One minute you're sitting there, quietly reading your in-flight magazine. Then the woman behind you stands up and vomits all over your shoulder.

The steward came running back with a giant aerosol spray. Chemical sweetness filled the air. It made everything worse. People were gagging.

"Can we lend you something to wear, sir?" said the steward. "Or do you have something in your hand luggage?"

Poor man, thought Tess. She looked out of the window, and now, through wisps of cloud, she thought she could see a grid of buildings way down below. Paris, she thought. Paris.

When she next looked up, the steward was closing the overhead locker. In his hands was a brown leather jacket.

• • •

"Oh," said George.

"What?" said Rhys.

"I can't find the map."

"What map?"

"The street map of Paris. So we know where we're going."

"Where are we going?" said Mo.

"I don't know," said George, "without the map."

They were sitting so close to each other they could have been in a commuter train in the rush hour. The Paris flat—lent to Rhys by his cousin Megan, who was spending three months in North Carolina—had turned out to be more of a cupboard. For one person, it was perfect: an attic room with a dark blue sofa bed, a tiny table with two chairs, a galley kitchen along one wall, and a minuscule shower room with just enough space for a toilet. But as temporary accommodation for four musicians, their bags, a saxophone, a double bass, a keyboard, and a full drum kit, it was proving something of a challenge. Tempers had frayed.

"What I don't understand," said Walter, "is why you're acting so surprised. You lose everything all the time."

George opened his mouth to disagree.

"There might be a girlfriend somewhere," said Walter, "if only you could remember where you left her."

It had been hard enough getting all their stuff up five flights of stairs in the first place. But once they were inside, out of breath, things had got progressively worse. Walter, who was six feet four inches and sixteen stone, couldn't fit into the shower room. Rhys had tripped over a trailing cable and smashed headfirst into a cupboard, which now had a crack on the glass door. Mo was busy dropping cigarette ash all over the white rug. George had an uneasy feeling that the studio apartment wouldn't look quite so bijou once they'd left it.

"So where we playing?" said Mo.

"When I find the map," said George, "I'll show you."

"You could just tell me," said Mo, "if you could remember."

"And once we get there," said Walter, "what are we going to play?"

George, leaning forwards from the sofa, upended a carrier bag and shook its contents out on the floor. "You know what we're playing. We're playing our own stuff."

"Just checking," said Walter.

"Look," said George, "there's no problem, all right? Everything's under control."

"There's a terrible smell coming from that bag," said Rhys.

George, who had forgotten where he'd stuffed the dark blue hoodie, crammed everything back.

"Have a look in your jacket pocket."

"I've already looked," said George, rifling through the pockets of his brown leather jacket.

"What you have to do," said Rhys, "is retrace your steps."

"Or go and buy another map," said Mo.

"I don't speak French," said George. He quite often had

an expression of panic on his face. It was when he realized that the bits of life he'd successfully ignored were squaring up to hit him.

"Which reminds me," said Mo.

"Oh, here we go," said Rhys.

Mo ground out his cigarette in a coffee cup. "So this Englishman gets a job in Wales."

"I knew it. I knew he was going to have a go."

"And this man says to his Welsh friend, 'How am I going to fit in? I don't know a word of the language.'"

"Which part of Wales is this?" said Rhys. He came from Swansea. You wouldn't want to live anywhere else, he said. In London, he felt like James Joyce in Croatia—artistic but exiled.

"So his friend says, 'That's easy. Everyone you meet, you just say, *Bore da*.'"

"It means 'Good morning,'" said Rhys, articulating carefully like an enthusiastic schoolteacher.

"So off he goes to Wales. And on his first morning, he wakes up and goes out to buy a paper. And the first person he meets, he says, '*Bore da!*' So this person smiles back and says, '*Bore da!*' And he thinks to himself, Brilliant. Second person, the same. '*Bore da!*' he says. '*Bore da!*' they say. So he carries on down the street getting all these nods and smiles. And by now he's feeling pretty confident. He sees a car and a pair of legs sticking out underneath. So he bends down and says, '*Bore da!*' There's no answer. So he bends down a bit lower. '*Bore da!*' he says. Finally, he gets right down to look under the car and shouts, *'Bore da!'* And this voice shouts back, 'Fuck off, you Welsh git!'"

Walter laughed.

"Every time," says Rhys. "It's like an obsession with you, isn't it?"

"No different from you going on about deep-fried Mars bars," said Mo.

"Kevin Bacon to Morgan Freeman," said George.

They all looked at him. He did this sometimes—emerged suddenly from the shadows like a Shakespearian messenger delivering a vital line.

"I don't know if I like this game," said Rhys. "I've never really been that keen on films. I'd rather read a book—let my imagination run riot."

"Have you ever thought," said Mo, "about getting help?"

"I don't understand," said Walter, shifting his weight sideways so suddenly that Mo nearly lost his balance and fell off the sofa, "why you always have to start with Kevin Bacon."

"Six degrees of Kevin Bacon," said George.

"No. You've lost me."

"Like six degrees of separation. The idea that everyone in the world is connected to everyone else through just five people."

"Nah," said Walter.

"Try it."

"Me and Tony Blair."

"I bet someone in your law school knows Tony Blair," said George.

"Of course they do," said Mo. "They're all in it together. One big club. Rich man's conspiracy."

"Yeah, right," said Walter gloomily. He was tired. Most evenings he drove a cab round southeast London. His girlfriend Sonya had given birth to a little boy when he was in his second year at Manchester. Walter had finished his degree, worked for two years in an abattoir to build up savings, and was now putting himself through law school. His own father had disappeared when he was a few months old, and he was determined to keep his family together. But he still found time for the band. Walter looked like a bigger version of Charlie Parker. He played like him, too, standing almost motionless, eyes expressionless, as if the saxophone just happened to be under his fingers as he breathed.

"Anyone?" said George.

"Remind me again," said Rhys.

"Get from Kevin Bacon to Morgan Freeman in as few moves as possible," said George. "So Kevin Bacon was in a film with X, and X was in a film with Y, and Y was in a film with Morgan Freeman."

"That's easy," said Mo.

"Go on, then," said Rhys.

"Well, give us a moment," said Mo. Sometimes, when he was cornered, his Glaswegian accent sounded even thicker than usual. "I can't just reel it off. I have to get my head together."

"Think about the films Morgan Freeman has been in," said George.

"*The Shawshank Redemption,*" said Walter.

"And *Se7en,*" said Rhys, all lit up with excitement that he'd remembered. Then he shuddered. "Dark, that film. Very dark."

He stretched out his legs. Rhys had very thin, very long legs. Because he normally wore black jeans, he looked like a child's stick drawing, complete with scribbly black hair and a wobbly mouth. You might have thought, misled by his wasted appearance—white skin, dark shadows under his eyes, hunched shoulders—that Rhys had a drug habit. Sometimes, onstage, it looked as if the double bass was holding him up. In fact, as long as he remembered to eat, Rhys was quite healthy. His problem (and this was an unusual health problem) was reading. Once he got caught up in a book, he couldn't put it down. He regularly stayed up until three or four o'clock in the morning, ignoring his burning eyes and aching neck. "It's the words, you see," he'd say. "I'm addicted." Luckily for Rhys, he worked in a secondhand book shop.

Mo played drums. Or rather, he didn't so much play drums as attack them. He provided a standard rhythm if you needed one. But give him a solo, and he was a frenzy of energy, like a barking dog, ears streaming, chasing a squirrel up a tree. He produced a sound like machine-gun fire, a rapid volley of percussion that was almost as deafening as the applause that followed. Mo was fiery in appearance, too—short red hair, light brown skin, and ginger stubble that glowed in the sun. He'd been brought up by foster parents in Glasgow, which hadn't been a particularly happy experience for any of them. Mo had set the garden shed alight when he was ten. Inside was a petrol mower. When it exploded, neighbors thought Bearsden was under terrorist attack.

Mo screwed up his eyes. "Gwyneth Paltrow."

"What about her?" said Walter.

"She was in *Se7en*."

"So go on, then," said Rhys. "How does that get us back to Kevin Bacon?"

Mo glared at him.

"There was Brad Pitt, of course," said Rhys.

George was beginning to regret starting the game at all. "Just one more year to go," he said to Walter, hoping to change the subject, "and you'll be finished."

"I don't think it works like that. I think being a lawyer means working twenty-four/seven. Forever."

"Think of the money," said George.

"Is that enough?"

"From the sound of it," said Mo, "it'll be plenty."

"What about you?" said Walter. "What are you up to these days?"

"I'm not up to anything," said Mo.

You never quite knew with Mo. Either he was maintaining a meticulously preserved front to hide a normal day job—delivering pizza or painting window frames—or he was involved in something illegal. Either way, George didn't want to know. It seemed safer to keep Mo at arm's length—especially in view of his pyromaniac tendencies.

"Which begs the question," said Rhys, "what has Brad Pitt been in?"

"Are we still playing?" said Walter, leaning his head back against the wall. "I need a beer."

"You should always finish something you've started," said Rhys. "No point leaving something halfway through." He leant forwards on the sofa to look sideways at Mo. "I thought you said you knew the answer."

"I do," said Mo. "*Sleepers*."

"Never heard of it."

"Brad Pitt was in *Sleepers*," said Mo. "Ask Robert De Niro. So there it is. Kevin Bacon is in *Sleepers* with Brad Pitt. Brad Pitt is in *Se7en* with Morgan Freeman. Forget about six degrees of separation. I've done it in one."

. . .

Tess was sitting in the beige reception area of an office building next to a roundabout somewhere on the outskirts of Paris. She was tired and miserable. Even her favorite dress (red rayon crepe print, designer label "Bijou," circa 1942) and shoes (brown snakeskin, two-inch heel, circa 1945) weren't lifting her mood. So far, this hadn't been the Parisian experience she'd been expecting. The hotel the night before, also in the industrial suburbs, had been small, cheap, and ugly. The all-expenses-paid dinner had been a thin piece of frying steak with hard greasy chips. Even the bread was stale. Back in her room, Tess had pushed open the window, but the hotel—part of a modern chain—was on a main road, and the sound of hundreds of cars rushing away from her as fast as possible had made her feel so lonely and homesick that she'd hurriedly shut it again.

She had spent the night lying stiffly on her narrow bed longing for the morning. But the morning had brought nothing but a battle with a lukewarm shower and a soggy croissant, flabby with exhaustion.

Now, sitting on a plastic chair, waiting to build bridges with the French suppliers of handmade paper, Tess could think of nothing but Tetley. If I had a proper cup of tea, she thought, I'd be fine. She wanted it so badly, she could almost smell it. She wrinkled her nose, imagining the steam on her skin. This, unfortunately, reminded her that she was wearing glasses. It shouldn't matter, she thought. Of course it shouldn't matter. But when you're small, round, and curvy, and desperate to make a good first impression, covering up half your face with old black plastic isn't the obvious way to go.

The receptionist on the opposite side of the room was ignoring her. Tess wondered how long the meeting would last. It depends, she thought nervously, clutching her brown vintage leather bag (big enough for a gas mask), on whether they know any English. If we're relying on what I can say in French, it's all going to be over in a few minutes. Sweat was sticking her dress to her back. I feel such *responsibility*. Everyone at Daisy Greenleaf is *relying* on me to get this right. You could say that people's jobs are *depending* on the way I handle this meeting. This filled her with such acute terror that her heart started racing.

On impulse, Tess pushed her glasses to the top of her head. Immediately, the room became comfortingly vague. Colors softened. Objects disappeared. She couldn't even see the receptionist.

Sometimes, thought Tess, reality is much too frightening.

There was a sudden commotion. One minute she was sitting on her hard plastic chair daydreaming. The next, all these people were standing in front of her in a corporate blur. Startled, she shot to her feet. This was it. Time for bridge-building.

"*Bonjour,*" said Tess, holding out her hand.

The president of the French paper company was a very small man—only a little bit taller than she was. That much Tess could see. But she was too shortsighted to make out much more than short dark hair, a white shirt, and a black jacket. Jacques Marceau. That was his name. Jacques Marceau.

She was still holding his hand. She tightened her grip.

"*Je suis très contente de vous rencontrer,*" she said. *Rencontrer*? Did that mean "meet"? It might mean something completely different. Like "hate." Or "kill." Tess's heart banged uncomfortably. A moment ago, all the French words she had ever known had been lined up in front of her, like birds on a wire. But now in a flash, just like birds, they flew off. No, no, she called. Come back! How can I conduct high-level negotiations if you disappear? I don't think *rencontrer* is right. Try again. Try again. She took a deep breath. "*Je suis très contente de faire votre connaissance,*" she said. And then quickly, because she knew the French were sticklers for politeness, "*Monsieur.*" She added, for good measure, "*Bonjour.*" And then, still shaking his hand, "*Bonjour, Monsieur.*"

Sweat trickled down her spine. There were so many people standing in front of her. Five, at least. But none of them said anything. Puzzled, she relaxed her grip. Her hand was smartly released.

Tess reached up and pulled her glasses down from the top of her head. She blinked. The room sprang back into focus.

Standing in front of her was a small woman in a white shirt and black jacket. Behind her, struggling not to laugh, was the receptionist.

"Good morning," said the small woman. "My name is Dominique Borel. I am the company lawyer. Shall we remind ourselves of the terms of our contract?"

. . .

"So do we start or what?" said Mo.

George didn't answer.

"George?"

They were sitting under a brick arch in the semidarkness of a small jazz club. The walls smelt of damp. This particular club, George had been assured, had a reputation for offering a warm welcome to visiting musicians. Unfortunately, no one had told the punters. Or perhaps Parisians didn't like jazz on Tuesdays. Or perhaps it was too late. Or too early. An elderly man sat in the corner, reading a newspaper. Otherwise, it was completely deserted.

Mo looked furious. The club owner had called his drum kit *la batterie,* thought George. That fits. Assault and battery.

"What we could do," said Rhys, "is treat it more like a rehearsal. Not bother about who's listening. Play for ourselves."

"We could've done that in London," said Mo.

There was an ugly silence. For a moment, tired of struggling with the feeling of hopelessness that threatened to overwhelm him, George fantasized about standing up and walking out. He had screwed up. This was his fault.

"I don't know about the rest of you," said Rhys, "but I'm looking forward to telling them back home."

"Telling them what?" said Walter.

"That I played in the same club as Charlie Parker when he made his Paris debut in 1949."

"Was this Charlie Parker's club?" said Mo, impressed.

"I've no idea," said Rhys. "But who's going to know?"

Al Haig, thought George. He was the piano player in 1949.

"George?" said Walter.

George straightened up. With a huge effort of will, he pushed away the black demons of failure. This was his band. He was responsible. So he played the first seven notes of "Oh, Lady Be Good!"

Rhys, on the double bass, joined in. Mo picked up the rhythm. Then Walter, on the sax, found the tune.

When George took them off in a different direction, following the new rhythm that arrived with purposeful stealth, like a cat in a dark alleyway, there was no hesitation.

The old man in the corner put down his newspaper. He looked up. He listened.

. . .

"You don't look too happy," said Colin as he took his plastic cup of cappuccino.

It was a Wednesday morning, full of spring promise. But Tess was the picture of misery.

"I'm sorry I haven't been bringing you your coffee," said Tess. "I've been away."

"Anywhere nice?"

She bit her lip.

"You can talk to me," said Colin, squinting up into the early sunshine. "Who am I going to tell?" He looked particularly tired that morning.

"They sent me to Paris to sort something out," said Tess. "But I made it much worse. So I think I'm going to be fired today."

Colin pulled his dirty black coat more closely around him. "How old are you?"

"I'm twenty-three."

Colin shook his head.

"I'm sorry," said Tess. "I shouldn't be burdening you with all this."

"What can you sort out when you're twenty-three? You've only just been born."

"They trusted me," said Tess, "and I blew it."

"What it sounds like to me," said Colin, "is that they sent someone very young to do their dirty work."

When you're sixty, or seventy, or whatever Colin is, thought Tess as she climbed the stairs to the office, people like me must seem very young. She stopped in the tiny toilet on the first landing. She wanted to comb her hair and make herself look presentable, as if a smooth parting would stop the axe from falling. Her face, in the mirror, looked back calmly. Oh, thank goodness the spare contact lenses arrived in the post, she thought. I couldn't bear to be fired wearing glasses.

"Morning," said Glenda, quivering with anticipation. "So how did it go?"

"Has he said anything?"

"Who?"

"Mr. Bankes."

"I haven't seen him," said Glenda. "He was working at home yesterday. So go on then. What happened?"

"Oh, Glenda," said Tess, her eyes filling with tears.

"What is it?" said Glenda, shocked.

"Tess?"

Tess swung round. There, filling the doorway with his healthy rotundity, was Oliver Bankes, founder and managing director of Daisy Greenleaf Designs.

"Oh," said Tess faintly.

"Do you have a moment?"

"But what happened?" hissed Glenda as Oliver turned and left the office. "Did you build bridges?"

No, thought Tess, scrambling to follow him. I blew them up.

"Shut the door, would you?" said Oliver.

The click of the catch seemed very final. They both sat down, facing each other over Oliver's enormous desk.

"So, how do you think it went?" said Oliver.

"It could have gone better," said Tess, wretchedly.

"Projection and evaluation," said Oliver. "That's the secret of business. Work out where you want to be and then, when you've got there, take a moment to look round and see whether you've achieved your objectives."

"Yes," said Tess.

"Like a mountaineer on top of Everest," said Oliver. "Master of all he surveys."

Tess bowed her head like a whipped dog.

"So," said Oliver, "let's do this as an exercise. What did you want to achieve when you went to Paris?"

"Mr. Bankes—"

He put up his hand. "As an exercise. As a useful exercise."

Tess said, miserably, "I wanted to build bridges."

"Excellent," said Oliver. "Excellent. There was a dispute. Each side had dug in. We needed to reach out and establish a dialogue. Do you think you achieved that?"

"I couldn't see—" said Tess, desperately.

"—how to achieve this?" said Oliver. "But you did nonetheless."

Tess stared at him.

"Now obviously, we still have to sort out the detail. But what you achieved, Tess, was a rapport. A rapprochement."

"A rapprochement? Is that what they said?"

"I spoke to the company lawyer yesterday."

"Oh," said Tess, hot with embarrassment.

"You obviously hit it off with her. She was telling me all about it. Laughing away. Said you had an unusual way of looking at things."

Tess suffered an acute memory of standing there, shaking hands, calling the diminutive Dominique Borel *Monsieur*.

"So overall I would say that was very well done." He narrowed his eyes, studying her thoughtfully, as if she'd turned into a valuable Old Master. "Carry on like this, Tess, and I think your future at Daisy Greenleaf Designs will be a particularly happy one."

Tess was bewildered. Had they got out of the contract? Or was Oliver going to pay up for handmade paper they couldn't sell?

"Do you understand what I'm saying?" said Oliver Bankes, leaning forwards over his gigantic desk.

"Yes," said Tess, who didn't.

"The sky's the limit, Tess. The sky's the limit."

• • •

"For a second gig," said Rhys, "that went pretty well, I think."

The band was back in the studio flat. Walter, taking up the whole of the sofa bed—which filled nearly all the available floor space—was asleep. Mo was smoking a cigarette out of the window, dropping ash on the white rug. Rhys and George, propped up against the wall, were drinking red wine out of small white coffee cups. They were on their second bottle. The first one had disappeared very quickly.

"It wasn't easy," said George.

"I'd agree with you there," said Rhys.

"More of a strip club, really."

"Was that what it was? I did wonder."

"I wasn't sure they were listening," said George.

"Well, it's a bit distracting, isn't it?" said Rhys. "When there are lots of pretty girls with their tops off."

"Dancing round poles," said George.

They fell into a reflective silence.

"Well, we've got another night lined up, haven't we?" said Rhys. "On Thursday."

"I hope it's a better place."

"Well, look at it this way," said Rhys. "It couldn't be worse."

George tried to focus on Rhys's face through a comfortable haze of alcohol.

"I mean there's no point in being negative, is there?" said Rhys. "You just make yourself miserable. That's what I'm always saying to Gareth. No point crying yourself to sleep every night. I mean, Kirsty's a lovely girl. But she's not the only one in the world."

"Kirsty?" said George.

"Long black hair," said Rhys. "Lives in Brixton. With Tess."

"Who's Tess?"

"You know Tess. She was at Lauren's party."

"Was she?" said George.

"Oh, for fuck's sake," said Mo.

George squinted in his direction.

"Tonight was shite," said Mo, his orange hair standing up in peaks. He looked like a flaming match. "We could've made more money busking."

George felt a wave of misery flood through him. Mo was right. The whole Paris trip had been a fiasco. And he was responsible. He'd been so sure this was the right move. A few nights in Paris, the jazz capital of Europe. It would make their reputations. Establish them as a band to watch. Instead, so far, they'd played first to an empty club and then to a group of middle-aged businessmen salivating over French strippers. George felt himself sinking into a drunken depression. Maybe he'd got everything wrong. Maybe they weren't good enough. Maybe they were playing the wrong kind of music. I don't know how you keep getting up again when everyone keeps knocking you down, he thought. No one's listening but you just keep playing. You've got to be mad—optimistic to the point of delusion. Or you've got to have something inside you that says, I don't care, I don't care what everyone else thinks. I'm going to do it anyway.

Someone once asked Thelonious Monk for advice. He said, I say, play your own way. Don't play what the public wants. You play what you want and let the public pick up on what you're doing. Even if it does take them fifteen or twenty years.

Mo flicked ash in the direction of the window. "We could do it now."

"Do what?" said George.

"It's the middle of the night," said Rhys. "You can't go out busking in the middle of the night."

"Why not?" said Mo. "There's folk about."

"Walter's asleep," said George.

Mo blew out a cloud of smoke. He looked like a dragon.

"I thought I might get up early tomorrow," said Rhys, "and go to the Café de Flore. That's where Sartre wrote his novels. Pen in one hand, cup of coffee in the other."

"Cigarette in another," said George.

"The great existentialist," said Rhys.

Mo picked up his coat. "I've had enough of this."

"Enough of what?"

"This geriatric conversation. Right in the middle of Paris, and all you can do is sleep."

George tried, and failed, to see Mo's face.

"Dinnae wait up," said Mo.

"Where are you going?"

To George's astonishment, Mo started jumping up and down in front of the window.

"Don't do that," said Rhys. "You'll wake the people downstairs."

Mo stared at his feet.

"What is it?" said George, his heart sinking.

"She won't mind a wee hole in the carpet, will she?" said Mo.

• • •

"Because what I'm suddenly realizing," said Tess, "for the very first time, is that I might actually be quite good at it. By mistake, really. I didn't think I was cut out for business. I didn't think I could do negotiations and deals. I thought you had to be like Dominic—you know, brilliant with figures and spreadsheets. And a business degree. But maybe it's something you just have a knack for. Like being musical. You're just born with it. Because he's so pleased with me. Really pleased. He's already given me a new title. I'm not assistant to the customer services manager anymore. I'm assistant customer services manager. And he's hinting, although he can't really come out and say it, that there's a strong possibility this could lead to promotion once Glenda leaves. Which would be incredible really when you think about it. Can you imagine? Those kind of offers don't come along very often."

Kirsty, who had been standing on her head, brought herself back down to the ground with a graceful stretch of both legs. "I thought you hated your job," she said.

Tess looked at her.

"I thought you wanted to throw it all in and open a vintage clothes shop in Brixton."

"That was just a dream," said Tess.

"A dream?"

"Well, it's not very realistic, is it?"

"Why?"

"I don't know anything about retail."

"You're selling stationery," said Kirsty.

"I work in customer services."

"Exactly."

"I don't know anything about opening a shop."

"You can learn."

"You don't understand," said Tess. "Because you've never had a job for more than five minutes. I'm on a career path. It would be stupid to throw it away."

"You're sounding like Dominic," said Kirsty.

"I think we should stop talking about this now," said Tess.

"Why? Because I'm getting too close to the truth?"

"No."

"What then?"

Tess raised her chin as if she would rather die than say another word.

"All I'm saying," said Kirsty, "is that being good at something doesn't mean you have to spend your whole life doing it. Shakespeare might have been good at growing potatoes for all we know. But I think we're all quite glad he concentrated on *Romeo and Juliet*."

"You're very tough sometimes," said Tess in a small voice.

"Tough?" said Kirsty, doubling over to hold her ankles. "I'm not tough. I just state the obvious."

• • •

George couldn't stop grinning. Because they wouldn't stop clapping. The club—a black cavern of a place—was big enough to hold a couple of hundred people, and they were all on their feet, whistling and shouting. Eventually, when he felt he ought to do something, George stood up and said,

"Thank you, thank you," which made the applause get even louder. Overwhelmed, he sat down again, the noise ringing in his ears. Now the club owner, a small dark man with a thin moustache, came onstage and took the microphone. He spoke in French, gesturing to each of the musicians in turn, pausing for more applause. Then he put the mike back on the stand and started clapping himself, turning to face them, and everyone in the audience was cheering and shouting as if they were going to carry on forever.

George looked over at his bandmates. Rhys and Walter looked bewildered, like window-shoppers unexpectedly caught up in a violent street protest. But Mo, his hair a hot flame under the stage lights, was reveling in it. Smiling from ear to ear, he gave George the thumbs-up.

"So, it's good?" said the club owner, putting his hand on George's shoulder.

The audience had settled back down at the tables, laughing and talking.

"Yes," said George. He felt like running round the club yelling and screaming and waving his arms in the air.

"You know there is a man from the newspaper," said the owner.

"A reviewer?" said Mo.

"He like the band. He is happy."

"You see," said Mo, "I always said it would come right."

"So you stay in Paris?" said the owner.

George said, "We have to get back. We're playing in London on Saturday."

"But you will come here again."

George nodded happily.

"And you stay and have a drink?" said the owner.

At the bar, Walter was standing next to a very pretty girl with braided hair and silver bangles. She had her hand on his arm.

"They always go for the sax player," said Mo. "No taste, any of them."

"Have you ever had a girlfriend?" said Rhys.

"Very funny," said Mo.

"Seriously. Because I've never seen you with anyone."

"I have a life outside the band," said Mo. "I don't spend all my time hanging round with you." He banged his hand on the bar, trying to get the barman's attention.

George looked up at the wall behind the bar. It was covered in black-and-white prints of famous jazz players. Will that be us one day? he thought. His mind drifted to his father, imagining him in the dusty house in Surrey drinking his single malt. I must ring him. I must ring him and tell him that Paris loved us.

"I was having an interesting conversation with Kirsty the other night," said Rhys. "About true love. Tess thinks everyone's born half a person. Half a soul. And then you spend the rest of your life searching for the other piece to make you whole. Very romantic."

"Oi, big man!" shouted Mo to Walter. "Tell the barman to get himself over here."

"But then she's a lovely girl," said Rhys, "as you know."

"I dinnae fucking believe it," said Mo.

Walter was walking back towards them. Behind him, the girl with the braids was staring after him with a glassy, shocked expression as if he'd just slapped her cheek.

"You turned her down?" said Mo.

Walter gave a little shake of his head as if he didn't want to talk about it.

"You turned her down?" said Mo again.

Walter looked at him. "I'm married."

"So?"

Walter turned away, disgusted.

"What?" said Mo.

"Leave it," said Rhys in a low voice.

"Leave what?" said Mo.

"You never get it, do you?" said Walter. "I miss them. I miss them both. I haven't seen my son for three days."

"It's not like he's gonnae disappear," said Mo. "He'll be there when you get back."

Walter glared at Mo with such intense fury that George put a hand on his arm. Walter shook him off.

"Take no notice of him," said Rhys.

"What's your problem?" said Walter, looking at Mo as if he wanted to hit him.

"There's no problem with me."

"You think this is all a joke," said Walter, still staring at Mo. "A big laugh. Well, it isn't. This isn't something I do just to piss away a few hours. I don't have a few hours. I work all the fucking time. And any time I'm not working, I want to be with my family. So this is serious. I'm not here to get out of my head. I'm not here to get laid. If that's what you want, fine. You go ahead. There's the whole of Paris out there. But you leave me alone. Because that's not why I'm here."

Mo, for once, was silenced.

"I think we're all a bit tired, to tell you the truth," said Rhys. "Maybe it's time to go back to the flat. What do you think, George?"

But George wasn't listening.

Walter's right, he thought. This is serious. Tonight was good. But the other two nights were a waste of time. The only way for the band to make it is to get the right people listening to us. I've got to find out where they are. I've got to get us into the places where they understand what we're doing.

Because, underneath it all, he had the sinking feeling that Walter had just delivered an ultimatum.

. . .

"She isn't pregnant," said Kirsty.

"How do you know?"

"I asked her."

Tess looked at Kirsty in horror. "When?"

"Just now."

"I can't believe you did that," said Tess.

They were standing in a queue at the wedding reception in Dorset, waiting to pick up their first glass of champagne. Behind them was the receiving line—Lily's parents, Tim's parents, a rather dazed-looking Tim, and a radiant, but not impregnated, Lily.

"Why else would you get married when you're twenty-three?" said Kirsty.

"Because you're in love?"

Kirsty frowned. "People in love don't get married. People who want babies get married. Or people who've been together so long they feel they ought to."

"How do you know?"

"Observation."

"You're the one who said the secret to happiness was finding the person who made you feel good," said Tess.

"I didn't say you had to marry them."

Kirsty was wearing a fuchsia-pink dress and black high-heeled shoes. She'd put her hair up under a black hat made of feathers and fine net, and you could see every angle of her face—the high cheekbones, the smooth forehead, the beautifully straight nose. As she stood, coolly surveying the crowd, you could imagine her being snapped by world-famous photographers, or standing on the catwalk, pausing for the rapturous applause of the front row. But Kirsty herself didn't seem to notice everyone staring at her openmouthed. She wasn't that interested in people who were drawn to her because of her looks. She ignored them. Tess loved that about her.

"George is playing today," said Kirsty.

"I know," said Tess. "You've told me three times already." She glanced back down the line at Dominic, who was shaking hands with Lily's father.

Tess wasn't enjoying herself as much as she thought she would. Lauren had given them all a lift from London in her brand-new Ford Fiesta—Ellie in the front, Tess sandwiched between Dominic and Kirsty in the back—and there had been a strange atmosphere all the way, as if someone had been diagnosed with a horrible illness no one was allowed to mention. They had arrived only in the nick of time—a combination of Saturday-morning traffic and getting lost behind hedgerows in Dorset—and had crept into the old stone church just as the bride arrived. Ellie, normally so laid-back, seemed tense and distracted. When Tess handed her the order of service, she had looked at it in some surprise, as if it was a set of instructions for a flat-pack wardrobe or a flyer advertising knife sharpening.

The ceremony had been endearingly simple. The wooden pews, which smelt of candle wax and old prayer books, were decorated with cornflowers and meadowsweet, and the dusty stone floor was smudged red and blue where the sun shone through the stained glass. Lily's wedding dress, made of silk and old lace (as Kirsty said later, not a meringue in sight), made her look delicate and very young. After the vows, the vicar, beaming from ear to ear, said, "Shall we give them a round of applause?" and everyone clapped. You could feel the relief—it was done, the promises were made, and the lovers were united. One small bridesmaid, quite overcome at the release of tension, sat down suddenly in the aisle, her dress, a puff of organza, collapsing round her like a parachute.

The reception was held in the grounds of a local country

mansion. Back in Lauren's new car, they swept up a graveled drive bordered by elm and ash, with gardens and fields stretching out on all sides as far as the eye could see, and there in front of them, its yellow ocher façade catching the afternoon sun, was a Georgian manor house so huge that for a moment, stunned by its beauty, no one said a word.

Kirsty stared out of the car window. "I sometimes wonder," she said, "what it must be like to live in a place like this."

"Quite frustrating, I should think," said Lauren, "if the only way you can make ends meet is to rent it out for weddings."

"Maybe I'll have to marry it," said Kirsty. "I won't inherit it, and I'll never be able to pay for it, so it might be the only option."

"Kirsty!" said Tess, shocked. Kirsty laughed.

"She's gone back in time," said Lauren. "To a Jane Austen novel."

Ellie, staring straight ahead, said nothing at all.

A young man in a black suit directed them to a field at the back of the house where thirty or forty cars were already lined up in neat rows, taking up just one tiny corner, like initials on a handkerchief.

Tess looked down at her pretty print tea dress (hand-sewn from a Butterick pattern, circa 1944) and wondered, with a hot rush of shame, whether she looked horribly shabby.

Inside the big white tent were huge blue and green floral displays, fanned out like the tail feathers of peacocks. Tess, holding her champagne, was standing on tiptoe trying to find her name on the enormous seating plan when Dominic appeared beside her.

"We're on table sixteen," he said. "Come on."

"Are we sitting with anyone we know?"

But Dominic, taking her hand, was already leading the way. Tess, trotting along behind him, felt about six years old.

There was a string quartet playing. As Tess stumbled past the cello player, who had the sad expression of an abandoned bloodhound, she wondered for a moment when the band would start. But maybe they won't, she thought. Maybe Kirsty got it wrong. She felt a small slump of disappointment.

Table sixteen was right over on the far side of the tent, a long way from the dance floor. Already seated was an overweight man of about fifty with thinning hair and a brick-red complexion. He had a white napkin tucked into his collar and was halfway through a thickly buttered bread roll.

"I think this is us," said Tess, smiling at him.

The red-faced man looked up angrily. "Who else could it be?"

The table was filling up. Tess found her name card and sat down next to an elderly gray-haired woman dressed in purple chiffon.

"Hello," she said. "I'm Tess."

"I had a dog called Tess once," said the gray-haired woman. "Went quite mad in the end. But then she never liked Basingstoke."

Tess tried to catch Dominic's eye, but he was sitting on the other side of the table, looking up at the vast dome of the tent like an amateur astronomer studying the night sky.

"So," said Tess, taking a deep breath, "have you come far today?"

Tess hadn't been to many wedding receptions. She didn't come from a big family and few friends, so far, had taken the plunge. But she decided, somewhere between the cold jellied chicken and the lemon syllabub, that wedding receptions were hard work. It might have been different if she'd been sitting near Kirsty, or Ellie, or Lauren. But she seemed to have been put on a table of people who were either deaf or socially incapacitated. "Organized walking tours provide the best of both worlds," said the tall, thin man in glasses who was sitting on her left. "You're keeping up with your general fitness levels while taking advantage of local points of interest. Of course you have to have the right footwear. And in the UK you have to expect rain. There's no point in being unrealistic."

Tess's face ached from the effort of smiling. She was just beginning to fantasize about disappearing under the table when no one was looking when the speeches began.

The best man started off with a joke about Tim's passion for jam doughnuts and a rather risqué story about his bicycle pump. Cheering and table-thumping followed the invitation to former Manchester University students to remember what happened to Tim's underwear on the charity run in the Lake District.

But then, without warning, the best man changed gear. The laughing died away. He talked about Tim meeting Lily in their second year at Manchester, and how they both knew, within weeks, that they couldn't live without each other. "They are," he said, "so clearly made for each other. They encourage each other, they support each other, they make each other laugh. Their happiness touches everyone around them. They make us understand that love is what's important, that love is what makes us into the people we want to be."

The vast tent fell silent. Tess felt her eyes filling with tears. And then the best man lifted his glass and said, "To the bride and groom," and everyone got to their feet and toasted Tim and Lily, who stood, awed and bashful, in the spotlight of public approbation.

People always say, thought Tess, you're much too young, you don't know your own mind. But you can't control when you're going to find your soul mate. If you're lucky, you find each other early. And, if you do, you have more time to spend together. You have your whole lives to get to know each other.

She looked across the table at Dominic.

The speeches continued, and there was more clapping and shouting and some tears. And then, when everyone thought it was all over, Tim's younger brother got to his feet. He stood there, swaying. His hair had flopped forwards over his forehead and his tie was undone. "What I want to say," he said indistinctly, his mouth loose, as if the words were boiled sweets he was having difficulty sucking, "what I want to say is that Lily is the right girl."

Someone shouted, "Hear, hear!" and everyone laughed.

"Because none of the others were right," he said.

There was a look of panic on Tim's face.

"And there were a lot of them," said his brother.

There was a stunned silence.

"But it's not just about the sex." He frowned. "I mean, I'm not saying Lily's no good in bed. She probably is. I mean, she looks like she is. They're probably having great sex."

Lily went bright pink.

You could have heard a pin drop.

Next to Tess, the elderly gray-haired lady in purple chiffon straightened her shoulders. "In my day," she said, "sex wasn't talked about at all."

Tess nodded, unable to speak. From what she could see of the top table, Tim's brother was being manhandled to the floor in a kind of headlock.

"I succumbed," said the elderly lady, "only when I absolutely had to for the purposes of procreation." She smoothed one of her purple sleeves. "Of course, that may be why I'm famed for my needlepoint. You can get a lot more done if you're not having sex all the time."

. . .

"Do you want a beer?" said Walter. "I don't mind driving back."

They were sitting on the black instrument cases at the back entrance of the tent, waiting to start their first set.

George looked at him.

"I'll drive us home," said Walter.

George shifted, as if easing the tension in his neck. "We said we were staying the night. Leaving tomorrow morning."

"It might be nice," said Rhys, "to have a bit of a party."

"I want to get back," said Walter. "I told Sonya I'd try to get back."

There wasn't much noise from inside the tent. The speeches seemed to have stopped.

"Where's Mo, then?" said Rhys. "It's time he was here. We're on in a few minutes."

"It might be good for business," said George, "to stay on."

"It's not going to make a lot of difference, is it," said Rhys, "whether we're back for breakfast or lunch?"

"It does if you're six years old," said Walter.

George looked down at his feet.

"Sunday's the only day we have," said Walter. "It's the only day we have together as a family."

The silence grew longer.

Walter stood up so suddenly that one of the cases fell over. He loomed large, blocking out the light. "You think I'm not committed because I want to get back and see my son."

"I didn't say that."

"But you're thinking it."

"We agreed to stay on," said George. "It's important. For the band. You know how it works. Everyone's in a good mood. You chat to them, they like you, they remember you, they give you more work."

"I want to get back," said Walter.

Rhys looked from one to the other.

"Fine," said George. "But leave us the van."

For a moment, Walter glared at him. Then he turned and walked off in the direction of the house.

"We're on in ten!" shouted Rhys.

But if Walter heard, he gave no sign.

They sat there, staring at the flattened grass.

George rubbed his forehead. "He said it was serious. In Paris, he said the band was important to him. But ever since we've been back, he's been making excuses. Couldn't do Friday night in Shoreditch. Couldn't do the new club in Peckham. Couldn't rehearse last Sunday. He didn't really want to play here, but I said we couldn't let them down."

"Maybe it's Sonya," said Rhys.

George said, "He's going to leave the band. I know it."

"You don't know it."

"I do."

"So don't push him."

"I just want him to come out and say it."

"No, you don't," said Rhys. "Once he's said it, that's the end. There's no going back."

• • •

Outside the tent, there was a sudden flurry of women and girls in wedding-guest finery—silk bows and hats and ribbons—and, in the middle of them all, Lily in a short pink dress clutching her bridal bouquet. She turned her back, holding the flowers high in the air.

"Go on, then," said Kirsty.

"I'm not going to catch it," said Tess.

"You should," said Kirsty. "You're next in line."

Tess, who might normally have come up with a cutting response, opened her mouth and shut it again.

Lily threw the bouquet. It was caught by a small girl of about five. There were pursed lips. Where was the mother? Why wasn't she controlling her child?

"Whoops," said Kirsty.

They heard the rumble of the engine before they saw the car—a dove-gray Porsche that rolled, magnificently, to a stop. Out got Tim. Everyone cheered.

"A Porsche?" said Kirsty.

"Rented," said Tess. "For the day."

"You know," said Kirsty, "Lily and Tim make marriage look almost attractive."

It was time for the bride and groom to leave. As word spread, the guests spilled out of the vast white tent, and there were hugs and kisses and tears, and then the newly married couple climbed into the car, and everyone shouted good-bye, and the engine purred loudly, like a deeply satisfied cat, and they were gone.

"That's that, then," said Kirsty.

Next to them, a short wiry man with orange hair was lighting a cigarette.

"You're Mo," said Kirsty.

Mo looked up with narrowed eyes.

"I'm Kirsty. A friend of Rhys."

"Brixton Kirsty?" said Mo.

"That's right."

"I've heard a lot about you."

Most people say, All good I hope, or, Don't believe a word of it. But Kirsty didn't bother.

"So where's George?" said Kirsty.

Tess's heart skipped a beat.

Mo shrugged. "Around. We're on in ten minutes."

"I might go and find him," said Kirsty.

"You do that," said Mo.

Mo looked after her as she sauntered back towards the tent. It was hard not to. Kirsty had a way of walking that hypnotized anyone in the immediate vicinity.

"So who are you, then?" said Mo.

"I'm Tess."

Mo frowned. "I've heard about you, too." His face cleared. "You're the one that believes in soul mates."

Tess was mortified. "Don't you?" she said, to cover her confusion.

Mo laughed and blew out a cloud of smoke. "It's a load of crap."

Tess knew, even as she opened her mouth, that it would be far more sensible to stay silent. "Why do you think it's crap?"

"Do you not know where it came from?"

"It's an old Indian legend," said Tess.

"It's from Plato," said Mo. "The *Symposium*. Ancient Greeks sitting round telling stories. One of them says, we used to be round, like bubbles, with four legs, and four arms and two faces. Three different sexes. Bobbing around like ducks on a pond. But then we got too full of ourselves and tried to gate-crash heaven. So Zeus punished us. Split us all in half. Drew the skin tight to stop us leaking. Which explains the navels. And ever since we've been wandering around looking for the other half. Women looking for women. Men looking for men. A male half looking for a female half. It's just a joke."

"A joke?" said Tess, faintly.

"That's all. A memory of complete bollocks."

Mo blew out smoke as he dropped his cigarette to the ground and stubbed it out.

"Were you at Manchester?" said Tess, as a way of filling the silence.

"I was," said Mo.

"Classics?"

"No," said Mo. "Theoretical physics."

. . .

By the time Tess had pushed her way back into the tent, the dance floor was full. She couldn't see the band, but she could hear them. Her heart lifted. It was 1940s jazz—the kind of music played by Charlie Parker and Dizzy Gillespie and Max Roach. Not swing, but bebop. She stood there, entranced. I had no idea the band played this kind of stuff, she thought. And now, in her head, she switched to old black-and-white clips of New York nightclubs with men in evening dress and women in glorious gowns that clung to their waists and hipbones and made them look at once unapproachable and wantonly desirable, and she thought, Sometimes, I wish I could go back in time. I want to live inside the films of the 1940s and wear the clothes, and drink the cocktails, and powder my nose from a mirrored compact. My grandmother says, you're forgetting about the war. No food, no hot water, everyone tired and hungry and smelling of old sweat and boiled cabbage.

But listen to the music. Listen to it.

Dominic was sitting at table sixteen with his fizzy mineral water.

"Shall we dance?" she said.

Dominic frowned.

Oh, thought Tess, I forgot. He hates dancing. I've never seen him dance. At parties, he just leans against walls looking impossibly cool. So she sat down next to him and listened to the band and daydreamed about swing dancing and girls being pulled between legs and around ribs and over shoulders so their little flared skirts flipped up and their sensible waist-high knickers were exposed, and she thought, You'd think Dominic would like dancing, really, because it's just two people moving in concert, which is the same thing as sex (which he's very good at) except that with sex you've got no clothes on, and she felt so bitter at the missed opportunity (the dancing, not the sex), and so angry that something she loved had been dismissed quite so casually, with just a disapproving frown, that she said, in a sudden rush, "Do you know what I really want to do?"

"What?" said Dominic, leaning forwards so that he could hear over the music.

"I want to open a vintage clothes shop."

"A vintage clothes shop?"

"In Brixton," said Tess.

"There's nothing wrong with having a dream," he said.

"But it's not just a dream. I could do it. I could open a shop."

He had the same expression he wore when she suggested eating spaghetti hoops on toast—incredulity mixed with a certain amount of pity.

"It's something I really care about. I love vintage clothes. I think you should spend your life doing something you're really passionate about."

Dominic smiled. "You should also think very carefully about throwing away a perfectly good career."

"But it's not what I want to do," she said, longing for him to understand.

"Glenda's going to retire soon."

"So?" said Tess, desperately.

"Have you thought about that?" said Dominic. "You could be head of customer services in a couple of years."

"But what if I don't want to be head of customer services?"

"Why wouldn't you?" said Dominic, puzzled.

Tess felt almost light-headed with misery. When she looked up, the elderly lady in the purple chiffon was beckoning at her from across the table. Tess stood up and went round to where she was sitting.

"That young man you're talking to," said the elderly lady.

"Yes?" said Tess.

"Is he yours?"

"Yes," said Tess, sadly.

"I just wanted to say," she said, "that if my husband had looked like that, I might have had sex more often."

Tess grabbed the nearest glass and was about to fill it to the brim with warm white wine when Kirsty appeared by her side. Tess's heart lurched. She only had to look at Kirsty's face to know that something was badly wrong.

"What's happened?"

"We need to go," said Kirsty.

"Go?"

"I've got someone to give us a lift back. We need to get Ellie home."

"Why? Is she ill?"

Kirsty's eyes were dark. "She asked Lauren if she was having an affair. And the stupid, stupid, stupid woman said yes."

2003

Dad?"

"Hello?"

"Dad?"

"Who's this?"

"Dad, it's George." He didn't want to add, "Your son."

"George? Everything all right?"

George found himself gripping his mobile hard as if it might slip through his fingers, crash to the floor, and break into tiny silver pieces. He said, "Fine. Everything all right with you?"

"How's your brother?"

"I don't know. I haven't spoken to him recently."

"Consultant cardiologist."

"Yes," said George.

"Job comes first. I remember it well."

So do I, thought George. He had a sharp memory of being ten or eleven, sitting alone on the brown shiny leather of the wing chair, the clock in the hall of the empty house ticking away for hour after hour after hour after hour.

"They say there'll be attacks in London," said his father. "Al-Qaeda."

"Do they?" said George, struggling to focus.

"Suicide bombers," said his father.

"I didn't know. I didn't hear that."

"In the news. In the news tonight."

You couldn't complain, of course, as the son of a surgeon, that you never saw your father. Even if he was the only parent you had. That would have been selfish.

"And what about you, Dad? Work all right?"

"Mostly private practice now," said his father.

You just sat there, in the wing chair, and waited for him to come home.

"We played in Paris," said George.

There was silence at the other end.

"It went well, I think," said George. "Particularly in the last place."

"Heat wave in Paris, of course," said his father. "Lots of people dying. Particularly the elderly. Or those with compromised immune systems."

George shut his eyes. Rage rushed through him, burning red, and then—just as suddenly—disappeared. He said, "I'll try and come down soon."

"Well, you know where I am," said his father.

For a long time after the call ended, George sat and stared into space. It happened every time. He would think of his father and feel sorry. So he would ring him. And then he would wish he hadn't. He would be left with this feeling of nothingness, of not existing, as if his body was a shell with the person inside sucked out. His father blotted out his reality. His father erased him. His father deleted him.

George shivered. His hands were very cold. There was a pain twisting in his gut.

. . .

"Walked out?" said Tess.

Kirsty shrugged.

"I don't believe it," said Tess. "You were only there a week."

"Believe me," said Kirsty, "that was quite long enough."

"What happened?"

"Hmm," said Kirsty, pretending to consider, "was it the hand down my bra or asking me if I liked it up the arse?"

"Oh, Kirsty," said Tess, shocked.

"It's all right. I made him pay me an extra week. I said I'd made secret recordings of everything he'd said and I'd post them to his wife."

"I'm so sorry. I thought men like him had disappeared."

"Men like him will never disappear," said Kirsty. "They're always around. Like thrush. Or athlete's foot."

"So what are you going to do now?"

"Find something else. There's always another bar."

Tess, who was halfway through chopping an onion, paused to wipe her eyes. "What about looking for something different?"

"Like what?"

"Well, something that suits you better."

Kirsty picked up a stick of celery and brushed the leaves against her hand. "I'm all ears."

"What about an art gallery?"

Kirsty frowned. "Why?"

"Because you're always going to exhibitions, and it's something you know about." Tess looked at her beautiful friend, leaning against the battered kitchen worktop like a butterfly on a rubbish tip. "And because you're a bit like a work of art yourself."

"Well, thank you. But I don't think that's the reason they employ gallery assistants."

"Isn't it?" said Tess.

"I'm not sure I'm ready for a proper job. How do you do a serious day's work if you've been out all night?"

"I don't suppose," said Tess, "you could chop up a few potatoes, could you?"

Kirsty straightened up and looked round vaguely for a knife. "Is Ellie definitely coming?"

"I don't know," said Tess. "Last night she said she wasn't. But she rang me this afternoon and said she was. So I've got no idea."

"She doesn't seem to be getting any better."

"It was true love," said Tess.

"Women beware women," said Kirsty. She had found a knife, and was now wandering round the kitchen. "Who else apart from Rhys?"

"I do love Rhys. I can't believe there was a time when I didn't know him."

"You have to trust me," said Kirsty, opening a cupboard, "to introduce you to all the right people. So who's coming?"

"Akash. And your new boyfriend."

"Oh yes," said Kirsty. "I'd forgotten about Rudolf Nureyev. But not Dominic?"

"You know not Dominic," said Tess. "He's on his training weekend." She looked up. "What are you looking for?"

"The potatoes."

"They're in the basket."

"Oh."

"They're always in the basket."

"How would I know?" said Kirsty. "I never cook anything." Then she said, casually, "Could this meal stretch to one more person?"

"I suppose so," said Tess. "If we give everyone a bit less. And put lots of cheese on top. Why? Have you asked someone else?"

"Yes," said Kirsty. "I thought it was time you met George."

"George?"

"Your soul mate."

"I wish you'd stop saying that." Tess glanced up at the clock. "Have I got time for a quick shower?"

Kirsty laughed. The doorbell rang. Tess looked at Kirsty in panic.

"Go on," said Kirsty. "Go and get ready. I'll entertain Akash. Or my ballet dancer. Or your soul mate."

This is ridiculous, thought Tess, as she ran up the stairs to her attic bedroom. It's *pathetic*. It's *childish*. Why do I even *care* that George is coming? It's because Kirsty has built him up into this mystical ideal. She's painted a picture of romantic perfection. I'll probably hate him. He'll burp loudly or drink too much or smell of old socks. He'll have extreme views about education or recycling or dangerous dogs. He may even like Tom Cruise. For all I know, he's one huge joke that Kirsty has been building up for months because she *knows* I'll hate him, she *knows* he's someone I wouldn't touch with a barge pole, and she'll just sit there laughing the whole evening, watching the expression of horror on my face. Which would be *fine,* Tess thought hastily, because I don't even *want* to like him, because I love Dominic, and have done for years, and I can't think of anyone I want to be with more.

She stood in front of the mirror, panting. Her face was quite pink. Oh, look at my hair, she thought miserably. It's gone all crinkly because I didn't dry it properly this morning. She rubbed a smudge of black mascara from underneath her left eye. I'll get changed. I'll put on my black dress (rayon crepe with fitted waist, label Lo Roco, circa 1944) and some red lipstick. Lipstick always makes it look like you've made an effort. Not that it *matters,* she reminded herself, as she fastened the narrow belt and smoothed down the skirt. I don't need to impress *anybody*.

But when she was pulling on some rather beautiful sheer stockings, she was so cack-handed with nerves that she ripped a ladder from ankle to knee.

"You look nice," said Kirsty as Tess walked into the kitchen, heart fit to burst. "This is Tom. Just started dancing with the English National Ballet."

"Oh," said Tess, trying to pin an expression of great interest on her face but finding that the extreme emotion of not meeting George had produced, instead, a sort of agonized grimace.

"Are you all right?" said Kirsty. "You look a bit flustered."

"I'm fine," said Tess. "I'm just a bit worried about the cooking."

"I would help," said Tom, "but I've broken a bone in my foot. I can't really stand for lengthy periods."

"Oh no," said Tess. "And you're a dancer."

"That's how he did it," said Kirsty. "Landing from a grand jeté."

"I went to three different casualty departments," said Tom, "before they diagnosed it correctly. I didn't even get an X-ray until I told them I was in agony day and night."

"I tell you what, Tom," said Kirsty. "I think we ought to pour Tess a glass of wine and let her get on with it."

"Teaching hospitals, too," said Tom. "Major London teaching hospitals. You do wonder what's happening to the NHS."

"Red or white?" said Kirsty.

Tess had just taken a welcome glug of wine when the doorbell rang again. She jumped so violently that most of the contents of her glass slopped onto the floor.

"Are you sure you're OK?"

"The neighbors," said Tess. "They're going to be so disturbed with all this coming and going."

"It will remind them of their youth," said Kirsty, "before they had all those children."

It's not ideal, thought Tess, hastily heating oil in a pan, having to meet new people when you smell of fried onions. But we're not going to eat anything tonight if I don't get on with it.

"Tess!" said Akash. "The love of my life! The woman I adore! How are you?" And Tess felt herself being gathered up into a huge bear hug.

Akash, who had met Tess in one of their first history lectures at Manchester (he had leant over with an expression of panic and said in a stage whisper, "But who the hell is Charlemagne?"), was short and stocky with a physique that managed to look both muscular and fleshy. He was famous for doing everything to excess—sex, alcohol, seafood, partying, chocolate, debt, flattery, and cocaine. There was, apparently, a billionaire father in Munich who asked no questions and paid off his credit card at the end of every term. But Tess wondered how much of it was true. He had, after all, been the only one of her friends to get a first-class degree, which would have needed hours of late-night study, a clear head, and an intimate acquaintance with university libraries. And once, years ago, she had called round to see him unexpectedly and found him in a tartan dressing gown and bed socks listening to Elgar's "Nimrod."

"Mmm," he said, leaning over the pan. "So what are you rustling up for supper tonight?"

"Shepherd's pie," she said. "The vegetarian version. In your honor."

It had been a relief, with Dominic away for the weekend, to cook something easy.

"Shepherd's pie!" said Akash. "Food of the gods!"

"Glass of wine?" said Kirsty, coming into the kitchen.

"Well, do you know," said Akash, "I think I might. Just this once."

"You are a complete fraud," said Kirsty. "Come and meet Tom. He's a ballet dancer."

"How splendid. Where did you find him?"

"Backstage at *The Nutcracker*."

"All tights and torso?" said Akash.

"Hands off," said Kirsty. "He's mine."

The doorbell rang again.

"Shall I go?" said Akash.

"I don't suppose," said Tom, appearing in the kitchen doorway, "you have any ice?"

"You're drinking wine," said Kirsty, "not gin."

"For my foot," he said. "I think it's a little swollen."

Kirsty disappeared to open the front door.

Tess, overwhelmed, said desperately, "Why don't you go and sit down and I'll bring you some?"

"And a footstool," said Tom, "so that I can put my leg up. That's what the physios say. Always raise your leg when you're sitting down."

Tess was straining to hear who had arrived in the hall below.

"It's so difficult," said Tom. "You need to keep moving. But at the same time you have to let the body heal. It's a matter of finding the right balance between rest and exercise."

"I know what you mean," said Akash. "There are days when I'm completely torn."

There were footsteps on the stairs. "That's because there aren't any women in *The Two Towers*," said Kirsty, coming into the kitchen.

"Oh, Ellie!" said Tess, turning round, wooden spoon in hand. "You came!"

If Ellie normally looked like a young boy strolling through the sun-dappled English countryside, she was now the picture of a waif from a Dickens novel. Her skin was gray. There were dark circles under her eyes.

"Ellie!" said Akash, enveloping her in a hug. "The love of my life! The woman I adore!"

Tears filled Ellie's eyes.

"Put her down," said Kirsty. "She needs a drink. Red or white?"

"I don't suppose I could have some ice, could I?" said Tom.

"Are you OK?" said Tess to Ellie.

"Sort of," said Ellie, shakily.

"How's the new flat?"

"It's quite nice, in a strange sort of way. I don't know any of them, so they leave me alone."

"She's renting a room in Stockwell," said Kirsty to Akash.

"St. Ockwell, as we prefer to call it," said Akash. "You can make most parts of south London sound a lot nicer with just a tiny bit of effort. Like Penge," he said, putting on a French accent.

"Dominic likes Penge," said Tess. "He says it's up-and-coming."

"Well, it might be," said Akash, "but can any of us wait that long?"

"I'm feeling a bit light-headed," said Tom. "I think I should go and sit down."

"You do that," said Kirsty.

"It might be nice," said Tess bravely, "if you all went and sat down. There isn't really enough room to cook with everyone in the kitchen."

"Well, really," said Akash. "How to make your guests feel welcome."

"After all," said Kirsty, "I did tidy up the living room today. Sort of."

"But, Ellie," said Tess, "could you stay and give me a hand?"

Akash tapped his nose conspiratorially. "Girl talk. Come on, Tom, they can't wait to get us out of the kitchen so they can discuss us."

"I'm a girl," said Kirsty. "Don't I count?"

"Yes, you do," said Akash, as if talking to a child. "You've got a degree in maths."

. . .

Once she and Ellie were alone, Tess carefully tipped chopped celery and carrots into the pan and said, "So how are you really?"

"I don't know," said Ellie. "I don't think I can feel anything anymore."

"Have you heard from her?"

Ellie nodded miserably. "She keeps leaving me messages. Saying we've got to talk. But what's the point?"

Tess looked at her. "You can't forgive her."

"No," said Ellie, and it was so final that Tess could see the words THE END written in the air. She moved the pan off the heat and came and sat down next to Ellie at the kitchen table.

"I'm sorry, Ells. I really am."

Ellie looked up, her mouth trembling. "I thought it was forever. I said to her, you know I love you completely, don't you? You can't ever leave me, because if you do I'll fall apart." Tears ran down her cheeks. "And she said, why would I ever leave you? You're everything I've ever wanted. And I thought she meant it. I thought she was telling the truth."

"She was," said Tess.

"So what went wrong? Why did she find someone else?"

"I don't know," said Tess. She leant out and took Ellie's hand. "The only person who can tell you is Lauren."

"No," said Ellie.

"Maybe not now," said Tess. "But in a while. You've got to talk sometime."

"I can't," said Ellie.

"What about all your stuff? Is it still in the flat?"

"It doesn't seem important."

Tess nodded. Part of her wanted to say, Maybe it was just a fling. A momentary lapse. Maybe this other woman doesn't mean anything at all and Lauren still loves you with all her heart and soul. But she wasn't quite sure she believed this. She had never forgotten the conversation with Lauren at the party about soul mates. She had thought about it again and again, half-fascinated, half-horrified by Lauren's cool analysis. If I hadn't met Ellie, Lauren had said, I would have met someone else. There's no such thing as soul mates. Love is about habit and shared memories. If that's what you believe, thought Tess, maybe it isn't that hard to end one relationship and start another. You just pick up the axe, swing it round your head, and let it fall.

She said, "Do you want me to go round? I could pick up your clothes, at least. You can't carry on in other people's cast-offs."

Ellie smiled in a wobbly kind of way. "*You* do."

"That's different," said Tess. "That's vintage."

"I don't want you to have to take sides. That wouldn't be fair."

"Lauren would understand," said Tess. "I knew you way before I met her. She'd know I'd want to look after you."

"But you wouldn't talk to her," said Ellie.

"Not if you didn't want me to."

"I don't want anyone talking to her."

"I promise."

Ellie said, her voice all broken up with tears, "The worst thing is that I keep going over and over everything that happened. I keep thinking, What did I do wrong? Yes, we were arguing. But no more than anyone else. Just stupid things like where to go at the weekend and the pink lampshade on the landing and buying monkfish. Nothing serious. I didn't think she was unhappy. I would have seen it if she was unhappy. So maybe she just stopped loving me. Or maybe I changed. Perhaps she started to see me as I really am. And she didn't like what she saw."

Tess said, "It isn't your fault. You keep trying to blame yourself, and there's nothing to blame yourself for."

"But I love her," said Ellie, crying.

"Do you need a hand in here?" said Kirsty, coming into the kitchen.

Tess looked up, her eyes full of tears.

"Ellie, my love," said Kirsty, "let's go and get you cleaned up. Then I'm going to make you a cup of black coffee. I don't know why, but you can't cry when you're drinking black coffee."

"I've got to do some cooking," said Tess, suddenly realizing that all she had done so far was fry a few vegetables and put the peeled potatoes in water.

"Or I could do the cooking and you could go and talk to Tom," said Kirsty.

"That bad?" said Tess.

"Bored, bored, bored."

"So he won't be moving in, then?"

"If he moves in," said Kirsty, "I move out."

Once she was on her own again, Tess whipped around

the kitchen as if she were on wheels, and managed to get everything in the oven in record time. She grated extra cheese, made a salad dressing, and refilled the grinder with black peppercorns. She put on the kettle for Ellie's coffee, and was just about to skid through to the living room at the front of the house to ask if anyone wanted more wine (Oh, she thought, I completely forgot about ice for Tom's foot) when the doorbell rang.

George.

"Akash!" she shouted.

No one answered. And Kirsty was still mopping up Ellie in the bathroom.

Tess took a deep breath. She opened the ugly front door of the flat (white plywood with peeling paint) and walked very slowly down the stairs, holding firmly on to the banister. When she reached the bottom, a small red plastic tricycle skidded to a halt. Brown eyes looked up at her.

"Hello!" she said.

The little boy stared. Through the stained glass of the front door she could see the outline of a figure.

"I'm going to open the door," she said to the small boy. Or perhaps to herself.

When the cold night air hit her, she found herself facing a bunch of pink carnations.

"Tess!" said Rhys. "You look shocked. Weren't you expecting me?"

"Of course," said Tess in a high voice. "Come in."

"I'm afraid I've got bad news. George won't be coming."

"Oh?"

"Terribly ill. No way he could come."

"Oh dear," said Tess, shutting the front door.

"Food poisoning, I think," said Rhys. "Hasn't got off the toilet since lunchtime."

Tess, turning towards the stairs, found herself falling headlong onto the brown and orange tiles. She lay there, winded. On its side, wheels spinning, was the small red plastic tricycle. For one horrible moment, Tess thought she'd landed on top of the small boy and flattened him. She sat up. Her wrist hurt. One of her brand-new stockings had a gaping hole.

"Are you all right?" said Rhys.

"I think so," she said.

"Here, let me give you a hand," he said, putting his hands under both elbows and pulling her up to standing. "Who does that belong to, then?"

"The little boy who lives downstairs," said Tess, who now felt slightly shaky from shock.

"Can you manage the stairs?" said Rhys as if she were someone's grandmother.

"Really," said Tess, "I'm fine."

Kirsty appeared in the open doorway of the flat and looked down at them both.

"Rhys!" she said. There was a small pause. "Where's George?"

"Sick as a dog," said Rhys. "Can't move for throwing up."

"Oh," said Kirsty. "How unpleasant."

"He would have come, of course," said Rhys, "but he didn't think it was a good idea under the circumstances."

Tess, whose wrist was now hurting quite badly, wondered whether all this was just an elaborate excuse. Maybe George had got fed up of being pushed to meet her. Maybe he, like her, had felt uneasy about being set up.

"Flowers!" said Kirsty. "How kind!"

In the kitchen, Rhys, standing under the harsh strip light, looked even whiter and thinner than usual. His black hair, sticking out in all directions, was a cartoon impression of someone who'd just been electrocuted. Looking round appreciatively, he said, "Lovely. I don't know how you girls manage. It's always so welcoming here. Our house is never like this."

"It's because you never clean it," said Kirsty.

"Very possibly," said Rhys. He caught sight of Ellie, sitting woebegone in one of the kitchen chairs. "Ellie, *bach*," he said. "How are you?"

"I'm all right."

"Very sorry to hear about what happened. Shocking news."

"So what have you been up to?" said Tess, who had glanced at Ellie's face and seen her eyes well with tears. "How's the band?"

Rhys hesitated.

"Go on," said Kirsty.

"Well, not as good as it could be to tell you the truth."

"Oh?"

"Bit of tension."

"Tension?" said Kirsty, interested.

"Not all pulling in the same direction."

"Tell us everything," said Kirsty, handing him a glass of red wine.

"Oh, you don't want to hear about the band," said Rhys.

"Yes, we do."

Rhys didn't wait to be asked again. He was clearly desperate to talk. "The problem is," he said, "that George is pushing us. Which I understand, of course." He sat down at the kitchen table and put one long black leg over the other. He was wearing Doc Martens. It made his feet look ridiculously big, as if he'd stepped into lumps of black tarmac. "But he's taking it too far. He says it's now or never. Either we make an effort, or we just give up. He says there's no point playing at it. He wants commitment." Rhys stopped and shook his head. "But Walter's got a family, and he's studying law, and when he's not at home or in the library he's driving a cab. So he hasn't got the time. And the more George pushes him, the worse it gets. And then Mo's off God knows where, all hours of the day and night, and won't tell us what he's up to. George thinks he's working undercover for MI5."

Tess's eyes opened wide.

"Not seriously," said Rhys.

"And what about you?" said Kirsty.

"I'm just piggy in the middle," said Rhys. "Trying to keep the peace."

Tess said, "But you want the band to make it?"

Rhys looked at them all—from Tess, to Kirsty, to Ellie. For a moment he didn't reply.

Oh, poor George, thought Tess. Poor George.

"I'm not sure, to tell you the truth," he said. "I thought I did. I mean, I love playing. And I think we're good."

"You are," said Kirsty.

"But recently—" He stopped.

"What?" said Tess.

"I want to be a poet," said Rhys, in a rush, and then hung his head as if he'd just admitted to having a secret love of Spam.

"But that's a good thing."

"No, it isn't," said Rhys, looking wretched. "Because I can't do both. Not the way George wants it now. It was all right before. I could write my poetry, and work in the bookshop, and play in the band. But now we're booked every other night. And it's not as if you can just get up and play. You have to rehearse."

"Talk to him," said Tess.

"But that's the point, isn't it?" said Rhys. "I don't think he'd want to listen, the mood he's in. It's bad enough worrying about Walter and Mo. I don't think he'd want to hear about me, too."

Tess looked at him with great sympathy.

"So what are you going to do?" said Kirsty.

"I've got no idea," said Rhys. He took a deep breath and raised his glass. "But I tell you what. It's been going round and round in my head, and I'm getting to the point where none of it makes sense. The more I worry, the worse I feel. So I'm not going to think about it anymore. Tonight, I'm going to forget all about it."

"Cheers," said Kirsty. They clinked glasses.

"Oh," said Tess, suddenly remembering her duties as host. "I've got to check the food. Can someone lay the table in the front room? And find out if Akash and Tom want any more to drink?"

"Have you met Akash?" said Kirsty to Rhys as they left the kitchen.

"I'm not sure I have," said Rhys.

"Brace yourself," said Kirsty.

Alone again, Tess reassured herself that the shepherd's pie hadn't burned, tore lettuce leaves into a large white bowl, and found some rather tatty paper napkins in a kitchen drawer. Her wrist was still hurting, but she managed to ignore it. She found herself thinking instead about the George she hadn't met, trying to fit the new information she had just been told into the impression she'd already formed. She couldn't quite squash it all together. Kirsty had said he was arty and old-fashioned. Ellie had said he was kind and thoughtful. Lauren had said he was a bit of a dreamer. And now Rhys was describing him as some kind of hotshot manager who was pushing the band to fame and fortune. Who was the real George?

"And I was in absolute agony," Tom was saying to Rhys as she joined them all in the living room. "Gritting my teeth to stop myself crying out. You know when they say, on a scale of one to ten, how bad is the pain? Well, I said to them, ten, ten, ten."

"Tess, my angel," said Akash, "where have you been? I've been so worried, I've taken to drink."

"It'll be about another five minutes," said Tess, putting a napkin at each place on the table and realizing, rather belatedly, they all said *Happy Christmas*. "Shall I get some water?"

"Water?" said Akash. "What's that?"

"Do we need another chair?" said Tess.

"I'll give you a hand," said Rhys, following her back out to the kitchen, where she loaded him up with the bowl of salad while she filled a jug of water at the sink.

"I think Kirsty's finding Tom a bit hard going," she said. "When she saw him in *The Nutcracker* she thought he was full of repressed passion. Now she thinks it was probably constipation."

Rhys frowned. "You have a boyfriend, don't you?"

"Yes," said Tess, rather guiltily, because she hadn't thought about Dominic all evening.

"So where is he, then?"

"He's on a training weekend."

"Training for what?"

"Accountancy," said Tess.

There was a small pause. "Well, look at it this way," said Rhys. "It's like unblocking drains. Someone's got to do it."

Tess was relieved that the shepherd's pie, when she finally

brought it out of the oven, looked quite professional with its little blackened peaks of potato and cheese. By now everyone was sitting round the table with its festive napkins and French bread and salad, and she felt a sudden lifting of responsibility because the evening had taken on a life of its own and had decided to flow by in a haze of collective silliness.

Rhys, who looked less ill in the kindness of candlelight, was testing Tom on his knowledge of the bones and tendons of the human foot, which left Kirsty free to argue with Akash about parental responsibility in *Finding Nemo*, while Tess and Ellie discussed the glory of McQueen meeting the queen. By the time they'd finished the lemon meringue pie she'd made that morning, the empty wine bottles were standing in a thick crowd like teenagers wasting time on a street corner.

"Cheese, anyone?" said Tess, coming back into the living room with Tesco's finest.

"Is your wrist OK?" said Kirsty. "It looks a bit swollen."

"It does, doesn't it?" said Tess, who had drunk enough red wine to look at her own body with a sense of curiosity rather than ownership.

"Rice," said Tom.

"Rice?"

"To stop the swelling."

"Raw or cooked?" said Tess, wondering whether you had to eat it or paste it on like wallpaper glue.

"Rest, Ice, Compression, Elevation," said Tom. "That's

what they should have said, of course, when I first went to A & E."

"Have we got any ice?" said Tess.

"We've got lots of ice," said Kirsty.

"But I thought you said—" said Tom.

"I could make you a sling," said Ellie.

"Or a bandage," said Rhys. "You could wrap it round to give it a bit of support."

Akash had his head on the table. He seemed to be sleeping.

"I'm only wearing a sling," said Tess, "if it's made of silk. A red paisley silk scarf."

Kirsty laughed. "Do you want me to get it for you?"

"Yes, please," said Tess, beaming. "It's on a hook behind the door in the box room."

Tom said, "I thought there wasn't any ice."

"You know, you're very alike, you and George," said Rhys.

Tess blushed. "What do you mean?"

"Well, you're both quite eccentric, aren't you?"

"Am I?" said Tess, not sure whether to be pleased or offended.

"I think George is probably the nicest person I've ever met," said Rhys. "I mean, there's no side to him, put it that way. He's not always trying to get one over you. He'd just as soon someone else got the glory. That's why I feel so sorry about the band. If anyone deserves success, it's George. He's worked so hard. And he's good. But of course you know that."

Tess opened her mouth to say, Tonight would have been the first time we'd ever met, but Rhys said, "I've never quite understood why he hasn't made it already, to be honest with you. You don't get talent like his very often. But he doesn't like making a fuss. He doesn't like standing up and shouting. And you've got to, haven't you, in this business? If you just sit there quietly, they'll walk all over you."

Tess thought about this.

"I mean I have wondered," said Rhys, "whether it might be better for George to go his own way. You see that happening, don't you? Musicians start off in bands and then go solo. I mean, it's hard, because you have to do it all on your own. You haven't got any backup. But it might be the answer. He can't give up. It would be a tragedy if he gave up. He's got to play. I mean, it's his life."

"Here," said Kirsty, coming back into the room with the vintage scarf.

"Kirsty," said Tom, from the other end of the table, "I'm feeling very tired. I think I need to go to bed."

"Shall I call a cab?" said Kirsty, looping the scarf under Tess's arm and tying it with an expert flourish round her neck. "You and Akash can share. You're going in the same direction."

"Did someone call?" said Akash, squinting upwards from the table.

"I ought to be making a move myself," said Rhys, "or I'll miss the last tube."

"You're staying," said Kirsty to Ellie.

"Am I?" said Ellie.

"It's a female conspiracy," said Akash.

"It always is," said Rhys.

. . .

When Tom, pouting, had been helped downstairs and he and Akash had disappeared off in a minicab, Rhys wound his scarf round his neck and hugged Kirsty and Tess good-bye.

"A memorable evening." He sighed. "If only I could persuade Gareth to stop crying at the mention of your name, you could come round to us."

"It doesn't sound like it's going to be any time soon," said Kirsty.

"I'll keep working on him," said Rhys.

Back in the living room, Ellie was slumped at the table, weeping. "I hate her," she said, her face pulled into a grotesque grimace of pain. "I hate her for making me go through this. I love her so much. How could she do this to me?"

Tess put her arms round her.

"Come on, miss," said Kirsty. "Time for bed. You can have the side by the wall."

While Kirsty was settling Ellie into her huge double bed, Tess began to gather up some of the glasses. But it was almost impossible with only one hand.

"Tom didn't look too happy," she said when Kirsty came back into the room.

Kirsty laughed and poured them both another glass of wine. Oh dear, thought Tess happily, it's going to be one of the late ones. Going to bed at dawn. But Dominic need never know. She thought of him in his glorious nakedness, lying peacefully in a hotel somewhere in Berkshire. For a moment, she almost missed him. She looked around at the wreck of the table. "I'm going to have a horrible headache in the morning."

"You can't spend your life worrying about tomorrow," said Kirsty.

"I'm sure you're right. But I always do."

"As John Lennon once said, life is what happens to you while you're busy making other plans."

"But if you don't make plans," said Tess, "you end up drifting."

"What's wrong with drifting?"

"You could end up miles from where you want to be."

Tess imagined herself like an empty green wine bottle, bobbing around on a glassy sea.

"That's the point," said Kirsty. "Go somewhere new. Look around and see if you like it."

Tess stroked the stem of her wineglass. "But what if you don't like it?"

"Then you drift on somewhere else," said Kirsty.

Tess looked disbelieving.

"Plans," said Kirsty, "are set up by people who are frightened of change."

"I'm not frightened of change."

Kirsty smiled. Tess dropped her eyes.

"If you think plans are such a bad idea," said Tess defensively, “why do you keep trying to get me and George together? Maybe we should just drift about and see what happens.”

“Let fate take over?”

“Yes.” Tess lifted her eyes again.

“OK,” said Kirsty. “From now on, you’re on your own.”

Oh, thought Tess. I don’t think I meant that to happen at all.

2004

The afternoon was gray and tired by the time George arrived at the law firm. He was, as usual, late. He raced through the revolving door, stared wild-eyed at the list of company names, and stood panting as the glass lift rushed him upwards through space and light. This was a bland Holborn building that had been gutted and refurbished. It now resembled a futuristic film set. George felt increasingly uneasy. The collar of his white dress shirt was way too tight. His bow tie was strangling him.

"I'm the pianist," he said to the receptionist on the sixteenth floor.

"This way," she said. Her accent was Polish.

They walked down shallow steps to an enormous black and silver reception room. Way up above was a glass and chrome gallery with plate-glass offices behind. There wasn't a lawyer in sight. Two black-shirted waiters were setting up at the central bar. The grand piano gleamed. Otherwise, the place was deserted.

George, who had been imagining a room full of cross solicitors looking at their watches, took a deep breath. "Can I warm up?"

"You are cold?"

George mimed playing a keyboard.

She looked at him expressionlessly.

He gave up. He said, "What time do people get here?"

"It start at six," she said.

The trick to playing at formal receptions arranged by your booking agent, George had discovered, was to ignore the party. You played for yourself. If people clapped, you dug out that style of music from your repertoire and continued until the next break. But generally you pretended the audience didn't exist. And they did the same with you.

He sat down and adjusted the piano stool. He stretched his hands to either end of the keyboard. It was an impressive instrument.

George began to play.

A gray-haired man put a hand on his shoulder. "Can I get you a drink?"

George looked up. He blinked. The room was full of people shouting and laughing. There was a party going on.

"Thelonious Monk," said the gray-haired man. "It sounds like 'Brilliant Corners.' But different. Yours?"

George smiled.

"I haven't heard jazz like this for a long time." He studied George's face. Then he looked across to a young woman standing in the curve of the piano. She had bony shoulders, dark shiny hair, and bright eyes like a sparrow. "Your idea, Stephanie?"

"He came recommended," she said. Her voice was high and clear.

"He's been playing for an hour. I think he deserves a break."

"There's food," said Stephanie, "if you're hungry."

George's empty stomach lurched.

"Come on," said Stephanie.

George followed her across the room through the crush of people, brushing against black cocktail dresses and expensive suits smelling of new cloth. Stephanie had very thin legs. She was wearing black shoes with stiletto heels.

"That," she said, as they reached a long table laden with tiny bites of pastry, "was the senior partner. And he liked you. Which makes me look good."

She was assessing him. It should have been uncomfortable, that open stare. But there was something endearing about it. She reminded him of a quick and clever child who'd been allowed to stay up past her bedtime. He waited for her to finish. She had freckles across her nose. She said, "You've got a nice face."

He smiled.

"I always make up my mind about people immediately," she said. "I find it saves time in the long run."

• • •

In the second set, George found it harder to concentrate. He kept looking up from the keyboard. Once he studied her rear view for several minutes. She was wearing a black dress that shimmered blue and green as she moved. He imagined holding the curve of her hips. He wanted to see her face again, and his heart beat fast when she came back to the piano. But she wasn't alone. She leant casually against a tall, dark-skinned man with black eyebrows as if she knew him very well. George found himself throwing in virtuoso runs he didn't even know he could do. He played "'Round Midnight." He took so many risks with the rhythm that it was like teetering on the edge of a rope bridge over a chasm. When he stopped, there was a crowd round the piano. They cheered him. They whistled and clapped.

George looked at Stephanie. She smiled.

At the end of the second set, he went to the bar. She came up beside him. She seemed both exotic and fragile, like a bird with exquisite plumage.

"You didn't ask," she said, "how I found you."

He said, "What are you doing later?"

"My sister," she said, "heard you play. At a club. And I thought, Well, the senior partner's party. What could be better? It might get me noticed. So I said we ought to book you. Although it was a bit of a risk. As I hadn't heard you myself."

He looked at her.

"Mergers and acquisitions," she said. "Very competitive. We go out to dinner when the party's over. All of us. The junior associates have been sharpening their elbows for months."

He studied his beer.

"You give up easily," she said. "It doesn't go on all night."

George, who wasn't used to playing these games, was lost.

She said, "How old are you?"

"Twenty-seven."

"I thought so," she said. "I'm the older woman. By two years. Does that bother you?"

By the end of the final set, the crowd had thinned out. George stood up. When people realized he had finished, there was another round of applause. He bowed his head. Then he looked around for Stephanie, but she was nowhere to be seen. The gray-haired man had gone, too.

George shut the lid of the piano.

As he walked past the reception desk, the Polish girl said, "Stop, please." She handed him a white envelope. Inside was a business card. Stephanie had crossed out all the contact details and written down a mobile number. Next to it she had added, in thick black italics, "Round midnight?"

From that very first night, George was dazzled. Stephanie was like a diamond tiara, glittering with the assurance of a valuable asset. She had a quick intelligence. She had no patience for people who couldn't keep up. In Stephanie's flat, when he lay in her bed watching her get dressed in lacy silk lingerie—and he could see every knuckle of bone in her spine—George thought he must be a curiosity, a plaything to amuse her. Why else would she be with him? He had nothing. He had achieved nothing. His value to her could only possibly be as some kind of cautionary tale—look how rubbish your life will be without cutthroat ambition.

But as the weeks passed, and she showed no signs of tiring of him, he grew puzzled. It made no sense.

"You're her project," said Rhys. "Women like hopeless men. They like training them."

"You work crazy hours," said Walter. "So does she. It's perfect."

"I can't see the problem," said Mo. "She buys you dinner. She lets you have sex with her. What are you worried about?"

Six weeks after they met, Stephanie invited friends back from work. It was a Friday night. George, who had been playing at one of his favorite clubs in Soho, turned up at midnight. Everyone was drunk. Empty wine bottles stood to attention.

"So you're the musician," said a red-faced man with a blond moustache.

All eyes were on George.

"Is that a living these days?" said one of the women in a superior drawl.

The red-faced man laughed.

There was a small, mocking pause.

"He does a lot more living than we do," said Stephanie.

You wouldn't want to be on the wrong side of her, thought George, looking at her taut, furious face.

Later, in bed, as she sat astride him, pinning his hands to the mattress, Stephanie said, "I want to see more of you."

"I don't think that's possible," said George.

She bent down and kissed him very slowly on the mouth. She said, "Move in with me."

• • •

"Is this what it's like," said Tess, "being twenty-five?"

Dominic frowned.

"It seems such a huge age," said Tess. "Halfway through my twenties. Half of fifty."

"Logically," said Dominic, "it's not going to feel any different to being twenty-four. Nothing's changed."

"Yes, I know," said Tess. "But it feels so significant."

Her words hung in the air as they often did when she was trying, and failing, to enthuse Dominic with a big thought.

It was ten o'clock in the morning. They were lying in Tess's bed, which was a mess of shiny wrapping paper and birthday cards that she had so far persuaded Dominic not to clear up. There was one from her mum in Leigh, and another from her grandmother in Poole. Already on her bedside table was an enormous card from "All at Daisy Greenleaf Designs" in a rather alarming shade of purple. Kirsty was out, not surprisingly, so they had the flat to themselves. Dominic had given her a huge bunch of red roses, breakfast in bed, and a languorous physical exploration that had left her feeling slightly light-headed. Sex was often strung out for several slow hours on a Saturday. Tess imagined they might have a bath together once they'd read the papers. We can walk around naked if we want to, she thought. There's no one here. We can make love on the living room floor. She began to daydream a sexual marathon that took in every room of the flat and was just wondering whether the kitchen table would support their weight when Dominic said, "It's the right time to make financial decisions."

She groped her way back through a fog of erotic imaginings. "What?"

"In your midtwenties. Pension plans definitely. Possibly even a mortgage."

Rather sadly Tess felt the pulse of sexual desire diminish to a pleasant memory.

"It's a mistake people make," said Dominic. "They leave financial planning much too late. If only they looked at the graphs they would realize."

Tess stifled a yawn.

Dominic said, "My parents are downsizing."

Tess had a mental picture of his mum and dad as doll-house people, complete with painted hair and big feet.

"They're putting the house on the market next month."

Very slowly, Tess began to piece these random announcements together. She looked up at Dominic, who was leaning against the wall staring into the middle distance like a man in a deodorant ad. "So what will you do?" she said.

He said nothing. She pushed herself up from the pillows so she could see his expression. "Are you going to be homeless?" she said.

"It'll take a few months to go through. Although Croydon prices are holding up well at the moment, so it should be a fairly straightforward sale."

"But where will you go?" She had visions of Dominic huddled in a doorway like Colin. "You could always stay here," she said. And then added, out of fairness to Kirsty, "For a while."

He said, "Or we could look for somewhere together."

She stared. For a moment, she couldn't quite be sure that she had heard right. He sounded so diffident. Then she realized, with a sudden shot of clarity, that he was worried she might refuse.

"Really?" she said, bouncing up and down on the bed with excitement. "Do you mean it? Move in together?"

He looked almost pleased.

"But where?" she said. "Where would we look? Round here? Or somewhere closer to the middle? There's Islington. Or west London. I don't know anything about west London. But there's Portobello Road. And the Notting Hill carnival. Or east London. You can get a warehouse in east London. And there are galleries and vintage clothes stores. Oh, where would we go? Where would we go?"

"If you're making an investment," said Dominic, "you pick an area where prices are about to go up. Like Penge."

Only a tiny pinprick in the bubble of joy. "But if you're just renting," said Tess, "you can be a bit more careless. You can pick a place just for fun."

Dominic frowned. "But you should use the rental period as a time for thoroughly researching the area where you want to buy."

"Yes," said Tess.

There was a little pause.

"You really want to buy with me?" said Tess.

Dominic said, “It makes financial sense.”

“What about romantic sense?”

He looked as if he didn’t quite understand.

“Buying somewhere together,” said Tess. She stopped, unable to put it into words. “It’s huge. Is this what you want?”

“Not immediately, of course,” said Dominic. “We’d have to start saving for a deposit.”

“Oh,” said Tess.

“Which might take a year or two. And a lot of careful planning. We’d have to review our outgoings and make some economies.”

“But this is what you want,” said Tess.

“I’ve been thinking about it for a while,” said Dominic. “I’ve done a few spreadsheets.”

He’s serious, she thought. He’s really serious.

Dominic reached out his hand and stroked the top of her arm. He said, “You look cold.”

She was sitting there naked on top of the sheets. In the drama of the moment, she hadn’t noticed her skin going blue. Dominic pushed back the duvet. She stared down with some surprise. What had they just been talking about?

But she succumbed happily. She never refused an invitation.

. . .

Stephanie’s flat had a white carpet. George had to leave his shoes by the door.

"When you take your shoes off," she said, "put your keys on the hall table."

He nodded.

"George? Are you listening? When you take your shoes off, put your keys on the table. That way you can't lose them. You won't be in a panic every time you leave the house."

To his intense surprise, George found that Stephanie's method worked. Even in the early hours, as he stood just inside the front door setting down the keyboard in its zipped black bag, he found himself taking off his shoes and putting his keys on the hall table. Always, for a moment, he stood there, amazed. There were his keys, subdued, obedient. Chaos had been vanquished.

Stephanie planned everything in meticulous detail—her wardrobe, the laundry, the cleaning woman, work commitments, their social life, the weekend. Every Sunday afternoon, they stood in the kitchen and wrote the week's appointments on a large wall chart. George, who before he met Stephanie had only ever halfheartedly scribbled incomprehensible notes in a thin black diary, looked on in astonishment.

"So at the moment," Stephanie would say, "we have Tuesday night when we're both free. Shall we go to the new Indian brasserie?"

The band was in a mellow phase. George and Walter, without saying a word, had called a truce. George, recognizing Walter's impossible daily timetable, was trying to ease the band's workload by concentrating on clubs and music venues where they could play their own stuff. That was, after all, what would eventually make their name. But sometimes they performed just for money. They had to pay the rent.

One Saturday night, the band was booked to play at a silver wedding anniversary in Hampstead. They arranged to meet at the tube station high on the hill. When Mo got out of the lift and saw George standing there—hair tamed, black tie in a neat bow—he narrowed his eyes in shock. "What's wrong?"

"Wrong?"

"You're early."

"Am I?" said George.

"You're never early." Mo walked around him, studying him from all angles as if he was a piece of sculpture. "Right clothes, right place, right time. What's going on?"

"Nothing's going on," said George defensively.

"So she's got you trained, has she?"

George looked down at his well-polished shoes.

"You want to be careful," said Mo. "Your life won't be your own."

Would that be so bad? thought George. It wasn't so great when I was in charge.

One Sunday evening as they stood in the kitchen filling in the wall chart, Stephanie said, "Have you thought about giving up your job in the shop?"

She was writing up a dental appointment, so he couldn't see her expression.

"Because it occurs to me," said Stephanie, "that you could

spend more time managing the band if you didn't have to spend half your life selling guitar strings."

"I need the money," said George.

She turned round. "No, you don't."

George shook his head. "I can't live off you."

"It's only temporary," she said. "Until you make it big."

"That could be years."

"Now you're being silly," said Stephanie.

George looked at her helplessly.

"Sometimes," said Stephanie, "you have to grab hold of a good offer. Or it might disappear."

He said, "I'll pay you back."

"Of course you will," said Stephanie briskly. "Now shall we have a cup of tea?"

When George handed in his notice, Rajesh said miserably, "Are you making enough from the band now?" Everyone who worked in the shop had dreams of making a living from performing.

On George's last day, Freya brought in a layered white cake. On the top she had drawn an octave of keys with black icing. She said, hugging him, "Will you remember us all when you're famous?"

"Famous?"

"You're going to make it, George," said Freya. "Out of all of us, you're going to make it."

When he left the shop for the last time, George turned round and looked back. He felt free.

"Do you remember Miles?" said Stephanie one evening.

She was standing in the bathroom in a lacy black camisole screwing a tiny silver earring into one delicate earlobe.

George, who was always disarmed by the sight of Stephanie in a state of undress, shook his head.

"The senior partner? The night we met?" Stephanie turned back to the mirror. "He's got a little girl of about five. Second marriage. She wants to learn the piano. He wondered if you'd be interested in teaching her."

"Teaching her?"

"Well, you could, couldn't you?"

George looked doubtful.

"She's five. It's just about putting fingers on keys."

He always backpedaled when he heard that note of irritation in her voice. "I could try."

"You can read music, can't you?"

George could. He had plowed his way through all the grade exams. He'd even done a teaching diploma. Then, at the age of seventeen, with a desperate courage he didn't know he possessed, he'd told his piano teacher he wanted to play jazz.

"A waste," said the teacher with pinched lips, "of talent."

His father, who had studied classical violin from the age of five, looked at him with incredulity. "Jazz?" he said, managing to inject a lifetime of scorn into that one single word.

"I'm just not sure I'm cut out to teach," said George.

Stephanie turned to face him. He was always fascinated by the color of her eyes—a warm hazel with flecks of green. She stepped forward to where he sat on the edge of the bath and stood between his legs. He could see the slight curve of her breasts against the black lace. "You never know till you try," she said, her hair brushing his cheek.

Miles, the senior partner, lived in St. John's Wood, in a double-fronted Edwardian house with a large front garden. A pink magnolia was in exuberant flower. George, who was normally oblivious to his surroundings, looked at the tree and felt a strange, joyful energy. The pace of his life was speeding up. Stephanie had woken him to change. He thought of the years he'd spent in the music shop in Soho, and he felt sorry for the person he'd once been—downtrodden, depressed, defeated. The band is going to succeed, he thought. We're going to make it. For a moment, the applause deafened him.

The door opened. Miles said, "George! How good to see you! Come and meet Lucy."

The pile of the carpet was so deep that George felt as if he was sinking into sand.

Lucy was a serious child with long, straight brown hair cut into a full fringe at the front. She eyed him warily. George squatted down and took one of her small hands. He examined it carefully. "Well," he said, "this is good."

Lucy was still watching him, but with more interest.

"You've got just the right kind of hands for a piano player," said George. "I can tell that straightaway."

"I can play," said Lucy.

"Can you?" said George. "Can you show me?"

Lucy scrambled up onto the piano stool. George drew up one of the dining room chairs.

"I'll leave you, then, shall I?" said Miles. He had the smile of a man who sees his hunch vindicated.

But George didn't even notice. He was watching Lucy's tiny fingers on the fat white keys.

Word spread. Before long, George had ten pupils.

"You're good with children," said Stephanie.

"I like children," he said. "They see things very clearly."

Stephanie put her head on one side and looked at him. "I suppose they do," she said.

Because of Stephanie's contacts, there was a sudden increase in offers of lucrative work for the band, as well—at country houses, Oxford colleges, the Inner Temple. This was serious money. But it left no time for their own music, for experimenting like they had in Paris.

"Tell me what you want me to do," said George.

"It's the age-old problem," said Mo. "Do you starve in a garret or go commercial?"

"I think we should go for a balance," said Rhys.

"Walter?"

Walter looked at him with cold eyes. "You manage the band."

"I want to know what you think."

"I need the money," said Walter.

"Fine," said George. "We'll take the bookings. We can review it in a couple of months."

He turned his back. He knew Walter was angry. But it was the luck of the draw. He hadn't asked Stephanie to support him. But he wasn't going to turn down her help.

"Had you ever thought," said Stephanie one morning, putting on her coat, "about getting a singer? It might make you more versatile. If someone wants to book the band for weddings. You know, Frank Sinatra. Fly Me to the Moon."

"We don't play that kind of music," said George.

"But you could," said Stephanie.

The silence grew.

"Oh well," said Stephanie lightly. "It was just an idea."

But George thought she shut the door behind her with more force than usual.

. . .

"You're looking very thoughtful this morning," said Colin.

"Am I?" said Tess. She blinked. "Oh, I forgot. I bought you a piece of toast."

"For me?" said Colin.

"I wanted one anyway," said Tess. It was a lie. She'd bought Colin a piece of toast because she was beginning to worry about him. His cough was worse. He looked even thinner. But she didn't know how to help. She'd once nervously asked if he'd like her to find out about hostels and he'd looked right through her as if she didn't exist.

"So what's on your mind?" said Colin, opening the thin paper bag with agonizing slowness.

"Oh, you know," said Tess. "Work."

He looked up. Even in a face so overgrown with hair and beard, she could still see the light of mischief in his eyes. "Work?"

"Yes."

"Nothing to do with that young man of yours?"

"What young man?"

Colin bit into his toast. He chewed slowly. He said, "Are you telling me there's no young man?"

Tess went pink.

"Aha," said Colin, taking another bite.

But I wasn't thinking about Dominic, thought Tess. I was thinking about Kirsty. And the way she looked when I said I was moving out. It's the end of an era. I've been living with her since I was nineteen. All through university, then three years in Brixton. And now it's all over. And I feel sad and guilty, because I've had to choose between them, and Dominic won.

Colin said, chewing carefully, "So what's he like, then?"

Tess had a mental image of Dominic, blond hair falling forwards, poring over the rows and columns of a figure-packed spreadsheet. "He's very good-looking."

Far better looking than I deserve, she thought. He should be with someone size 4, five feet ten inches, with waist-length blond hair and eyes as blue as a California sky.

Colin didn't say anything.

"And he's very organized," said Tess. "And logical. Good with money." She paused, watching Colin eat the last of his toast. "We're going to move in together. As soon as we can find somewhere."

Colin sucked the butter off the tips of his fingers one by one. It was a curiously elegant gesture, as if he was a restaurant critic appreciating the fine taste of white truffles. He said, staring off into the middle distance, "You don't sound very excited."

She hadn't expected criticism. She thought he was on her side. She said, "I'd better be going. I don't want to be late."

Colin said, "Don't rush into it. Not unless you're sure."

"I am sure," said Tess.

"You don't get second chances," said Colin. He looked at her directly. "They say you do. But you don't."

Tess hesitated. More than anything, she wanted to sit down next to him on the cold, dirty pavement and ask him how he knew.

But she didn't.

. . .

"It's been more than two years," said Ellie.

"It hasn't," said Tess.

"It has. July 2002."

"And you haven't spoken to her all this time?"

Ellie shook her head.

"And then she just sent an email. Out of the blue."

Ellie nodded.

They were in a small crowded pub in Argyll Street in the West End. Outside, like a weary stagehand throwing buckets of water onto the stage in *King Lear,* the storm crashed rain against the windows.

"So what are you going to do?"

Ellie looked at her. "I've got no idea."

"And what did she say again?"

"Hi, Ellie. Just wondered if you wanted to meet up. Let me know. Lauren."

"You know it word for word," said Tess.

"I think I've read it a hundred times."

"So where is she?"

"I've got no idea."

"Aren't you in touch with anyone who still sees her?"

Ellie shook her head. "I thought we had a lot of friends in common. But we didn't. It's just that her friends and my friends ended up at the same parties."

A row of suits blocked the light. Every conceivable style, thought Tess. She wondered, looking at a fat man's pin-striped back, what had possessed him to buy double vents. "Maybe something's happened to her," she said. "Sometimes when there's a crisis you think of someone you used to be close to."

"But do I want that?"

Tess didn't know how to answer.

Ellie looked bewildered. "I mean, part of me thinks, OK, a lot of time has passed, maybe now I could face seeing her. But another part of me thinks, What for? This woman destroyed my life. She cut out a whole year when I couldn't function at all. You remember what it was like. So why would I want to see her again?"

"Curiosity?" said Tess.

"I'm not sure that's a good enough reason. I'm not sure I'm strong enough. I feel pretty good. I've got a new relationship. I've got a job I love. But I'm frightened. I'm frightened of risking it all."

"Then don't," said Tess.

Ellie smiled. "I know. It seems so simple, doesn't it?"

"Excuse me," said a young man with a shiny red face, "but is this seat taken?"

"Yes," said Tess, firmly.

As he backed off, rebuffed, Ellie said, "Liar."

"I don't want him eavesdropping," said Tess. She sipped her drink. "It sounds to me like you want to see her."

Ellie didn't answer for a long time. Then she said slowly, "I want to ask her whether I made the whole thing up. A grand illusion. Whether I fooled myself that something was there when it wasn't. Maybe she never loved me at all. Maybe none of it was true."

"You didn't make it up," said Tess.

"How do you know?"

"Because I saw you together. You were very happy."

"But if she loved me," said Ellie, "why did she hurt me?"

Because she didn't love you enough, thought Tess. She had an affair because she didn't have the guts to tell you face-to-face that it was over. I've seen it happen so many times. Forget what people say. It's what they do that's important. Actions, as my grandmother has always said, speak louder than words.

But she could say nothing of this to Ellie. For some reason, even after all this time, Ellie needed to believe that Lauren had loved her with a burning intensity that matched her own. This was the story Ellie had made of the past, and she didn't want to let it go. And there was I, thought Tess, imagining that I was the romantic one.

Tess leant across the table and held Ellie's hand. "I'm not defending her. But I don't think she meant to hurt you. Maybe even now if you asked her why she did it she wouldn't be able to tell you."

Ellie didn't say anything.

"You loved each other very much," said Tess. "Lauren knows what she did was wrong. And that might be why she wants to see you. All this time has passed, but she still wants to ask you to forgive her."

"I can't forgive her," said Ellie.

"I know," said Tess. "And that's why I don't think you should see her. Let it go. It's all in the past. Leave it all behind."

After a long time, Ellie nodded.

"You don't have to reply to emails," said Tess.

Ellie looked up, her eyes full of tears.

"You can just delete them," said Tess.

• • •

"You know Kate, don't you?" said Oliver Bankes.

Today Oliver was wearing a purple shirt and a shiny dark blue tie. George found himself thinking of chocolates wrapped in brightly colored foil.

"No," said George. "I don't think I do."

"Katherine Bankes, my cousin."

George shook his head.

"Ah," said Oliver. "That's strange. I thought you knew Kate." He frowned. "How did I get your name, then?"

"I'm not sure," said George.

"Perhaps it was someone Kate knows. One of her friends. She has a lot of friends."

"That could be it."

There was a rather mournful pause.

"Maybe she knows my girlfriend," said George. "Stephanie."

"Stephanie! That's it!" said Oliver excitedly. "They were at school together." He gave an exaggerated sigh, blowing out the air in his cheeks. "Terrible when there's something on the tip of your tongue and you can't remember it. Maddening. But we got there in the end, didn't we?" He beamed at George like a proud father. "Right. Let's get down to it. My mother's eighty in a couple of months. Said she didn't want a fuss—just a small dinner. With the family. So we're keeping it simple. But I was talking to my sister at the weekend." He paused. "Do you know Isobel?"

"I don't think so."

"Shame. You'd like her. Really down-to-earth. Lives in one of those great big double-fronted houses in Peckham. Black iron railings? Yew tree?"

George shook his head.

"You'd know it if you saw it. Anyway, Isobel said, What about a pianist? And I thought, What a fantastic idea. What do you think?"

"Sounds good," said George.

"But could you do it?"

"Well, yes," said George. "If I'm not already booked."

Oliver's face fell. "I see what you mean."

"Have you got a date?"

"Well, it would be her birthday," said Oliver.

George waited. Oliver looked at him expectantly.

"And when's that?" said George.

"Ah," said Oliver, "terribly short notice, I'm afraid. December fifth. It's a Sunday. We were thinking, during lunch and tea?"

"Fine," said George. "I'll get that booked in."

"You can do it?"

"I was looking at the calendar this morning. I know I'm free that Sunday."

"Well, isn't that good news?" said Oliver, delighted. Then he frowned. "One slight problem."

"Oh?"

"It's in Essex."

"I can do Essex."

"Can you?" said Oliver gratefully.

"Maybe the train?" said George.

"Well, there we are, then," said Oliver. "No problem at all." Suddenly his face stretched into a scowling grimace as if he'd been hit by severe indigestion. George stared, alarmed. "No," said Oliver, "it's no good. I've forgotten her name."

"Stephanie?"

"Stephanie! That's it!" His face burst into smiles. "She said you could play absolutely anything. Is that right?"

"Well, yes," said George, "within reason. I play jazz, mostly. But anything your mother particularly wanted—"

"Sinatra," said Oliver.

"Sinatra," said George.

"You know, Fly Me to the Moon. Strangers in the Night. That kind of thing. Stephanie said you could do that."

There was a small pause.

"You could do that, couldn't you?"

"Yes," said George slowly, "I can do Sinatra."

"Splendid," said Oliver. "We're all sorted. I'll send you an email with all the details." He stood up. "Let me show you out."

The office beyond Oliver Bankes's small glass cubicle was completely deserted. There was a red paisley scarf draped over the back of one of the chairs.

"Not usually—" said Oliver. "Ah," he said, as Glenda appeared in the doorway, freshly lipsticked, looking as if she'd kissed a vat of pink icing. "Worried for a minute where everyone was."

"Well, here I am," she said brightly.

"So we'll look forward to meeting in a few weeks." Oliver turned to George to shake hands.

"Yes," said George.

"Nice work if you can get it."

George stared.

"My Way. That kind of thing," said Oliver.

. . .

"It's a lot of money," said Tess.

"Not really," said Dominic. "Not if you think of them as an investment."

"Are they, though?"

"Le Creuset?" said Dominic. "Of course they are."

They were standing in a department store in the West End. A whole set of Le Creuset cast iron cooking pots was on special discount. It was a bargain. It was a once-in-a-lifetime opportunity.

"But do we need them?" said Tess.

"Yes," said Dominic. "We can't last much longer with a few battered saucepans borrowed from your mum."

I notice, thought Tess with unusual asperity, that your mother didn't offer us any of her old stuff, despite the great Croydon downsizing. "But shouldn't we put the money towards the deposit?"

"I think the odd impulse buy is fine."

Tess looked down at the cooking pots. In her rather fractious state of mind, they reminded her of hollowed-out Halloween pumpkins leering at her with evil intent.

"Don't you like the color?"

"Yes," she said.

"And you like the price?"

"Yes," she said.

"We won't get this chance again," said Dominic.

"No."

"So let's do it," said Dominic.

She felt extraordinarily tired.

. . .

They couldn't have been more welcoming. George played for an hour on the rather beautiful Steinway in the drawing room of an Edwardian mansion in the Essex countryside before they insisted he stopped and had something to eat. He ate poached salmon and warm buttered shrimps and potatoes cooked with garlic and cream with a sprinkling of chives on the top. He shook his head when Kate Bankes tried to give him a large portion of passion fruit pavlova.

"I'll be too full to play," he said.

"Well, maybe later, then," she said. "I don't want Stephanie thinking we starved you."

He liked Kate. She seemed straightforward—no hidden agendas.

"I can give you a lift home if you like," she said. "If you can wait till everyone's gone."

"Thanks," he said, "but I need to get back. The train's fine." Somehow he thought Stephanie might not like it, he and Kate Bankes alone in the car.

He played twice more—once while they had coffee and then later when it was time for tea. They were a big and boisterous family. Small grandchildren raced up marble staircases and between the legs of priceless chairs. A flatulent Labrador dozed. One of the cousins, who was heavily pregnant, laughed so much she became dizzy and had to be fanned with a copy of the *Times*.

"That was lovely, dear," said an elderly aunt as he sat waiting for his cab back to the station. "Just right. Mary loved every moment of it."

"It was a pleasure," said George.

"So good to hear all the old songs."

"What was your favorite?"

"I've always loved Strangers in the Night." She sighed. "Love at first sight. So romantic."

He smiled.

"And For Once in My Life. How does that go again? It was Tony Bennett, wasn't it, before Sinatra?"

"And Stevie Wonder," said George. "That's the one everyone remembers."

"But I still love Sinatra the best. I remember it was playing on the radio when we first moved to Haslemere. I stood there in the kitchen and I thought, Yes, it's true. If someone really needs you, it makes you strong. You're as brave as a lion. You can do anything." She stopped, laughing. "You wait till you get to my age. You'll be all silly and sentimental too."

George felt a moment's sadness. He didn't feel anyone really needed him. In fact, he felt infinitely replaceable.

She leant forwards. "So tell me more about yourself. You live in London? Like Kate?"

George nodded.

"I don't think I could manage that at all," she said. "Much too much of a country bumpkin these days."

"It's very busy if you're not used to it," said George. "Lots of traffic and people."

"Absolutely. The only noise I hear these days is the dawn chorus." She put her head on one side and looked at him. "So are you married, dear?"

George shook his head.

"Why not?" she said, with the bluntness her generation was allowed.

"I'm not sure I've met the right person yet," he said.

And then realized what he'd just said.

"George?" called Kate. "Your cab's here!"

"Are you all right, dear?" said the elderly aunt. "You've gone quite pale."

Outside, in the cold December air, George staggered to the car like someone who'd been kicked in the shins.

. . .

Southwark Playhouse was full. Tess, who was late, crept into her seat seconds before the lights went down. At the last minute, Dominic hadn't been able to come. Some crisis at work. Although, she thought, Dominic would never use those words. He didn't see the world in the same terms as everyone else. Panic is counterproductive, he said. When people flap about like headless chickens, that's the time to slow everything down. Look at the problems calmly. Use cold, hard logic. Tess felt, sometimes, as if she had blundered onto the bridge of the starship *Enterprise*. Although he's right, of course, she thought. I wouldn't deny that for a second. You can't surf through life on a wave of emotion. Extreme feeling gets you nowhere.

In the darkness of the theater, a lone saxophonist spilled sound into the empty space.

Tess flinched. The impact was so sharp that she felt the music pouring down inside her like neat gin. Tears pricked the back of her eyes. What's wrong with me? she thought. She tried to be rational. It must have been the ridiculous rush to finish work and race for the tube, no time to stop and say good night to Colin, hunched in the icy December drizzle. It must have been because she'd skipped lunch and had nothing but a bag of salt-and-vinegar crisps. It must have been because of the night before, arguing with Dominic about Penge (I don't want to live in Penge), or because of Glenda at work, all wet pink quivering, saying, "So can I buy a hat?," or because of her mother, on the phone, saying, "But are you sure you want to move in together? Really sure?"

It must have been the hormonal buildup that had been knotting her reason all week, clogging her thinking, sending her into a small vortex of panic. It must have been all of these things. It must have been all of these things that made her bow her head in the darkness, as the saxophonist played, and start to cry.

Oh, the relief of weeping when rationalizing the causes doesn't help at all.

But when the stage lights came up, and the play began, she quickly used both hands to wipe the evidence from her face.

Behind her, slightly above her, George—whose old

friend Alex had stepped in at the last minute to play the saxophone solo—couldn't concentrate. He watched the actors moving around the stage, walking from side to side like little people in an architect's model, but he wasn't listening to what they were saying, or thinking about what they were doing. He was wondering, with some anxiety, why no one in the band was talking to him. Something was going on. But he didn't have a clue what it was.

. . .

Tess was lost. If this was the right ward, where were you supposed to go? She glanced into a room to her right, but on the bed lay a man she didn't recognize, with a bald head and so much flesh it seemed to be flopping over the edge of the mattress. There was no one around to ask. For a moment, she wondered whether she should be there at all. As she hesitated, a woman in blue overalls with a kind face came out of a storeroom to her left.

Tess said, "Excuse me, but I'm looking for someone."

"Go and ask the nurses, dear," said the woman, pointing up the corridor.

So Tess ventured further in, feeling guilty for bringing her outdoor dirt into a place that was trying so hard to keep clean. She found an official-looking alcove with a desk and telephones, but there was no one there. Just when she was about to turn round and take her teeming bacteria back outside again, a woman in a dark blue tunic appeared as if by magic behind the desk and said, "Can I help?"

"I'm looking for Colin," said Tess.

She had been walking back from Dickins & Jones in Regent Street, where she had spent a very happy lunch hour choosing earrings for Kirsty's Christmas present. It was cold and sunny, the sky pale blue. And then, just as she neared Daisy Greenleaf, she saw the ambulance. She ran. When she got there, the paramedic was closing the rear doors. He wouldn't tell her anything to begin with. She had to plead with him. Then, at last, he said she should try Guy's Hospital. So she had rung every day until they said he could have visitors.

"Oh Colin," said the nurse. "He's down to your right, in the bay at the end."

She was busy. She turned away.

But I wanted to ask you, thought Tess, how he is. Because I'm frightened of what I will find.

The bay was filled with bright clear winter light. Tess's anxious glance took in four beds, all occupied by men in various states of undress. She looked at the first bed, but it wasn't Colin. The man propped up against the white pillows—his eyes shut, gaunt but clean-shaven—was only middle-aged. She walked to the end of the bay. To her left was an Asian man flanked by small children and a smiling woman in a purple coat who nodded at her in a friendly way as if they already knew each other. To her right was a thin black man lying down flat with a young white woman holding his hand. Tess turned back to face the entrance of the bay. The only other bed was empty, with someone in a green dressing gown—young, with blond hair—sitting in a chair by its side.

Oh, thought Tess, confused and embarrassed. I'm in the wrong place. She was walking back the way she had come when the man in the first bed opened his eyes. She stared. He coughed, a terrible sound that shocked her and made her rush forwards to the end of his bed, where, because she didn't know what to do, she stood in hopeless confusion. After a while, the coughing stopped. His eyes closed again.

Tess said, "Can I get you some water?"

The man nodded, but slowly, as if even that small movement tired him.

Tess filled the plastic cup from the jug, spilling water all over the narrow table across the bed, and leant forwards to hand it to him. But he was too weak to lift his arm to take it from her. She said, "There's a straw in the cup. I'm going to put it on your mouth. All you have to do is drink." He gave a small nod. And it was only then, once she could see him drinking, that she thought, It's Colin, it's Colin. Her heart contracted and she felt like crying. Because the man in the bed wasn't seventy, or sixty, or anything like it. The man in the bed was probably in his late forties—the same sort of age her dad would have been had he lived. Without the huge gray beard, and the matted mess of wiry gray hair, you could see that he was skeletally thin. There were deep lines scored on both cheeks. Laughter lines, thought Tess. But when did I ever see Colin laugh?

When he'd finished drinking, Tess took the cup and straw away and set it back on the table in the puddle of spilled water. She looked around for something to wipe it with. But there didn't seem to be anything at all in Colin's little bay—no tissues, or fruit, or papers to read. She bit her lip. She said, "Can I sit down?"

His eyes opened again. They didn't look like Colin's eyes. They were opaque like dirty glass. Tess pulled forward the gray plastic chair and sat down.

Colin didn't say anything for a long time. He shut his eyes again, and she wondered if he'd gone back to sleep. She felt awkward and hot, stuffed into her clothes like a homemade toy filled with too much foam. You are a body in a bed, she thought, and I am a body in a chair, and some giant hand has just flopped us both here until the action begins again. She longed for a cup of tea. I think I might feel less strange, she thought, if I had a cup of tea.

He said, with great effort, "When?"

She leant forwards. "What did you say?"

But he didn't repeat it.

Eventually she said, guessing, "When did you come in here? On Wednesday. Five days ago."

After a while, Colin said, "What took you so long?"

His eyes were still closed. Was that a joke? It was hard to tell. He's probably drugged up. That's why he's so sleepy. Tess looked over at the next bed, where the woman in the purple coat was visiting her husband, and she envied her all the children. It must be so much easier visiting someone if you can bring in children. It gives you something to talk about.

She said, "It's nice and light in here. Great big windows."

Colin didn't react. Why would he? Who wants to talk

about hospital architecture when they're ill? There was another long gap when neither of them spoke, and then Tess said, desperate to fill the silence, "Colin, is there anything you need? Anything I can bring you?"

Still he said nothing.

"Anyone I can contact?"

Colin's face cracked into a frightening expression she couldn't read—anger or laughter or extreme pain. In panic, she half-stood and said, "What's wrong? What's happened?" desperately looking round for a cord to pull or a button to press or a nurse to call. Then she saw that the skin beneath his eyes was wet. Oh, she thought, creased and folded inside with an anguish that hurt like a vicious punch to the stomach, please don't cry. Please don't cry. She sat down on the chair and leant forwards, taking hold of the hand lying nearest to her. It was very cold.

"What do you need, Colin? What can I bring you?"

A nurse appeared at the end of the bed. She said, "Sorry to disturb you, but I need to take some blood."

"Shall I go?" said Tess.

"I'll be about ten minutes, if you want to stay."

But Tess couldn't stay. She had reached the limit of what she was able to bear. She turned to Colin. She said, "I'm going now. But I'll come back tomorrow."

As she left the bay and walked back to the nurses' station, she found there were tears running down her face.

• • •

"What?" said George.

Rhys couldn't meet his eyes.

"Someone tell me."

Walter said, "Man, this is hard."

"What's hard?" said George.

"Spit it out," said Mo to Walter.

But Walter just stood there.

"You've got to tell me," said George. But he knew what Walter was going to say. He leant back against the wall, needing its support.

"I can't do it anymore," said Walter. "I'm sorry."

George had known it was coming. But it didn't make any difference. It felt as if Walter had punched him in the ribs. "That's OK."

"I don't know if I'm doing the right thing."

"I know," said George.

"It's the money. And the security."

George took a deep breath. "You've got a son to look after. I can see that." After a while, he said, "Do you know anyone? Anyone who's as good as you?"

"You might have a problem there," said Mo.

"I know," said George. "You don't get many sax players like Walter."

"No," said Mo. "I meant, you're going to need more than a sax player."

"Why?"

Mo looked over at Rhys.

"No," said George.

"I'm sorry," said Rhys.

"Why?"

"I don't know how to say this," said Rhys. "But I've been doing a lot of thinking. And I want to go home."

"Home?"

"Back to Swansea. I'm ever so sorry."

"Right," said George. After a while, reeling like a boxer who's been hit on the chin, he said, "It's not that far. Swansea. You could come down for gigs."

"Not really," said Rhys.

"Four hours? Five hours?"

Rhys shook his head.

"But why?" said George. "What's the problem?"

"The thing is, you see," said Rhys, "I want to be a poet."

George looked at him in bewilderment. After a while, he said, "A poet?"

"I know what you're thinking. Where's this come from? But to tell you the truth, I've been writing for years. I just didn't tell anyone. It's not something you talk about, really."

"I never knew," said George.

"Well, that's the thing, isn't it? We all keep secrets."

"So is it my turn now?" said Mo.

George, on the ropes, looked up through the one swollen, bloody eye he could still see through.

"Time to call it a day," said Mo.

George said, "Why? Are you a spy?"

Mo stared. "A spy? Who says I'm a spy?"

George pictured Mo with a stirred martini and a Walther

PPK. But then he thought, Maybe not. Maybe they don't pick red-haired Glaswegians. He said, "So why are you leaving?"

Mo shrugged. "There's only two of us left."

George looked at him helplessly.

"You know I'm right. It's like cutting the front legs off a horse. No chance it'll run." Mo flicked his fag end to the floor. "And anyway it's time you learned to swim. Like throwing a baby in a pond. Best way to get it started."

George was down for the count. He said, with the small bit of breath he had left, "So what are you going to do?"

"Me?" said Mo. "I'm going back to school."

"School?"

"That's right." Mo looked round the room, belligerent, ready to take them all on. "I'm gonnae teach physics."

. . .

"Someone must care," said Tess.

"Like who?"

"I don't know. But everyone's got someone who cares about them."

Tess and Kirsty were in the launderette. It was the week before Christmas. A strand of tinsel, wafted by hot air from the dryers, was dancing about on the ceiling.

"Some people don't have anyone," said Kirsty.

"But that's so sad." Tess bit her lip.

"He's got you," said Kirsty.

"But I'm no one," said Tess. "I'm just someone who says

hello to him in the morning on my way to work. You need family when you're ill."

"He might not have any family."

Tess pulled her cardigan more closely around her waist. It was bottle-green, hand-knitted, vintage—but not quite warm enough. "He might be one of those people who went missing. Maybe his family has been looking for him for years."

Kirsty looked at her sadly. "You want him reunited with his loving family in time for Christmas."

"What's wrong with that?"

"Maybe Colin got out because he couldn't stand the sight of them. That could be his idea of hell—his whole dysfunctional family returning to haunt him."

Tess imagined the family, frowning and furious, standing round the hospital bed all different heights, stiff and officious like traffic wardens. "But what if," she said, "there'd been some kind of misunderstanding? Some terrible argument that everyone regrets? Maybe he was married. Maybe right now his wife is sitting in their living room desperately wanting to know where he is."

"You don't know," said Kirsty. "That's the point. If you dig up people from his past it might make the whole thing worse."

They sat watching their sheets tumble and flip in the dryers.

"I'm going to be away for a whole week," said Tess. "I hate to think of him without visitors all that time."

There was a pause. Kirsty said, "I'm back at work on Boxing Day. Do you want me to go?"

Tess turned to look at her.

"We'd have to visit together at least once before then," said Kirsty. "Or he wouldn't know who I was."

"Would you do that? Really?"

"My good deed for Christmas," said Kirsty.

"I'll bring you back an extra-big slice of Christmas cake," said Tess. Tess's mum's Christmas cake was legendary. In Manchester, Ellie used to hoard her piece for weeks, eking it out crumb by crumb.

"A corner," said Kirsty, "with all the icing."

"Done."

Someone opened the door onto the street. A blast of cold air whipped round, disturbing the dust under the benches and ruffling the pages of someone's abandoned newspaper.

Tess shivered. Kirsty said, "You should be wearing a coat."

"It didn't quite go with this skirt."

"You'd sacrifice warmth for fashion?"

"Of course," said Tess. "Doesn't everyone?"

Kirsty yawned. "How much longer will it be?"

"I don't know. We can check in a minute. But I don't want damp sheets."

Kirsty stretched out her legs. "Oh, I know what I forgot to tell you. Gareth's going to South America."

"Is he? Why?"

"To get over me, of course."

"That seems a bit drastic."

"Rhys says he's always wanted to travel. He's going to start in Argentina." She frowned. "Or maybe Patagonia."

"And Rhys is going back to Swansea."

"It'll be really weird," said Kirsty, "once they all go. End of an era. I spent so much time in Hackney. And now they're all leaving London and disappearing round the world."

Tess said, "Wales isn't round the world."

"But New York is."

"Who's going to New York?"

Kirsty said, "Didn't I tell you? George is going to Manhattan. His girlfriend got a promotion."

Tess's heart thumped uncomfortably. "What girlfriend?"

"She's a lawyer."

"When did all this happen?"

"It was really quick," said Kirsty. "I think she's quite pushy. She's the kind of person who gets what she wants."

It was ridiculous to feel sad.

"I think fate got a bit creative," said Kirsty, "and went off piste."

After all, she'd never even met George. None of this made any difference.

"Look at it this way," said Kirsty. "We can get a free holiday in New York."

Tess thought of all the films of New York she had ever seen—*Breakfast at Tiffany's, Manhattan, When Harry Met Sally*. She thought of the Chrysler Building, the Statue of Liberty, Central Park. She thought of the pictures of the planes flying into the Twin Towers. New York, thought Tess. George is going to New York.

"I don't think I'll have time for a holiday," said Tess.

"Why not?"

"I might be busy," said Tess in a voice that she hoped sounded bright and enthusiastic. "I might be busy buying a flat in Penge."

2007

Mum?"

"You sound excited."

"I've got some news."

"Oh good!"

"Not that kind of news."

"Oh."

"Mum, it's not fair. It really isn't. Every time I ring."

"Not every time."

"Have you thought that it might never happen? Maybe I don't want to get married."

"Of course. If you don't want to. I just thought, now that you and Dominic have bought the flat and got yourselves settled and done all that DIY—"

"We bought the flat to get a foot on the property ladder. As an investment. You know that."

"It was very sensible."

"And we've only had it two years and it's already gone up in value. So Dominic was right."

"He's good with money."

"About Penge. Right about Penge. Mum, what are you doing?"

"I'm just putting the milk back in the fridge."

"Don't forget to shut it. Or everything will go off like it did last week."

"And how are his parents?"

"They're fine."

"Still in Croydon?"

"Still in Croydon."

"And his sister? Still with the violent husband?"

"Mum, he's called Enric."

"I know he is. But I find it very hard to remember the names of people who sound unpleasant."

"Dominic hasn't heard from her for a while. Which is probably a good sign. She only ever gets in touch when things are going wrong."

"It must be so hard having a daughter in Cyprus."

"Catalonia."

"London's bad enough. And we're only an hour to Charing Cross."

"So do you want to hear the news?"

"Go on, then. What's happened?"

"You know my boss?"

"Mr. Bankes?"

"No, my immediate boss. Glenda."

"Oh yes."

"She's retiring."

"Well, that's nice."

"She's going to Swanage."

"Oh, just down the road from Gran. How lovely. So you

won't lose touch. Every time you visit Gran, you can pop in and see her."

"There's a bit more to it than that."

"Is there?"

"Glenda's retiring."

"I know, darling. You just said so. She'll be by the sea."

"Which means that someone has to do her job. Mum, are you listening?"

"Someone's just put something through the door. I think it might be one of those charity bags you're meant to fill up with old clothes. But I don't really have any old clothes to give away. I'm wearing them, mostly."

"So, Glenda's retiring."

"Yes."

"And when she retires, someone has to take over."

"Right."

"Take over the job. Head of customer services."

"Not you."

"Yes!"

"Tess. You're going to be head of customer services?"

"Yes!"

"But you're only twenty-eight! That's the kind of job people get in their forties!"

"I know. Isn't it wonderful?"

"What does Dominic say?"

"He's very proud of me. I've got a bigger salary. And he says that if we go on at this rate we might be able to afford a house before too long."

"A house?"

"Maybe even in Beckenham."

"Oh, Tess. What wonderful news. When did you hear?"

"This morning."

"I'm so proud of you. Really. Can I tell everyone?"

"Who?"

"Well, Toby's mum for a start. She's always going on about Saint Martins and Toby's installments. Head of customer services. Your father would have been so proud. Are you coming home to celebrate?"

"Just me, or both of us?"

"Both of you. Dominic's family now, isn't he?"

"Let me ask him. He's pretty busy at work."

"I know, darling. He works very hard."

"He's ambitious."

"And so he should be. So he can look after you."

"I can look after me."

"Well, not if—"

"Mum?"

"I'm just saying. Not now. But at some point. I did hope when you were doing all that decorating that you might be getting ready for a new arrival."

"You can't help it, can you?"

"Ten years."

"Nine."

"Nearly ten years. Isn't that enough time to make up your minds?"

"It's not about making up our minds."

"Isn't it?"

"No. And I know you're making a face."

"You're imagining it."

"I've got to go now. Supper's nearly ready."

"Is Dominic cooking for you?"

"Dominic always cooks for me."

"What is it tonight?"

"Something to do with aubergines. And lemons."

"How exotic. You're so lucky to have him."

"Mum, what's that noise?"

"It's the washing machine."

"It sounds like it's about to explode."

"It always does that on the spin cycle these days."

"Shall I ask Dominic to have a look at it when we come down?"

"Would you? Such a lovely man. So practical."

. . .

Sometimes, when he and Stephanie were both in the brownstone in Greenwich Village, George felt that he was entirely alone. The house was absurdly big for two people. It had been bought, George knew, not so much as a house as an in-your-face display of success. After several high-profile deals, Stephanie had become ridiculously popular. The presidents of US companies asked for her by name. She was a luxury brand—something you could drop into the conversation to prove you meant business.

Now she wanted to flaunt this hard-won fame by spending money as publicly as possible. She looked well on it. Her credit-card thinness made clothes look stunning. Her bony legs showed off shoes to perfection. Her skin glowed, her eyes shone, and when she shook her head, every single hair of her shiny brown bob settled back into neat, obedient symmetry.

George, meanwhile, was torn in two directions. On the surface, he was enjoying his new luxurious existence. When his elder brother, who had flown in for an international conference on heart surgery, came round to the house for dinner, George relished every moment of his obvious astonishment. George opened bottles of champagne as if they were Coke. He name-dropped. He mentioned plays they had seen, dinners they had been to, private views they had enjoyed. He reveled in the fact that his father would soon know that George—hopeless, dithering, indecisive George—was leading the kind of life that a hospital consultant could only dream of.

Still, sometimes, George worried what Stephanie saw in him. He wasn't rich or successful. He wasn't witty or brilliant or even particularly good-looking. Perhaps, he thought, that was the point. He didn't cause problems. He didn't make trouble. Stephanie wanted to concentrate on her work. She didn't have time for complicated relationships. So George—supportive, helpful, and quite happy to pick up dry cleaning—was ideal. They had efficient and reasonably satisfying sex twice a week. He accompanied her to the parties and lunches she had to attend. He listened admiringly to her tales of confrontation and killer blows. He didn't challenge her, or contradict her, or try to change her.

But inside he was terrified.

He kept it secret, this desperate mouthing for air. Stephanie's rich and influential friends had no idea. After all, she managed his PR perfectly. From the very beginning, she dressed him in cashmere suits and silk ties and handmade shoes. She dropped hints about his astonishing musical virtuosity. Tentatively, parents began to ask whether this gifted performer and composer had ever thought about teaching. Because Stephanie's friends were lawyers, not musicians—and because George was British, which made it harder for anyone to check out the truth of the stories Stephanie told—no one asked too many questions. Within twelve months of moving to New York, George was having to turn people down. I'm afraid I can't take anyone else on, he would say. I just don't have enough time. He was a good teacher, which helped. He was patient and kind and brought out the best in his pupils. The children loved him.

He should have been happy.

But, for the first time in his life—or rather for the first time since he was two years old and had scaled the piano stool in order to press all the black keys, one by one—George had stopped playing. He ran through the pieces he was about to teach his pupils. He reminded himself of scales and arpeggios. From time to time he picked out a half-forgotten tune. But, for the most part, the grand piano stood lonely and unloved in the second-floor living room, its lid firmly shut.

To begin with, when they first moved to Manhattan, George had spent his evenings in jazz clubs. He listened to what was going on. He was excited by the possibilities. Alone in the house when Stephanie went to work, he started playing with ideas. New York moved to a different beat. It had a percussion so different to London that the old rhythms didn't seem right anymore. He worked hard. He got so involved in composition that he had to buy a large old-fashioned alarm clock that rang shrilly when it was time to go and teach.

But the harder he worked, the less confident he became. He had no idea if any of it was any good. He researched the market. He bought magazines. He read online interviews with jazz promoters and festival directors. He listened to clips on YouTube.

"George," said Stephanie, "shut the door, please, when you're playing."

He screwed up his courage and recorded a CD. He put this together with a photograph, a biography, and press quotes, ready to send out to booking agents.

"It's all a bit strange and discordant, that new stuff, isn't it?" said Stephanie.

One morning, as usual, George made a cup of coffee and went upstairs to start his day. He had a whole morning before he had to shrug off his secret jazz ambitions and go out to teach Chopin and Bach to the offspring of wealthy New York attorneys. But he didn't even get as far as the piano. He stood in the doorway and looked at the great shining curve of black lacquer and it was like staring at the dishwasher or the microwave. He didn't want to play. It was strange and frightening, this lack of desire, like not breathing, or not eating, or never feeling thirsty.

He told no one. Who was he going to tell? His old friends—the down-at-heel musicians whom Stephanie so despised—were on the other side of the world. He didn't answer emails from London. There was, at the same time, too much and too little to say.

The mail-out to booking agents stayed in his desk drawer.

"Are you sick?" said Stephanie impatiently one Saturday morning. She was putting on mascara in the hall mirror. She was anxious to go shopping. There was a lot to do. "Do you need to see a doctor?"

"I don't think so," said George.

"So what's wrong?"

"I don't know."

"George," said Stephanie, "everybody gets down sometimes. But you don't just give in to it. You fight it. If you're depressed, go and see Dr. Mishkin. He'll give you some Prozac."

George looked at her like a kicked dog.

"Now what?" she said. "You look terrified."

He shook his head.

"If you're ready to go, can you get your coat? We'll never get everything done otherwise."

"I was thinking of going home for a bit," said George.

Stephanie turned round and looked at him. "Going home?"

"Back to London."

"What about your pupils?"

"They could manage without me for a few weeks."

"They're studying piano, George. Of course they can't manage without you."

"I just feel," said George desperately, "that I might play again if I could visit some of the old clubs. See what's going on."

Stephanie looked at him. "Aren't you getting a bit old for all that?"

"I'm thirty."

"Exactly."

George opened his mouth and shut it again.

"All I mean," said Stephanie, speaking slowly and clearly, "is that you can sit around dreaming of fame and fortune when you're in your teens. But by the time you get to our age, the game has changed. It's time to get serious." She stopped and looked round her at the tall ceilings, the paintings, the elegant lamps. "I mean, this didn't just happen by itself, George. I worked for it. We worked for it. And we've got to capitalize on the time we have now to make the most money we can. That's what happens in your thirties. You make your fortune."

George looked at her.

"I'm very proud of you, George. You're teaching the children of some of the wealthiest families in New York. And I don't think you find it too exhausting, do you?"

"But I've stopped playing," said George.

"Well, maybe because you've woken up to reality. As you've said yourself, it's very hard to make money out of performing. But you can make a very nice living from teaching. As long as you charge enough. Which you do now. Thank goodness."

"But if I'm not playing, what's the point?"

"Oh, George." Stephanie shook her head. "Sometimes you sound like a child."

A child? thought George.

"I think you should see someone. A shrink. That's what everyone does here. I think you need to talk out what's going on in your head. I mean, personally, I think you're fighting against growing older. And I think all men do that to a certain extent. They want to remain little boys. Which is, you know, perfectly understandable." Stephanie frowned. "Although slightly alien to women. Because we quite relish being adults. But still, it's something I've heard a lot about, this male immaturity, and I think it would be a good idea to have a few sessions and bring it all out in the open." She looked at her watch. "But right now, we've got to go shopping. You need new socks, and I've got to pick up my jacket."

"I don't think—"

"George, can we leave this now? I think we've covered what we've got to say."

It was at moments like these, when Stephanie was particularly impatient, that George found himself wondering whether their relationship was really working. Would I be happier alone? Should I get out now before it's too late? And the thought would jiggle at the back of his mind all day, small but hugely significant, like a crucifix dancing from the rearview mirror.

But Stephanie always seemed to know when she had gone just a little bit too far. Much later, after supper and fresh mint tea, George would come back into the bedroom after cleaning his teeth to find her stretched out on the bed wearing nothing but black garters and Chanel No. 5.

"We're a team, George," she would say, her tiny breasts flirting with his mouth. "We're a team."

As the months passed, George's longing to go home intensified. He couldn't get London out of his head. He fantasized about the late-night café round the corner from the house in Hackney, where the four of them used to go after gigs. A full English at two in the morning, steam on the windows, the smell of bacon fat and boiled milk and buttered toast. We were good, thought George. The band was good. And now what am I doing? Sitting around in luxury houses teaching the kids of wealthy lawyers.

Two years after they arrived in New York, George's dissatisfaction had reached the point where he knew he had to take action. But then three things happened in quick succession.

One afternoon at four thirty, George went to the Upper East Side for his regular weekly lesson with William, the fourteen-year-old son of a wealthy divorce lawyer and his extremely unfriendly wife. The maid let him in as usual, and George walked up the sweeping curved staircase to the main living room, all blond wood and white walls, which looked out over Central Park. Everything was ordered, empty, and silent. George always felt, in their modern and minimalist house, that he had become suddenly deaf.

When he turned round, there was William's mother.

"Can we talk?" she said.

George stared at her. She had never before shown the slightest interest in having any kind of conversation with him. Mostly she looked just past him as if she wasn't sure whether he was sufficiently well connected to be visible.

"Please sit down," she said. "I asked William to wait five minutes."

So George sat down.

"We need to talk about my son," she said.

George was lost. He liked William. He was a competent pianist who practiced fairly regularly and seemed to enjoy the lessons. What was there to talk about?

"Tell me," she said, "are you pleased with William's progress?"

"Yes," said George. "He's doing well."

"How well?"

"Pretty well."

She gave him a tight little smile. "Could you be more specific?"

"His technique is good," said George. "He's coping with advanced pieces. He has a musical ear."

She said, impatiently, "Is he better or worse than your other pupils?"

"I'm not sure I quite understand," said George.

She looked at him with irritation. "Next month there is a public festival. William is playing. I want to know if he will be the best one there."

She's poisonous, thought George. He felt angry and cornered, protective towards William.

"I didn't know," he said slowly, "that this was a competition."

"Of course it's a competition," she said scornfully. "Life is a competition."

All the words George wanted to say spit in his mind like a fistful of sparklers. He longed to walk out, to turn his back on her snobbery, her stupidity, her small-mindedness. But instead he sat there, rooted to the spot. Is she right? he thought. Her words reverberated round his head. If life is a competition, am I winning or losing?

Later, as he walked through the park after the lesson, trying to clear the fog in his mind, he weighed up what he had as if balancing evidence on old-fashioned scales. I'm not playing, he thought. I'm not performing. So I'm losing. But, on the other hand, I'm making easy money. I'm living with a beautiful woman in a beautiful house in one of the richest cities in the world. That sounds like winning.

In his pocket, as he walked, he fingered random coins. Should I flip a quarter? Heads I win, tails I lose?

He was angry with himself. He hated thinking of his life as bookkeeping, as a record of profit and loss. New York is changing me, he thought, as he looked up at the clear blue sky through the trees. I used to live in a muddle but know exactly what I wanted to do. Now my life is a model of order and I have absolutely no idea where I'm going.

The second thing that happened was a charity dinner to raise money for cancer research. George found himself sitting next to a woman in her fifties with swept-up dark hair just beginning to go gray. She was easy to talk to. George found himself thinking up stories about his childhood in Guildford to make her laugh—his father's insistence that the heating should never be turned on until December, ice inside the windows, sheets so stiff they made a sound like cracked glass whenever you turned over.

He said, "And what about you? Where did you grow up?"

"I grew up in California," she said, "where the sun always shines."

"And what do you do as a job?"

"Well, I've raised four sons."

George smiled. "That sounds tiring."

She laughed. "It was. It still is." She took a sip of wine. "When I was younger, I was a dancer."

"What kind of dance?"

"The ballet." She looked at him, her eyes bright, gauging his reaction. She said, "I was good."

George didn't doubt it. "So what happened?"

"You can't dance forever. It's something you do when you're young."

George searched her face for signs of regret. But she was quite calm.

She said, "You know, if you asked anyone around this table whether they were still doing the one thing they were desperate to do when they were young, I think they'd all pretty much say no. I loved to dance. But then it was time to stop. And I had my sons. And I think I've been very blessed."

Soon afterwards, she turned to talk to the guest on her right. George swallowed his red wine. He refilled his glass. He would have continued down the bottle had he not caught sight of Stephanie's disapproving glance from the end of the table.

Much later, when they were back home in bed, George lay on his back and stared into the darkness. He felt as if he was sitting in the back of a New York cab, looking out at total gridlock, with no idea how long he'd be stuck, or what was holding him up, or even whether he should stay put or get out and walk.

The third thing that happened was that Stephanie made him supper. She very rarely made him supper. Generally, they went out to eat. If they didn't, it was George who raided the deli and found enough ingredients to assemble some kind of picnic. But this one Thursday night, George got home to find Stephanie in the kitchen peeling potatoes.

"You're home," he said, surprised. She never normally got back before eight—later, if she was in the middle of a deal. He took off his jacket and put it on the back of a chair. "Is everything all right?"

"Oh, do hang it up, George, please," she said.

He went back out to the hall and hung his coat in the cupboard. Somewhere right at the back of his mind was a tiny pilot light of hope. Had something gone wrong? Something at work? Did this mean they could go home? And then, filling his head with celestial brilliance like a shaft of sunlight after a storm, the solution came to him. It was as if he'd been sleeping and something had jerked him awake. Manhattan suited Stephanie. But it didn't suit him. Yes, it had been an experience. But now, after two years, it stifled him. It appalled him. It reduced him to zero. We should go back, he thought. After what she's done in New York, Stephanie could walk into any job in London. And back home, in the grit and grime of London clubs, I could feel my way to playing again. And if Stephanie won't come back, he thought, if she won't understand that I can't live here anymore, I'll go without her. Because I have to get out. I need to breathe again.

For one brief, glorious moment, George felt intense relief. The shackles fell. The chains were loose. He was free.

Back in the kitchen, George opened the fridge. "Would you like a drink?" he said. He thought a glass of wine might make it easier for her to tell him what had happened.

"No, thanks," she said.

Something in her voice made him look up. "Are you sure?"

She nodded, smiling. His heart beat faster.

"I'm pregnant," she said.

George stood there, holding the bottle of wine, as if someone had sprayed him with ice and immobilized him forever.

"I found out this morning," she said. "I was wondering why I felt so tired. Ten weeks, apparently." She looked at him. "You've got that panicked look on your face."

"Were we trying?"

"No, of course not. We're in the point-three percent."

"The what?"

"The point-three percent perfect use failure rate of the combined pill."

"Oh."

"Although when you think about it, we wouldn't have wanted to leave it much longer, would we? I'm thirty-two."

George put down the bottle of wine. "No."

"I'm going to have to watch my diet from now on," she said. "No soft cheeses."

George felt as if his head was full of mascarpone. He tried to think clearly. "Have you told them at work?"

She frowned. "Of course not. I've only just told you."

"Of course," said George.

"There's a lot to plan," she said, turning back to the sink and picking up the knife.

George, whose world had just exploded, tried to pick up

recognizable fragments from the rubble. "Will we go back to London?"

"Why would we do that?"

"I don't know. I just wondered if you wanted to."

"No," she said, cutting a potato in half. "There's nothing for us in London."

"No," said George.

"Thank goodness we've got space for a live-in nanny."

George felt for a chair behind him and sat down heavily. "So is there anything you need?" he said. "Anything I can do?"

She turned round and looked at him. "Well, there is one thing."

"What?" said George.

"You could ask me to marry you."

"Oh," said George. "Oh yes. Is that what you want?"

She laughed. "You are funny," she said. "Of course that's what I want. I told you," she said, and the knife glinted in her hand, "we're a team."

. . .

"I'm not sure you have quite the right experience," said Tess.

Although to be fair, she thought, she's only just out of university. And, really, there isn't a lot of experience that's relevant to selling badly dyed handmade goods at inflated prices. Except, perhaps, for a thick skin.

Opposite her, staring with the huge eyes of a Disney faun, the young woman looked as if she might burst into tears.

"What made you think of applying?" said Tess.

There was an awkward pause.

"What was it about Daisy Greenleaf," said Tess, helpfully, "that made you want to work here?"

It was quite exciting taking on a new member of staff. Her number two. But I have to be very careful, thought Tess, to choose wisely. This particular candidate could speak Spanish, which might come in handy if they ever did business in South America. And she had an A-level in maths, which would be a definite bonus on the days that Oliver asked for ballpark figures. But was there anything about her that made her stand out from the crowd?

The young woman blushed bright red. "You have such a wonderful range of goods," she said.

"Do we?" said Tess, astonished.

"Oh yes," said the young woman. "I love the notelets from Jaipur. And the little memo pads from Zimbabwe. And your mission statement on the website is really inspiring."

One of Oliver's less embarrassing efforts. "But you haven't really worked in customer services before, have you?" she said. "Or marketing?"

The young woman hung her head.

Oh dear, thought Tess. I really ought to bring this to a swift conclusion. She won't last five minutes with Oliver barking at her across the room. But she didn't want to be unkind. After all, she could just about remember being interviewed for the job herself, lying about the fluency of her French as Glenda quivered supportively across the table.

Where had the time gone? This, for some reason, made her think about the backbreaking hours she'd spent in the flat over the past two years, stripping the Anaglypta wallpaper and burning off curls of deep maroon gloss. Every weekend, it seemed, had been spent painting the skirting boards. She hadn't minded making curtains or learning how to put up roller blinds. But sometimes she had wished that Dominic's decorating standards weren't quite so high. Personally she would have been quite happy with a quick spray of stain blocker when the upstairs radiator had leaked onto the hall ceiling. But Dominic had insisted on pulling off the lining paper and starting all over again.

"Goodness me," her mother had said, standing in the kitchen, stunned at the extreme cleanliness of the paintwork. "It's like an operating theater."

"It's just very new," said Tess defensively.

"Oh, I'm not criticizing," said her mother. "I think your Dominic's extraordinary. He only wants the best for you, doesn't he?

He does, thought Tess. Like the time he bought me an art deco Bakelite wireless set from a car boot sale. He doesn't like clutter. He'd be all white and minimalist given the chance. But he knew I'd appreciate an old radio—one that probably broadcast Neville Chamberlain telling Britain the country was at war. "I have to tell you now that no such undertaking has been received." Small gestures like that mean so much. He doesn't need to tell me that he loves me. He shows me he loves me by all the things he does.

Tess frowned. Although I did think, once we had our own place, that we would be wandering about naked from room to room, throwing ourselves into sex on bare floorboards and unbridled passion on the IKEA flat packs. But it hasn't really worked out like that. Once there's absolutely no reason not to—no possibility of a flatmate slamming through the front door, or an overnight guest bursting into the bathroom—you seem to lose the urge. Perhaps that's why people dress up as nurses and policemen. You have to pretend everything's naughty or it seems too normal to bother.

With a sudden rush of embarrassment, Tess realized that she was in the middle of an interview.

"So," she said, clearing her throat, "perhaps you'd like to tell me a little bit more about yourself. What are your interests?"

"Interests?"

"Hobbies," said Tess.

The young woman took a deep breath. "I love vintage clothes," she said.

Tess looked at her properly for the first time. "Do you?"

"They're so beautifully made. And I like the history of them. And thinking about who wore them, and what their lives were like. Do you know Cornucopia in Pimlico? I spend hours in there. Every Saturday if I can. And charity shops. You have to look quite hard sometimes. But I found a 1930s black silk satin evening dress by Jeanne Lanvin in Camberwell a few months ago."

Tess stared. The young woman bit her lip. "I mean, I wouldn't wear them to work. That wouldn't be appropriate. . . ." She trailed off, horrified that she'd said so much.

Tess leant forwards to study the CV. "Helen, isn't it?"

The young woman nodded.

Tess looked up. "When can you start?"

2008

As in Mia Farrow?" said his brother on the phone from London.

"We just liked the name," said George.

Stephanie liked it, he thought, more honestly.

"And how's it going? Getting any sleep?"

"Not much," said George.

But he didn't mind. Sometimes in the early morning hours, when Mia stared at him as if trying to memorize every line and angle of his face, he had a feeling of complete calm. Her eyes anchored him to the present. This was important, this moment of communication, and nothing else really mattered. Of course, when Stephanie appeared, furious (as she always was first thing in the morning), and stomped around replumping cushions and crashing crockery into the dishwasher so loudly that Mia began to cry, the mood was broken. But once she'd gone to work in her tailored black suit, looking surprisingly untouched by motherhood, George and Mia settled back into their long day of busy nothingness, staring at each other in mutual wonderment, falling asleep to the rhythm of each other's breathing. Stephanie would appear again at around seven PM—a slightly shorter working day because of the new baby—and look around at the chaos with irritable disbelief, and George would try hard to think of all the small achievements and pleasing milestones they had managed, with extreme cleverness, to pull off while she'd been at the office. He wanted her, like him, to have the joy of reveling in her small daughter's astounding progress. But when it came to it, when he looked at his wife's taut, angry face and opened his mouth to describe what this small magical person had done, there seemed nothing to say. Stephanie would snap, "So what have you been doing all day?" and George, suddenly tired, would say, with deferential apology, "Oh nothing, really. Nothing at all."

"Fresh air is very good for babies," she said one evening. "It helps them sleep."

He nodded.

"Really, George," she said, "it must be possible to get out to the deli at least. It's only just down the road."

"Yes," said George. "We'll do that tomorrow."

Two days later, they made it. At the deli, in the brightness of red and gold packets and light shining from cellophane wrapping, he was overwhelmed by kindness. Mia was admired and loved, and they wouldn't let him pay for anything—the pasta, the pancetta, the Parmesan. Every single woman in the shop was either smothering him with advice or patting his arm and telling him what a wonderful father he was. When he staggered out into the sunshine, he felt as if he'd joined some secret society he hadn't even known existed. Until you have children, he thought, you don't realize they're the focus of most people's lives.

"George?" said Stephanie one evening.

"What?" He had been watching Mia sleeping.

"Do you think you're becoming a little obsessed?"

George jumped guiltily. "Am I?"

"She doesn't need you to check she's breathing."

"No," said George.

He tried to ration himself after that. Or, at least, to stare at Mia only when he thought Stephanie wasn't looking.

. . .

"It's always so clean here," said Kirsty suspiciously.

"It's Dominic," said Tess. "He doesn't like mess." She felt embarrassed. The flat was so tidy and polished it looked as if someone had soaked it in Tide and hung it on the line to dry.

"I don't think anyone likes mess," said Kirsty.

Tess frowned. "But you never clean anything."

"That's because there's a big difference between not liking mess and actually being bothered to do anything about it." She flopped down onto the sofa. "So what's new?"

Kirsty was wearing a short purple dress, cinched in at the waist with a black leather belt. It clung to her body, with just a slight flare midthigh. She looked, as usual, effortlessly chic.

New? thought Tess. Nothing's ever new in my life. Unless you count an unexpected house coming onto the market in Beckenham. "Nothing, really," she said.

"You're wearing your glasses," said Kirsty. "That's new."

Tess put her hand up to her face. "I keep forgetting I've got them on," she said.

"I thought you hated glasses."

"I thought I hated lots of things," said Tess. "But I find, as I get older, that I don't." She looked at Kirsty. "What?"

"Nothing."

"You've got that 'Will you listen to her' look on your face."

"I just think you're a bit young to be saying, 'As I get older.'"

"Why?" said Tess. "It's true. I find sometimes that things I used to think were disgusting are actually quite nice. Like broccoli. And chicken livers."

"How about elasticated trousers?" said Kirsty. "And bi-focals?"

"Everyone's getting older," said Tess.

"But some people are doing it faster than others."

"It's called maturity."

"It's called sinking into middle age when you're not even thirty."

Tess opened her mouth to retaliate but decided not to bother.

"So how's your Polish journalist?"

Kirsty made a little face. "He's gone back to Poland."

"Really?" Tess felt sad for her.

Kirsty shrugged. "It's what he does. Follows the good stories."

"So when's he next coming back?"

"A couple of weeks," said Kirsty airily.

"You're not fooling me," said Tess.

"I'm not trying to," said Kirsty, opening her eyes wide.

"You quite like this one."

"I've told you I like him. But I'm not going to build my hopes up. We're never in the same country long enough for me to work out whether we even get on."

"It must be lovely to have the kind of job that takes you all over the world," said Tess.

"All you have to do," said Kirsty, "is resign from Daisy Greenleaf."

"I used to think I'd travel. And now look at me."

"In Penge," said Kirsty, grinning. But Tess looked so wistful she said, "So what's brought this on?"

"Tim and Lily are moving to Seattle."

"Are they?"

"They say it'll be really lovely for the children."

"Sleepless in Seattle," said Kirsty.

"The baby's going through the night now."

"Talking of babies," said Kirsty, "Rhys had an interesting bit of news the other day."

"He's having a baby?"

"I think he might need a girlfriend first."

"I thought you said there was somebody," said Tess, "who lived near Swansea. Somewhere quiet."

"The Mumbles," said Kirsty. "No, that's all over. This isn't about Rhys. This is about George."

"George?"

"Your soul mate," said Kirsty.

"You know, I never met him. Ever."

"You must have done."

"I didn't. We had so many near misses. But we never actually met."

"Even on Facebook?"

Tess, her glasses making her look like an intelligent owl, frowned. "He's not on Facebook."

Kirsty's eyes were full of mischief. "But you checked."

Of course I checked, thought Tess. It was natural human curiosity. I even looked on Twitter. There was someone called George in New York who liked 1940s jazz, but there was no photo. Just an egg.

She said, casually, "So what's George up to?"

"He got married. To that American woman. And they had a baby girl."

Tess's heart skipped a beat. "A baby girl?"

"George is besotted, apparently."

"I suppose he must be," said Tess, "or he wouldn't have married her."

"With the baby. He's the one looking after her. Full-time."

Tess pictured a man she'd never met standing on the Brooklyn Bridge (a random New York location she thought she remembered from *I Am Legend*) with a baby in a sling. "That's very progressive," she said.

"His wife earns a packet. So she goes out to work and he stays at home."

"What's she called?" said Tess.

"The wife?"

"The baby."

"I've no idea," said Kirsty. She looked at Tess more closely. "Why? Are you getting interested in babies?"

Tess thought back guiltily to that morning's conversation. Dominic had just got up and was stretching his rather bony arms above his head. (He looked slightly less godlike these days. In fact Tess had recently begun to wish that he'd put on his clothes a little faster in the mornings.) Tess, yawning, had asked him if he'd like a cup of tea and he'd smiled and said they were talking just like an old married couple and then, after a pause, added, "My mother keeps asking when she can buy a hat." Tess had looked at him anxiously. "I'm not quite ready yet," she said. Dominic said, "But we're probably the optimal age for babies, you know. Still young, but financially secure."

Tess stared into the middle distance. I don't want a baby, she thought.

"Tess?" said Kirsty.

"What?" she said, coming back to the present.

"Babies?"

Tess shook her head.

"Are you sure?"

"Yes," said Tess, firmly. "There's far too much I want to do before I settle down."

Despite all appearances to the contrary, she thought miserably.

2010

The house in Guildford was built on a downward slope. You stood like a skydiver in the road high above, wondering if falling was the only way in. The front drive was almost too steep for a parked car (would the bonnet end up on the sofa?). George and his brother had never been able to play a proper game of football at the back. In the long grass beyond the fence at the bottom of the hill, in the dip of the escarpment, was a graveyard of lost balls, cracked, damp, and deflated.

It had been bought as a temporary house. It wasn't particularly pretty—black Crittall windows, red bricks, and a tiled roof with a sharp ridge. George thought he could remember the year they moved in, when his mother stood on a stepladder painting all the walls white. But he wasn't sure. He would have been two or three. Perhaps he had created a memory with sunlight and the windows open and his mother conducting the Boomtown Rats with a paintbrush.

But then she left. She left when George was ten years old. She went to live in Cornwall with a man who made sculptures. In tears, she had tried to explain to George, her baby, that she had no choice, that she loved him but had to leave him.

I can't stay here, she said. I can't stay here. Looking back years later—when his mother had died and memories of summers in Cornwall had blurred to blue skies and seagulls—George thought she probably couldn't. Living with his father would have driven anyone mad. But at the time he didn't understand. She left, and he felt blank inside, like an empty room.

After that, he always stood back, watching what people did. Distance was comfortable. Taking part brought the danger of extricating yourself when things went wrong.

Once his wife had left to live with an artist in the West Country who couldn't support her, George's father forgot about the house being temporary. He didn't, after all, care very much about his surroundings. So there was no incentive to leave. As the years passed, the house—the white walls now gray—sank inexorably into a state of forlorn neglect. Paint peeled off the skirting boards. Damp patches appeared on the bathroom ceiling. Maggie, the cleaner, came twice a week. But her eyesight wasn't much good. Dust covered the books and the mantelpiece like soft gray felt. George's father didn't notice. After both his sons left, he lived alone for fifteen unremarkable years. He asked nothing of a home but a radio, bread and cheese, and a bottle of single malt. Life took place under the bright lights of the operating theater, where he ruled like a god. Home was just a waiting room for the hours in between.

His father hadn't wanted him to visit when he got out of hospital. "No need," he said on the phone.

"I want to see how you are," said George.

"Nothing to see."

The operation, according to George's older brother—who knew something about surgery, being a consultant cardiologist in a London teaching hospital—had gone well. But the long-term prognosis was poor.

"Poor?" said George.

His brother looked at him. "It's cancer."

As always, George was silenced. Both his father and his brother talked in the same way, supplying full stops where a comma would have been kinder.

So now, back in England for the first time in five years, George stood on wet red maple leaves, the lobes spread out like owl feet, and looked down at the green front door of his father's house. I have come, he thought, even though he asked me to stay away. I have come even though he will tell me nothing, give me nothing, share nothing of his thoughts. I am standing here on the pavement in the black cashmere coat that Stephanie bought me last fall, gathering up my courage to skid down a vertiginous drive into the house of a man who, at best, has only ever tolerated me.

It started to rain.

I am his son, thought George.

But it was only when he thought of Mia, his two-year-old daughter, and the way she opened her arms and laughed whenever she saw him, that he straightened his shoulders and began the steep and slippery descent.

• • •

"So how is he, then?" said Rhys.

They were sitting in the kitchen of the house in Hackney, drinking tea. Since George had last been there, someone had decided to paint the room blue. But they'd got only half-way. You could see the random sweeps where the roller had stopped, right in the middle of the wall above the cooker. George wondered what the interruption had been. A phone call? Running out of paint? The pub? Otherwise everything looked much the same. There was still no handle on the cupboard by the fridge and the wooden working surface—a recycled door—was a comprehensive history of ten years of cooking, complete with scorched rings, dents, and deeply gouged knife marks.

"Hard to tell," said George. "He seems the same. Says he's not in pain. I have no idea."

"It's not easy, is it?" said Rhys. "I think we're lucky, Gareth and I."

Rhys's parents lived on a smallholding in mid-Wales. It was windswept, uneconomic, and hard work. They were very happy.

"He didn't even want me to stay," said George. He thought of his father in the brown leather chair, listening to the ticking of the hall clock. He hated that clock. It made the emptiness seem even louder.

"He must be used to his own company," said Rhys.

He's certainly against the idea of mine, thought George.

"I think that's what happens in the end, to be honest," said Rhys, "if people live alone. They can't wait for you to go.

You're just sitting there, littering up the place. Once you've gone, they can turn on the telly and put their feet up."

George tried, and failed, to imagine his father putting his feet up.

"So go on, then," said Rhys.

"What?"

"Well, we've been here ten minutes and you haven't even shown me a photo."

"Of Mia?"

"Who else?"

George felt inside his pocket for his wallet. He drew out the picture of Mia and glanced down for a moment before he handed it over, just for the extreme pleasure of seeing his daughter's smile.

"Well, look at her," said Rhys. "She's beautiful. Doesn't look a bit like you."

But George just sat there smiling.

"I wish you could see yourself," said Rhys. "Just talking about her makes you light up."

"No one tells you it's like this," said George. "They tell you all the bad things. But nothing good."

"And you look after her."

"Stephanie's full-time. I'm still teaching. We have a babysitter who comes over two afternoons a week. But most of the time it's just me and Mia."

"How old is she?"

"She's two."

"You look well on it," said Rhys. He looked at George

more closely. "Quite prosperous, if you don't mind me saying."

"It's all Stephanie. Nothing to do with me."

"She's successful, is she?"

"Very," said George. She was unstoppable. New York suited her. "What about you?"

"Well, not successful exactly," said Rhys, after a pause. "And not in Swansea. As you can see."

"What happened?"

Rhys shifted uncomfortably. "I missed London. I can't believe it. All those years I spent longing to go home. And when I got there, I wanted to come back. I don't think I'm happy anywhere, to tell you the truth. I've become peripatetic."

George smiled. Rhys made the word sound so long, so full of carefully enunciated syllables.

"They took me back. At the bookshop. Got a few things published." Rhys pulled a face. "But I'm not what you'd call established."

"I thought you'd go back and find a nice Welsh girl and settle down."

"I'm not going to lie to you," said Rhys. "I was hoping the same thing myself."

George waited.

"There was someone," said Rhys.

"And?"

"It didn't work out," said Rhys. He stared into the middle distance, the scribble of his hair quite still, his thin face tragic.

So that's why you came back, thought George. He hoped Rhys might say more. But the silence lengthened.

"What about Mo?" said George. "And Walter?"

Rhys came back to the present. "Mo comes round sometimes. Knocks on the door at midnight and wants a bed for the night."

"Did he become a teacher?"

"He did. Secondary school in Essex."

"I can't imagine Mo teaching," said George. It would, he thought to himself, be like pinning a Catherine wheel inside a small cupboard and waiting for it to explode.

"Walter's got another two."

George stared. Had he been away that long?

"Twins. A boy and a girl."

"And he's a lawyer?"

"Working in the City. I can't help thinking it's a terrible waste." Rhys put his mug down on the table. He looked almost stern. "And what about you?"

George tried to make his voice sound light. "Not much."

"How much?"

George looked away.

"You're still not playing," said Rhys.

"I've just put it on the back burner for a bit."

I clear up Mia's toys. I make supper. I put on the TV. I do just about anything but play. Sometimes, thought George, I can't even hear the music in my head.

"You've got clubs in New York," said Rhys.

"Hundreds."

"So what's stopping you?"

An image of Stephanie came into his head. She frowned a lot these days when she looked at him. Of course they'd agreed that he would stay at home and look after Mia while she went out to work. But recently she'd seemed angry about the arrangement. She'd seemed angry with him. He felt like a painting that was being analyzed and found wanting—sloppy brushwork, indeterminate color, a lack of form and substance.

"Maybe it's the teaching," said George. "Too many scales." He picked up a spoon and drew in the spilt sugar on the table. He knew Rhys was watching him.

"You can't not play," said Rhys. "You were better than any of us." After a while, he added, "Maybe you need to find some other musicians. Start another band." And then he said, "Just go and listen to some of the people who are playing these days. See whether it inspires you." After a pause, he said, "There's a piano in the front room."

When George failed to respond to any of it, Rhys sighed. "There's a party tonight."

Now George met his eyes. "Tonight?"

"Kirsty. It's her birthday."

"I don't think so," said George.

"Why not?"

"I don't know," said George. "It's been so long since I've seen anyone."

"She's living in Kennington now."

"I might just have an early night."

"You'll never sleep."

He's probably right, thought George, gloomily. "I'm not in the mood."

"That's the thing about parties," said Rhys. "It doesn't matter if you're in the mood. You just stand there and let it happen."

George smiled.

"That's better," said Rhys. He seemed to be waiting for something.

"What?"

Rhys stood up. "Well, come on, then," he said. "If we're going."

. . .

Kirsty's flat was on Kennington Park Road, a fat, gray, traffic-filled thoroughfare that thundered from the Elephant towards the Oval. Some of the houses were Georgian, thin and elegant like shocked elderly ladies finding themselves unexpectedly in a greasy spoon. Kirsty lived in the basement of one of these houses. Her friend Rafael had gone back to Brazil for six months, and she was guarding his art collection from the south London burglars who didn't want it. One of the wooden carvings was of a nude man with an enormous erection. Despite this joyous state of affairs, his eyes were wide open with alarm, perhaps because his face appeared to be sliding down from his skull, his flesh long gloopy dribbles of runny icing.

When Kirsty opened the door and saw Rhys and George, she lit up with delight.

"You came!" she said happily.

"And why wouldn't I?" said Rhys.

"George," said Kirsty, and leant forwards to kiss him. "Is this a flying visit? I never did come for that holiday."

"You'd be very welcome," said George, who knew Stephanie would never allow one of his old friends to stay.

"We're having cocktails," said Kirsty. "Anything you like. Until it all runs out."

The flat was packed—so full of people you could hardly see the walls, which were hung with huge paintings that seemed to be almost entirely orange. They left their coats in a small study, which, piled with silk and leather and mohair, already looked like a charity shop in the King's Road, and then they were back in a crowd that was bursting with energy, screaming at itself from all directions. You could hardly hear the music, which sounded as if it might be breathy singing mixed with South American pipes. George, already displaced—at home but not at home—looked round with some anxiety. These were the kind of party guests who always made him feel uneasy—so ahead of the fashions that were about to appear in glossy magazines that they looked almost retro. He recognized no one.

"Drink?" said Rhys.

"Yeah."

"What do you want?"

"Anything," said George. He felt tired—jet lag, his father, too many impressions of a London he hadn't seen for four years, the noise of conversations from people he didn't know. Most of all, he missed Mia.

"George?"

He turned.

"You know Tess, don't you?" said Rhys.

. . .

This was George. She knew that. She recognized him, although she had never met him. All around him were people pressing into him, shouting over him, jostling him, and he stood there, looking at her, completely and utterly familiar.

She was shocked, from that jolt of recognition. But at the same time she was reassured, because he was exactly as she knew he would be. All those times she'd pictured him, she'd seen him like this—about five feet nine, five feet ten, brown hair, blue eyes. Pale skin like someone who never saw the sun. Fine lines round his eyes, as if he laughed a lot, or perhaps worried a lot. His face rough with stubble. There's nothing about him, thought Tess, to make you stop and stare—he's not fat or thin, or tall or short. There's no birthmark or piercing, no beard or tattoo. Even his clothes are unremarkable—a dark blue shirt, crumpled as if he's forgotten to iron it, or has worn it all day, or has fallen asleep on the sofa, the heat of his body making new creases.

But perhaps that's what he wants, she thought. Maybe he doesn't want to look conspicuous. (No one, after all, had ever suggested that George liked the limelight.) He stands back watching everyone, and the only thing that makes you look at him again is that air of awkwardness. There's a tension about him, as if he's waiting for something, or listening for something, as if he's not quite sure whether it's a good idea to say anything, or do anything, because the time might not be right, or it might not be welcome, or it might be better coming from someone else. It makes him look wary and vulnerable. At the same time, it's an invitation. His expression is saying, Say something and I'll know what you mean. His eyes are saying the same thing—Say something and I know it will be witty and clever and entertaining. And then, in recognition of all that brilliance, he will smile. His eyes will crinkle at the corners and the laughter lines round his mouth will appear.

And that's what makes George unusual, thought Tess. That's what makes him different. That's what makes him stand out from the crowd. He wants you to succeed. He wants you to shine. He wants you to be happy.

"I can't remember when you last saw each other," said Rhys.

There was no gesture that was appropriate. How do you greet someone you already know but have never met?

"Tess," said George.

I knew you would sound like that, she thought—warmer, deeper than you might expect from someone your build. But you sound puzzled. You sound confused.

"I didn't know," he said.

"What didn't you know?" said Rhys.

Around them was shouting and laughing, a roar and rumble of flirtation and gossip and grandiose claims of wealth and power and success.

Tess said, "Ten years."

George smiled, a huge smile that lit up his face. It transformed him.

"Ten years of what?" said Rhys, looking from one to the other. But no one answered. "I tell you what," he said, "I'll go and get some drinks."

Although, perhaps, they wouldn't have noticed if he'd stayed.

George said, "We did meet."

Tess shook her head.

"So how do I know you?"

They stood in a little self-contained bubble of delight, smiling at each other.

"But we did nearly meet," said George, "lots of times."

"Lots of times," said Tess.

"For years," said George.

"You were going to come to supper once," said Tess. "I cooked shepherd's pie."

"Did you?"

Tess nodded, her eyes shining.

She looks at me, thought George, as if she thinks I'm interesting—as if she thinks I'm about to make her smile.

"Rhys kept telling me I knew you," said George. "All the time. I almost believed him in the end."

Tess laughed. "And Kirsty tried very hard."

She kept looking at his mouth. She wanted to stand on tiptoe and kiss it.

George, lost, was staring at every inch of her face.

"Kirsty didn't tell me, though," said Tess. "This time."

George remembered to speak. "That's because she didn't know. I surprised her."

"A birthday surprise," said Tess.

George's smile disappeared.

"What?" said Tess.

"I didn't bring her a present."

"She won't want a present."

"Won't she?"

"I bought her a hat," said Tess.

"A hat?"

"She likes hats."

George was smiling again.

Tess said, "She looks wonderful in hats. She looks wonderful in everything."

"I didn't know," said George, "that you were so lovely."

Tess was silenced. George rubbed the stubble on his cheek. He had beautifully shaped fingers. He plays the piano, thought Tess. I remember now, he plays the piano. He said, "I'm sorry."

Tess smiled, a little uncertainly. "That's all right."

"I didn't mean to embarrass you."

"You didn't."

"I did."

Tess laughed. "Oh all right, then. You did."

"I just meant that all those years when we didn't meet, no one told me." His eyes didn't leave her face. "No one told me what you looked like."

"Would it have made a difference?" But then his expression was so sad that she stopped smiling.

They both looked down at their feet. He was wearing brown leather shoes, slightly scuffed.

He said, "You used to live in Brixton."

"Yes," said Tess, looking up again. "Kirsty and I had a flat together."

"Are you still there?"

Tess shook her head. "A bit further out. A bit less interesting."

She didn't mention Dominic.

"Where?"

"Penge," said Tess.

George shook his head.

"There's no reason why you should know it," said Tess. "Crystal Palace?"

"I think I know," said George.

"It's very suburban. All the houses look the same. But it's quite fast into central London." Why am I talking like an estate agent? "There's a garden," she said.

"You like gardens?"

Oh, come back, she said, calling out in her mind to a conversation that was rattling off the tracks, derailing into thick undergrowth. I don't care about gardens. I can't tell the difference between a dahlia and a delphinium. I want to know about you, George. I want to know everything about you. Do you like coffee? The smell of cloves? Martial arts films? Springer spaniels? Sag aloo? She opened her mouth to speak.

"Here we are," said Rhys. He was holding three shallow cocktail glasses, each one very full and decorated with white frosting round the rim.

"What is it?" said George.

"You've got me there," said Rhys.

Tess took a tentative sip. "Margaritas," she said.

"She's right, you know," said Rhys. "That's salt round the edge."

Tess felt George looking at her. She felt blurred and muddleheaded, as if she'd already drunk too much tequila. "Is Gareth here?"

"He's in Ecuador." Rhys frowned. "Or Peru."

"Is he ever coming back?"

"I don't know. There's something about the life out there that suits him. I never had him down as the adventurous type, to tell you the truth. But he's turned into a bit of a wanderer. Speaks Spanish like a native. I envy him, really. Not so much for what he's doing as for the fact he wants to do it. I've never really felt the urge. Although I wouldn't say I was particularly happy, really, just staying here. It's not very exciting, is it, just staying in one part of the world."

"But it's good to come home," said George.

"You feel that, do you?" said Rhys.

George smiled. "I never really intended to live anywhere else."

Tess said, looking up, her eyes taking in every angle of his face, "You live in New York?"

George nodded. "My daughter's got an American passport."

Tess, who had taken a sip from her glass, spluttered and coughed.

"You all right there?" said Rhys. "Need a pat on the back?"

Tess shook her head.

"So you've got no plans to come back, then?" said Rhys.

"No, I don't think so."

"It feels like everyone's all over the place, doesn't it?" said Rhys sadly. "I liked it when we were all in London."

"I suppose things have to change," said Tess.

"Somebody told me," said Rhys, turning to her, "that things probably will."

Tess, blushing pink, shook her head.

"Dominic's getting impatient."

"No," said Tess.

"No?" said Rhys.

"Who's Dominic?" said George.

"Nothing's fixed," said Tess.

"But you've got your flat," said Rhys.

"We might be moving soon," said Tess, miserably, "to a house."

"Well, that's nice," said Rhys. "Although I'd like it better if you came north. Last time I came down to see you, I had to take a tube, a train, and a bus. There's only a boat left, really."

"Once you get used to it, it's OK."

"Used to what?" said George.

"It's an investment," said Tess. "You find an area that's on the way up."

"We have those in Manhattan," said George.

"Do you live in one?"

George looked awkward. "No," he said. "No, the part we live in went up a long time ago."

"She's very successful, you see," said Rhys.

George's air of panic increased.

"Stephanie," said Rhys. "She's a lawyer." He drained his glass. "Well, I don't know about you two, but I fancy getting another one of these."

George nodded. Tess, who had gone rather pale, didn't say anything. Rhys plunged back into the crowd.

Tess and George stood there. The little bubble of intimacy had burst. Now they were two strangers, standing stiff and embarrassed, buffeted by the bags and shoulders and elbows of people pushing at them from every direction.

Tess said, "I ought to go and find Kirsty."

"No," said George.

She stopped.

"Don't go," he said. He made a visible effort to smile. "It's taken ten years to meet. Don't go yet."

There was a big gap between them now, opening up like a fissure in the earth. All the questions she'd wanted to ask seemed impossible. They jumped into the chasm in free fall, not a parachute in sight. She said, groping round for anything—anything—that might do, "So how long are you staying?"

"I'm not sure. My father's had an operation. That's why I came back."

"Oh, I'm sorry."

"Although it doesn't really help, me being here. My brother lives in London. In Hampstead. So he's keeping an eye on him."

"But you felt you should come?"

George nodded.

The roar of the party grew louder. They were surrounded on all sides by people's backs, barricading them in like wooden posts in a fort.

George said, "Who's Dominic?" just as Tess said, "So which part do you live in?"

George, leaning forwards, said, "What?"

"Which part?" said Tess.

"What did you say?" said George.

"He hasn't got the balls!" shouted a man with a beard.

"Which part?" said Tess.

"*Cojones,*" said a woman in a tight purple dress.

Quite suddenly, Tess felt like crying.

George said, "Can we get out of here?"

Tess looked at him, startled.

"I can't hear you. Let's go somewhere."

"I can't," said Tess. "It's Kirsty's birthday. I can't just leave. We haven't even had the fireworks yet."

It all seemed impossible.

"The back," said Tess. "There's a little courtyard at the back. Off the kitchen."

• • •

They forgot about Rhys, battling through bodies to get them margaritas.

It was slow going. Tess pinned a bright but vague smile on her face and kept nodding pleasantly, like the queen, to make sure she didn't get involved in any conversations. She wanted to reach out and grab George's hand as he shouldered his way through, but of course she didn't.

Because she didn't know him. She didn't know George at all. You can't grab hold of someone if you don't know them. So she walked in his wake, trying to keep close to him, fighting down an unruly mess of emotions that kept flooding through her, threatening to spill out of her mouth in a kind of animal howl.

Because she did know George. She knew him well. He was so familiar, so lovely, so obviously someone she should have met years ago. She understood nothing, but at the same time it all made perfect sense. This was George. He belonged to her. And she couldn't have him. She was shocked that the thought was so big, so bold, so brazen. It shouted at her in capital letters like a ten-foot explosion on a billboard. YOU CAN'T HAVE HIM. Because it was all far, far too late. He had a daughter. And a wife. Who was a successful lawyer. Who made millions.

Oh, thought Tess, her head huge with jealousy and wanton longing, and how could I think that I could have him anyway, living, as I do, with Dominic, who just happens, this weekend, to be visiting his parents in their downsized house in Croydon?

She was ashamed of herself. She had a bitter taste in her mouth, as if she'd chewed on a wizened stick of vanilla.

And anyway, she thought, her heart as heavy as stone as she watched George press down the handle of the French windows that opened, miraculously, onto the dark hole of the neglected backyard, he lives in New York. This man I have just met, whom I have known for a very long time, lives thousands of miles away. Which means, she thought—as she followed him outside onto the tiny patio surrounded by eight-foot walls that rose, like dark cliffs, around them—that quite soon he will be back on the other side of the world.

Tonight we talk. Tomorrow he leaves.

So, she thought, as he turned to face her, just a shadow of a man in the mean, hopeless, reluctant light that spilled out from the basement kitchen of the flat in Kennington, this is all completely and utterly pointless.

• • •

The minute I saw you, thought George, I knew who you were. I felt I'd met you so many times before. But I didn't know, until tonight, that you looked like this. Dark hair, dark eyes. A softness about you that makes me want to reach out and touch you. You seem so familiar. It seems like yesterday we were talking. But there weren't any yesterdays. So why do I feel that I know you? I even know your voice, as if we've spent hours talking. I know your expressions—every single one of them. That little lost look you have when a thought comes to you that makes you feel lonely and afraid. The way you bite your lip when you're anxious. The light in your eyes just before you smile. How do I know this if we've never met before? You have such a lovely smile. You make me feel like smiling, too.

George said, "I can't see you."

"I know," said Tess. "It's too dark."

His senses felt cheated of her.

A tiny light came on in the corner of the courtyard. Startled, George looked into the crowded kitchen. Kirsty waved but turned her back.

George could see Tess now. She was shivering. He wanted to take off his jacket and give it to her. But he wasn't wearing his jacket. It was somewhere inside, on a heap of expensive coats. He said, "You're cold."

"It's just the contrast," she said. "It was so hot in there." She rubbed her hands up and down her arms to get warm. George felt horribly selfish that he'd dragged her outside. They could hear the road, the cars hurtling south towards Brixton and Streatham and Penge. They could hear police sirens. Tess said, "How old is your daughter?"

"My daughter?"

"What's her name?"

"Mia. She's two."

Tess smiled. "That must be lovely."

"It is," said George, his face alight. "Have you got children?"

"Me?" said Tess. "Oh no."

"She's talking quite a lot now. Girls do, apparently. They're more advanced."

"Boys catch up, though, don't they?" said Tess, rubbing her arms again.

"I could go inside and get your coat," said George.

"You'd never come out again. The crowd would swallow you up."

"And get your drink."

"I'm all right," said Tess. "I don't need it."

They looked at each other.

George said, "I must have met you. We must have met somewhere."

Tess shook her head.

His eyes were anxious.

"You play the piano," said Tess.

"I did. I teach it now."

"You don't play?"

"No."

"Why?"

"Stephanie thinks it's an indulgence," said George. He felt an acute pain inside, like a pinch of electricity. Was that what Stephanie thought? She'd never said so. So why was he saying this? He had a sudden fear that all sorts of random words would fly out of his mouth, unfurling in a long stream like one of those party whistles with feathers on the end. "There are too many performers," he said, struggling to explain himself to Tess (or perhaps trying to explain himself to himself). "You can't make a living out of it. So there doesn't seem much point."

Tess looked confused. "But wasn't that always the case?"

George shook his head.

"You played when you were in London."

"I was younger when I was in London," said George sharply. "You've got to grow up sometime."

Tess said nothing.

The silence was like a huge gaping shark's mouth, waiting to eat them alive.

"I don't believe a word of what I just said," said George.

"That's a relief," said Tess. "I was beginning to hate you."

She smiled. He thought, She has beautiful even teeth. Everything about her is small and perfect. She said, "I don't think you should give up your dreams."

"No," said George. "You're right."

"It's what makes you unique."

He nodded.

There was a pause.

"I'm a hypocrite," she said.

He wanted to rush to her defense, even though it was Tess who was making the accusation against herself.

"I gave up on my dreams." She sounded sad and weary. "I always thought I'd open a shop selling vintage clothes. I've been collecting them for years. Ever since my grandmother told me stories about World War II. I've always loved them. Even if I opened a shop, I'd keep some of them back. Because they're so beautiful. But I don't want a museum. I want to make a living out of it."

"It's quite hard," said George, "to start up a business."

"Don't make excuses for me."

"But it is," said George. "You risk a lot."

She smiled. "Like when you give up a steady income to play jazz."

And now he smiled, too, and they were back together in a little circle of mutual understanding.

"I remember you playing at Tim and Lily's wedding."

George looked surprised. "You were at the wedding? I didn't see you."

"I didn't see you either."

We might have met, he thought, all those years ago.

She said, her eyes lit up, "Do you remember his brother's speech?"

George shook his head. He didn't remember any speeches. But he did remember arguing with Walter about driving back to London. I didn't understand then, he thought, what it was like to miss your child.

Tess said, "You were playing bebop."

"You know about bebop?"

"It goes with the clothes," said Tess. "Charlie Parker. Miles Davis. Max Roach."

"Thelonious Monk," said George.

"Round Midnight."

George looked at her, astonished.

"Straight, No Chaser," said Tess. "Brilliant Corners."

"I can't believe you know that."

"Didn't he used to get up and dance when he was performing?"

"He couldn't keep still," said George. "His whole body moving."

"Is that what you do?" she said, her eyes teasing.

"I'm far too repressed."

"Repressed?"

"Or maybe depressed," said George, the corners of his eyes crinkling as he smiled.

She laughed.

If I were with you, thought George, the realization coming to him with such clarity that he was blinded by its brilliance, my life would change completely. You understand. I don't have to fight to explain. You're already there, meeting me halfway.

"I was trying for a while," he said, tentatively, "to find something different."

"Different?"

"I don't know," said George. "Something beyond Thelonious Monk."

Her eyes were serious. "And what happened?"

"I stopped."

"Why?"

"I don't know," he said. "Life got in the way."

Oh, Tess thought, seeing the steel blade of a scraper underneath stubborn wallpaper, maroon gloss paint, chipped skirting boards, I know what you mean. She felt all the Sundays of her recent past collapse together in one resentful memory of DIY, time carelessly thrown on the scrap heap, never to be recovered. How did I let that happen?

Why did I behave as if what I did with my life just didn't matter?

After a while, she said, "I should have walked out a long time ago."

"From your job?"

There was a long silence.

"I'm sorry," said George.

Tess looked up. "No, it's a good question. I just don't know the answer."

George thought, I want to kiss her. What would she do if I kissed her?

She said, "I knew someone once, a long time ago, who said there were no second chances. He said, you think there are, but there aren't. That's always haunted me. What if he's right? What if you don't get another go?"

"Perhaps that's what happened to him," said George. "It doesn't have to happen to you."

"He was in hospital," said Tess. "And Kirsty went to visit him, because I was away, and when she got there, he'd gone. They'd tidied up his bed and he'd disappeared. As if he'd never even existed."

The French windows onto the patio opened suddenly.

"Oh," said someone. "I didn't realize there was anyone here."

"That's OK," said Tess.

"Came out for a smoke."

"We were just going in."

"Were we?" said George.

"I expect Rhys is looking for us."

More people were spilling out onto the patio. George and Tess stood side by side waiting for a gap in the party traffic.

Before he lost courage, George said, "Can we meet again?"

"When?"

"Before I go back."

Tess hesitated.

"Please?" said George.

. . .

"You see, I'm not really sure," said Rhys, "what I think about nachos. I mean, I think I like it. But it can get a bit soggy, can't it? If you have too much salsa. Or sour cream on the top. It's like you lose the crunch altogether, if you're not careful. And then it's more like porridge, isn't it? Not what you'd call a savory snack."

They were standing by the sink in the kitchen. Outside on the patio, revelers were writing their names in the dark with sparklers. From somewhere by the neon pink fridge came the sound of breaking glass. There was crushed birthday cake under their feet, sticking to the soles of their shoes. George was holding an empty beer can. Tess was staring at the floor.

"Of course, you can have too much cheese," said Rhys.

I want to say, Come back, thought Tess. Come back to the flat. We could talk all night. Dominic's not there. He's in Croydon. We could sit on the sofa and talk until dawn.

You could stay. You could stay with me. You could stay the night.

"You can become addicted, can't you?" said Rhys. "Even if it doesn't really agree with you. You should know better, but you do it anyway."

Screaming, a rush of light streaked across the darkness outside and exploded with a bang. There were staccato bursts of yellow, pink, and green and then a fierce fizz of orange. Tess looked up in shock.

"It can give you nightmares," said Rhys, "cheese."

Tess, dazed, watched as a bright blue anemone filled the sky.

"I like fireworks," said Rhys, following her gaze, "but I can't help thinking they're dangerous. You can have a lovely display, can't you, everything under control. But if you're not careful, they go off in all directions. Cause terrible damage. It's like the time Mo got talking to that man in the pub. You remember, George? Bought a whole load of rockets. Chinese, they were. Huge."

Now there was a burst of gold, like a giant dandelion.

"Massive explosions."

George leant out and put his empty can on the draining board. Tess, with big eyes, watched him.

"You couldn't really blame the neighbors for calling the police," said Rhys. "Fair do's. The whole back fence was burning for hours."

• • •

They found each other, in the end, by the coats in the study. The crowd was thinning out, leaving in its wake, like driftwood at low tide, the few who could no longer stand. Someone had made a bed from a tweed jacket and a red velvet cloak and was curled up in the corner, fast asleep, snuffling like a small pig.

They stood, tongue-tied and awkward.

"Are you leaving?"

Tess nodded.

George leant forwards. She thought he was going to touch her. But he didn't. He said, with sudden urgency, "Come to New York."

She made herself smile. She said, "Kirsty's always talking about it."

"So come."

Tess blinked hard. How well I've got to know your face, she thought, in just a few hours—that look of anxiety, the way you hesitate just in case you've misunderstood. But you haven't misunderstood. You know as well as I do what happened tonight.

He said, "Do you have to go?"

She nodded again and he smiled. But it wasn't a proper smile. It didn't reach his eyes. He said, "Maybe next time we meet, you'll have opened your vintage clothes shop."

Next time? She said, "Maybe you'll be playing jazz."

"We could combine the two. Vintage nights at a jazz bar."

"Where? Here or New York?"

"Anywhere," he said. He looked down at her dark eyelashes and the soft curve of her cheek. "Please. Just once. Before I go back."

Tess took a deep breath. "You could come round for supper."

"Yes," said George, his eyes not leaving her face.

She looked at him very directly. She said, "You could come round to the flat. And meet Dominic."

George felt a familiar emptiness inside.

They stood by the discarded coats, saying nothing.

. . .

"So you met him," said Kirsty.

"Yes," said Tess.

"Finally," said Kirsty.

It was Monday morning. Tess, in her numbed state, kept expecting something to happen. She thought the sky might fall in. She thought there might be some cataclysmic world event, like the new ice age from *The Day After Tomorrow*. But so far everything seemed completely normal. The West End was its usual tacky, crowded self.

"And what did you think?"

"Hold on a minute," said Tess. She stood up and said to Helen, "I'm going to take this outside."

As usual, Helen's eyes were wide with alarm, like Bambi surprised by a butterfly. Sometimes Tess looked at her assistant manager at Daisy Greenleaf and thought, Does she think of me as I used to think of Glenda—so much older that I seem like someone from a different country?

Outside on the brown stairwell, she straightened her shoulders. "OK," she said into her mobile.

"So what did you think?"

"Very nice," said Tess. She ignored the beating of her heart.

"Very nice?" said Kirsty.

"Yes," said Tess. "Very kind and considerate."

"You make him sound like a gynecologist."

"I'm just saying that he seems like a nice man."

"I don't know why I bothered," said Kirsty.

"Well, you didn't, really," said Tess. "You didn't even know he was going to turn up."

"I meant all the years before."

Tess had a sudden unwelcome memory of her journey home the night of the party. She had cried all the way. She couldn't help herself. She had leant her head against the dirty gray glass of the window of the night bus and looked out at the endless suburbia of southeast London and felt the heavy weight of desolation, of life without George. I don't know how it happened, she thought. But it did. And he felt the same way. I know he did. And now it's all over. He's gone. And there's nothing I can do.

"Didn't you even think he was good-looking?"

"Well, sort of," said Tess. "Ordinary looking."

"I thought you'd like that."

"What," said Tess, "ordinary?"

"No, the sort of disheveled, I-never-look-in-a-mirror sort of look."

"All men are like that, aren't they?"

"Dominic isn't," said Kirsty.

"Dominic has to look smart for his job."

"Dominic would iron his jeans if you let him," said Kirsty.

"What about you?" said Tess, desperate to move on from the topic of Dominic in case her mouth started trembling and she began to cry. "Did you have a good time?"

There was a silence.

"Kirsty?"

"What?"

"Did you have a good time?"

"I did," said Kirsty.

"How good?" said Tess.

"He's French."

"And?"

"He's an art dealer."

There was something in Kirsty's voice that made Tess listen harder. "You like him."

"Well, obviously," said Kirsty.

"No," said Tess. "You like him a lot."

"Maybe."

Oh, thought Tess. This phone call isn't about me at all. This phone call is about Kirsty. She said, "So when are you seeing him again?"

"In about five minutes."

Tess thought about this. "Where is he?"

Kirsty laughed.

Tess said, "It's Monday morning."

"So?"

"He's been there since Saturday night?"

"Yes."

"You'll wear him out," said Tess.

"I think he's rechargeable," said Kirsty.

. . .

A week after Kirsty's party, on Sunday morning, Tess was standing in the living room of the very neat, newly decorated flat in Penge, ironing a 1940s blouse with a small Peter Pan collar. She had the radio on. She was only half-listening. She was thinking about George.

She had been thinking about George all week. But today, more specifically, she was thinking about George's eyes and George's mouth. She kept trying to move out from the individual features into his whole face, but something kept going wrong. When she tried to see George's face, she came up with nothing but a blur, as if she was trying to watch the TV without her lenses in. It made her want to weep. Why was it so hard? Was he disappearing from her head? I don't have a photograph, she thought. If I can't see him in my mind, that's it. He's gone. He's gone forever. She pressed down into a seam with the V of the iron. A tear fell onto the striped cotton.

"It'll be ready at one," said Dominic, coming into the room and sitting down on the sofa.

"Oh," said Tess.

"If you like it pink."

She looked up. “I don’t,” she said.

Dominic picked up the paper. “I’ll leave yours in longer, then.”

She turned the blouse round. She pressed down with the iron. “Why do you never remember?”

“What?” Dominic flipped open the Money section.

“You never remember I like it well-done.”

He smiled. “Because you’re wrong.”

“How can you be wrong about lamb?”

“Very easily,” said Dominic.

Tess pulled the blouse away from the ironing board. For some reason it caught on the edge. There was the sound of ripped fabric. She stood there, shocked, still holding the iron in her right hand. “Oh,” she said.

“What?”

“I’ve torn it.”

“Well never mind,” said Dominic. “You can always mend it.”

Tess carefully put the iron down. With both hands, she held the blouse up to the light. There was a great rent in the bodice.

“It must have been getting old and thin,” she said in a quiet voice.

“That’s what happens,” said Dominic. “Things wear out.”

She looked at him, in profile, still reading the paper. Sometimes, recently, she had observed him like this and found herself thinking that he had quite an ugly face, really. His nose was too bony. His chin was pointed, like Mr. Punch.

"There's an article in here," said Dominic, "about domestic energy."

Tess didn't say anything.

"About switching suppliers," said Dominic.

. . .

Tess had just walked past the winged statue of Eros on Piccadilly Circus when it started to rain. She was tired. Oliver's ideas for expansion were all very well, but there were still only two of them in the customer services department. And this week had been particularly hard. She would have liked to sit alone, in a corner, thinking about nothing at all. She would have liked to stare out unfocused, like a fish in a glass bowl, at a world of magnified awfulness. But the office had been more than usually busy. Oliver had taken to sitting on the edge of her desk at five thirty PM—in his shirt and suspenders, swinging his short fat leg and exposing his bright red socks—to pick her brains about the new lines he was developing. Normally, she might have been flattered. Normally she would have listened attentively and made helpful suggestions. But this week she had wanted to shout, Go away! Leave me alone! I can't cope with this! I can't do your job as well as my own!

Tess rummaged in her bag for her navy-blue collapsible umbrella, which she now remembered was still sitting on the table in the living room in Penge, and thought, But time is passing. It's been nearly a fortnight since the party, and I'm managing to get through the days. I'm still alive. For a moment, she almost abandoned the idea of shopping. Dominic was away, on a client site somewhere in Dorking, staying in a hotel overnight. She had the flat to herself. She so desperately wanted to curl up on the sofa in old pajamas and thick wool socks and eat chocolate biscuits and cookie dough ice cream. The fantasy hovered in her mind's eye, a delectable temptation.

But unless I buy something for Mum this evening, she thought, it'll never arrive in time. The post is so unpredictable these days. She took a deep breath, put her head down, screwed up her eyes against the slanting rain, and battled her way towards Piccadilly. I could have bought something online, she thought, as she stood at the crossing, turning up the collar of her coat. But I always feel that's cheating. If you really want to know what something's like, you need to hold it in your hands.

She looked up. There in front of her was George.

There were car horns screaming and people shouting, because George and Tess were still standing in the middle of the road staring at each other. He grabbed her arm and pulled her to a traffic island. Safe in a sea of shiny cars wet with rain, she felt at the same time like shouting with joy and bursting into tears. A London bus lumbered past, throwing up a fan of dirty water.

George was holding her by both elbows as if he was worried she'd run away. She looked up at his face, wondering at his physical reality.

"But you're not here," she said.

"I had to stay."

His hair was plastered to his head. His eyelashes were dark with rain.

"What are you doing here?" she said.

A black cab came to a halt beside them. George banged on the side. "Where?" said the driver, winding down the window.

"Anywhere," said George. He held open the door. Tess was about to say, I've got to go shopping. It's my mother's birthday. But she didn't. She got into the cab instead.

The driver pulled back the small glass partition. "Where do you want to go?"

"Covent Garden," said George, sitting down next to her.

Your voice, she thought. I've heard it in my head for days. And now here you are. She could make no sense of it. It was like being at a wake when the dead man walks in.

The partition slid shut.

George was looking at her, hesitating.

She said, "Why Covent Garden?"

He smiled. "I've got no idea."

Your face, she thought. So that's what it looks like. And she smiled back, flooded with relief. There was a small rivulet of water running down her nose. She wiped it away. "You're still in London," she said.

"My father."

"Oh."

"He's OK. But he had to go back into hospital for a couple of days. So I stayed on."

"So you were here last week," she said. She thought of all the days when she and he were both in the same city.

"I was staying with Rhys. In Hackney. In Gareth's old room."

She nodded.

"But I have to go."

"Do you?"

"My flight's tomorrow."

"Tomorrow," she said, like a small child repeating important information.

"Heathrow. In the morning."

The detail made it so much worse. She said, in her head, Don't go. Please don't go. Out loud, she said, "I didn't know you were still here."

"I wanted to see you."

Her heart missed a beat. "Did you?"

"I wanted to thank you."

"For what?"

"After the party, I got talking to Rhys, and I've been playing again. All day, every day. When I'm not visiting my father. Because of what you said."

"I'm glad," she said.

"It all came back. My fingers remembered. It's better than it was. It's different."

"You mustn't stop."

"It's all because of you," George said. "It's because of what you said."

"You must carry on," she said, "when you get back."

She looked at the floor of the cab. It was either that or start weeping. The car ground forwards through the gray London rain. This moment, she thought, when I am so alive, is the worst moment of my life. I can see and hear and feel more than I have ever seen or heard or felt, and all I want is to be buried underground, under ten feet of clay, so nothing can ever touch me again.

Suddenly he was sitting forward on the edge of the seat, turning so that he faced her. He said, "I didn't just want to see you to thank you."

Tears came to her eyes.

"I haven't stopped thinking about you."

She shook her head.

"It's like you're under my skin," he said, "in my head, everywhere I look."

She said, "There's no point."

"Why?"

"You know why."

He said, "Just to talk."

"Talk about what?"

"About anything."

"About Mia?"

George flinched.

"We screwed up," she said, and now the tears were running down her face. "We should have met a long time ago."

"But you feel the same way."

"Of course I feel the same way," she said, almost angrily.

"We can't not see each other."

"It's just the way things happen. Life is shit sometimes."

"Please," said George.

The glass partition slid open again. "Whereabouts?" said the driver.

"Anywhere," said George, his eyes not leaving her face.

"Bow Street?"

"Fine," said George.

Tess opened her mouth to speak.

"Ten minutes," said George.

"It'll make it worse."

"Just a drink," said George.

Tess hesitated.

"Do you have to be somewhere?"

"No," said Tess. "Dominic's working."

And now that she'd said his name, there he was with them in the cab with the steamed-up windows.

"So you've got time," said George.

She bit her lip.

"Please, Tess. It's not finished. We've got to talk."

The taxi stopped. When Tess pushed open the car door, the cold evening air came rushing in all soft and slithery and cold like a silk scarf. It had stopped raining. She got out and waited, listening to the splash of puddles sliced by cars, and George leant into the front window and paid, and she thought, feeling tired and dazed with tears and misery, Is this what it's like? Is this what it's like, being in love?

. . .

She looks at me as if she hates me, thought George. She looks at me as if I'm making her unhappy. I don't want to make her unhappy. But we can't leave it like this. He said, "Keep it," to the cab driver, even though it was far too big a tip, and the car rumbled off and he turned round, and there she was, standing on the pavement, looking so utterly defenseless that he wanted to gather her up and hold her tight. But he knew it would be the wrong thing to do, after everything she'd said. So he stood in front of her as she stared down at the ground and the pain of loving her but not being able to have her twisted inside him like a fistful of razors.

He said, "Shall we go somewhere? A pub?"

"Anywhere," she said.

Now the pavement seemed to be full of tourists trying to go in the opposite direction, so George touched her arm and said, "Down here?" and they turned left, into a side road, and there was a pub on the corner looking dark and Dickensian with diamond-shaped windows and an air of historic gloom. George pushed open the door and his heart sank, because it was full of people and shouting and the low thump of rhythm and bass and the warmth of bodies and the smell of beer and old chips.

He was beginning to feel that this was all beyond him, that he couldn't manage anything like this at all, when Tess touched his arm, and he saw that a couple was leaving the tiny table just behind him, leaving space for two people, and he said, "You sit down. I'll go and get the drinks. What do you want?" but she just shook her head as if to say, It doesn't matter, it doesn't matter what you get.

He pushed his way to the bar and stood behind a young man with tattoos on his biceps who smelt of sweat and stale cigarettes and he waited while the barmaid, whose veins stood out like a long-distance runner's, dealt with order after order, and he looked back to the table where Tess was sitting and she was bent over like a child with a stomachache, or an old woman praying, and he thought, watching her, What are we going to do? What are we going to do?

"What would you like?" said the barmaid, shouting over the music.

Time, thought George. I'd like more time. He said, "Beer. No. Wine. What wine do you have?"

"White or red?"

Why do people keep wanting me to make decisions? "White. It doesn't matter what."

When he got back to the table, holding the cold glasses of wine, Tess looked as if she'd managed to take herself a long way from her surroundings. She didn't seem to notice the noise, or the music, or the constant to and fro of people walking past, banging into the table, knocking her chair. He said, "I bought you some wine. Is that OK?"

She nodded, as if she wasn't really listening.

He said, desperately, "Do you want to go?"

She looked up, startled.

"I feel I've forced you to come here."

"No," she said.

He took a large sip of wine. It was very sharp.

She said, “I’ve got a suggestion.”

George sat very still. There was a ringing in his ears. But it wasn’t because of the shouting of the drinkers, or the clinking of the glasses, or the thumping of the bass. It was because this was the end. He knew it. There was no hope. That’s what she was going to tell him. This was the end.

She said, “I don’t want to think about the future. I don’t want to think about your wife. Or Mia. Or Dominic. Or the fact that you live in New York and I live in London.”

He opened his mouth to speak, but she shook her head. She said, “I don’t want to think about any of those things.”

“So we won’t,” he said urgently. “We won’t.”

Her eyes were full of tears. He leant forwards to hold her hand but she shook her head again.

“And I don’t want to do anything,” she said, “that either of us will regret. No guilty secrets.”

She was looking at him with such pleading in her eyes that the fight went out of him.

She said, “We spend a few hours together. As friends. And then we say good-bye. And you go home. And I go home. And there will be nothing we have to lie about. Because nothing happened.”

Her voice had gone very quiet.

He said, helplessly, “Why?”

“Because we aren’t the kind of people who could do anything else.”

“Aren’t we?”

Tess shook her head.

"Are you sure?"

"Neither of us," said Tess. "We couldn't smash up other people's lives and be happy."

George said, bitterly, "Then I wish I was someone else."

She smiled, her lip trembling.

He said, "I'll never forget you."

Her face crumpled.

"I'm sorry. I'm sorry. I wanted you to know."

She said, "I do know."

And they sat at the little pub table in the noise of a Thursday night and there was nothing else left to say.

2011

I remember when we used to drink all night without eating," said Kirsty.

"I can't do it anymore. I get a headache in the morning."

"I don't expect Dominic likes it, either," said Kirsty, "if he can't cook for you."

Tess looked at her. "Can we just leave him out of it?"

Kirsty opened her eyes wide. "We're a bit touchy tonight, aren't we?"

"I'm not touchy."

There was a small silence filled with ruffled feathers.

"So do you want pudding?" said Tess eventually.

"No," said Kirsty.

"What?"

"When did I ever eat pudding?"

"I don't know."

"We've known each other for thirteen years. Have I ever, in all that time, eaten pudding?"

"Do you know what," said Tess, "I think we ought to ask for the bill. It's getting late."

She looked round the restaurant for their waiter.

"Tess? What's wrong?"

"Nothing's wrong."

"Yes, there is," said Kirsty.

"There's nothing wrong."

"Just saying it over and over again won't make it true."

"Look," said Tess, "I'm tired." She saw the waiter and signaled for the bill.

"Why don't we go and have a drink somewhere?"

"Because I have to get up in the morning," said Tess, putting her bag on the table and rummaging round for her wallet.

"So do I. I'm respectably employed these days, in case you've forgotten."

"So you won't want to be up late either."

Kirsty leant out and put her hand on Tess's wrist. "Stop a moment, will you?"

Tess looked up furiously.

"The whole night you've been sounding off about people. You're angry with Ellie. You're cross with Lily. You're fed up with your mum. And I can't say anything without you jumping down my throat."

"I'm just in a bad mood," said Tess.

"I don't want to sound like an A-level psychology student," said Kirsty, "but the only person you haven't slagged off is Dominic."

"So?"

"What's he done?"

"He hasn't done anything."

Kirsty gave her a long, hard look.

Tess took a deep breath. "Really," she said. "He hasn't done anything."

"So why are you so angry?"

"I'm not angry."

Tess picked up her empty glass, and put it down again.

"OK," said Kirsty. "I'm not sure this is the right time. But I've got some news."

Tess looked up.

"I'm moving to Paris."

"Paris? With Philippe?"

Kirsty smiled.

"But that's wonderful," said Tess. "Why didn't you tell me earlier? We could have celebrated. Had some champagne."

"I don't know," said Kirsty. "Maybe I was waiting for you to ask me why I looked so happy."

"Oh, Kirsty," said Tess, feeling wretched. Because Kirsty did look happy. She was all lit up inside. And Tess hadn't even noticed.

"What's even better," said Kirsty, "although I am, of course, delighted that I'll be sharing his flat, is that he's asked me to manage his new gallery."

Tess stared, openmouthed.

"I know," said Kirsty, laughing. "All those years of utter indolence rewarded by a proper job."

"But won't you have to speak French?"

"I know you won't believe me," said Kirsty, "but I've been taking classes. At the Institut Français, no less."

"Thursday nights," said Tess.

"Exactly."

"I wondered why you were never free."

Without warning, Tess felt her eyes fill with tears.

Kirsty leant forwards. "What's wrong?"

"Oh, I don't know. You going away, I suppose. I'm really happy for you. Philippe is wonderful, and the job sounds incredible. Managing an art gallery. It's everything you deserve. But I'm going to miss you. I'm going to miss you such a lot."

"It's only Paris," said Kirsty. "I'll probably be back every other weekend."

But they both knew that was a lie.

"I'll definitely be back for the wedding."

"What wedding?" said Tess.

"Your wedding," said Kirsty, "of course."

. . .

Tess usually got home to the flat before Dominic. He tended to work quite late these days. He said this was the time to put the hours in if you wanted to edge your way up the company ladder. Sometimes he even texted Tess and asked her to start making preparations for dinner. Nothing complicated, he said—just dice the onions, crush the garlic, skin some fresh tomatoes, and strain the stock.

Sometimes, after she'd finished all these preparations, Tess sat in the empty flat with the curtains drawn and the lights out. There was a faint glimmer from the streetlamp outside. She sat on the sofa and listened to the silence.

It was a relief to be on her own. It was only when she was alone that she allowed herself to think about George. This was because thinking about him made her lose all control. She cried a lot. She paced up and down. It made no sense. Why would she meet him when it was too late, when neither of them was free?

Because she knew, with complete certainty, that the joke, Kirsty's old joke, wasn't funny at all. As Kirsty had said all along, she and George were soul mates. She didn't care whether it was an Indian myth or a bit of fiction from Plato or something pulled from a children's fairy story. She and George were meant to be together. Without him, she was nothing—a half looking for a whole. Without him, life stretched out pointlessly like a long white road taking her somewhere she didn't even want to go.

This thought was so big and so cold that she would curl up on the floor in a tight little ball like a hedgehog or a cat, trying to make herself as small and invulnerable as possible. But this made no sense, either. There was no point scrunching up small trying to protect herself from a kicking. Because the blows didn't come from outside. The blows came from inside her head. She thought about George, and every single thing she remembered hurt her. She thought about his eyes, and the expression of anxiety that disappeared so quickly when he smiled. She thought about his voice. She thought about the way he frowned. She thought about his hands with his beautiful musician's fingers. Thinking about him was agony. But at the same time she welcomed this pain—the pain of thinking about George—because it was an exquisite addiction, allowing her to relive every moment of the time they'd spent together. And poring over it, piecing together the minutes and the hours, she knew that he had felt exactly the same way—that recognition, that realization, that they belonged to each other.

But then he had left. He had gone back to New York. At this point she wept, because missing George meant a desolate emptiness she had never felt before. I didn't know what falling in love meant, she thought. All those years listening when friends were talking about breaking up and getting back together, and I felt sorry for them, but also mystified, because the pain seemed so intense. I had never felt anything like that with Dominic. With Dominic, life trotted along like a good-natured Labrador with ripples of fat under the skin. There were no arguments. There was no jealousy. There wasn't much passion, either, which I didn't know at the time, because I thought, then, that sexual desire was the same thing. And I used to think, Why do people go on and on about love? It's so straightforward. You meet someone, you get on with them, you decide to spend time together, and then you buy a set of Le Creuset casserole dishes. It's so simple. What is there to talk about? What is there to say?

But that was before I knew what love was, she thought. That was before I knew what it felt like to miss someone with every beat of your heart.

So tonight, as she opened the front door of the flat, she hoped Dominic would still be at work. She hoped she would have time alone. She needed to think about George. There was a lot of post lying jumbled on the mat. That's the trouble with buying things, she thought. (And she and Dominic were always buying things these days.) People add you to their mailing lists and try to persuade you to buy a brand-new kitchen every year.

But she could see, as she bent to pick them up, that most of the letters were from estate agents.

Still with her coat on, Tess began to open the envelopes. "Ideally situated for the local schools," said one, "this immaculate detached home with loft extension and 100 ft garden is comprised of four bedrooms, two reception rooms, and designer kitchen with en suite to master bedroom." Another said, "Character residence in need of some refurbishment with three bedrooms, two bathrooms (one with Jacuzzi), and newly built conservatory." A lot of the houses were boasting, and many were rich in period charm.

After a while, Tess put all the estate agent particulars in a neat pile by the cooker.

She walked through the flat, taking off her coat as she went. She went into the little spare room at the back, overlooking the garden. Dominic was always threatening to turn this room into his study. At the moment, he had to make do with a corner of the bedroom. (The blank eye of the computer screen glared at them reproachfully from the moment they woke up.) But where would I put everything, said Tess, if I didn't have this room? You could put all the clothes in boxes, said Dominic. But he didn't push her. Perhaps there was something about her expression that made him stop.

Tess turned on the lamp by the little blue chair where she sat to sew sequins or mend seams. She looked round. There were two long black clothes rails hung with suits, dresses, skirts, blouses, and evening gowns. There were three racks of neatly paired shoes. On the wall nearest the window were hooks hung with hats, belts, bags, corsets, snoods, scarves, and sateen swimsuits. Gloves were laid out neatly on a shelf. She had several favorite pairs—white wedding crochet, pink ruched from Van Raalte, and elbow-length black leather from Hermès.

This was a carefully edited selection of all the 1940s clothes she had ever bought. There wasn't enough room to keep any more than this. So she had bought and sold with the skill and calculation of a dealer, ending up with the best, the prettiest, the rarest, the most unusual. She knew her market. But even this pared-down collection made her uncomfortable these days. She looked round the room filled with vintage treasures and felt as if she and an old friend had drifted apart. After all, it wasn't a business. She hardly wore any of the clothes anymore. If you're head of customer services for a West End company, you don't want to look too unusual. You don't want to risk offending your clients at important meetings. So maybe, she thought, it was just a weird hobby, like pinning dead butterflies to a board.

Her mind drifted to the house in Beckenham. Her head

was filled with snatches of conversation from the past few weeks when, numb with misery, she had been unable to defend herself at all.

"You don't need to move," said her mother. "You could just pack it all away. And then you've got a study. Or a nursery. Plenty of room for a cot."

"If we go for four bedrooms," said Dominic, "that's one for us, a study each, and a spare room for guests."

"I'm just saying," said Lily, "that you don't want to buy an enormous house on the assumption that you're going to fill all the bedrooms. Because sometimes it just doesn't happen. I know people who've had to wait for years."

"Beckenham?" said Helen, her assistant. "Is that near Croydon?"

Tess fingered a small Bakelite-and-bead purse. I don't think I can bear this, she thought. I am dying. And no one has noticed.

She heard the front door of the flat slam shut. She bent down and switched off the lamp.

At the end of the long hall, Dominic, still by the front door, was taking off his coat. He had taken to wearing a beige mac. It was practical. It protected him from rain. But sometimes Tess felt, in suburban Penge, that it made it almost impossible to tell Dominic apart from all the other commuters. I have a John Lewis account, she thought. I buy my cake tins from Lakeland. Maybe I should go the whole hog and paint the front door in Farrow & Ball.

"Sorry I'm late," he said.

"You're not, really," said Tess. "I haven't been in long myself."

Dominic was still wearing his blond hair slightly long. He had to keep shaking it out of his eyes. He put his rolled umbrella by the radiator and his brown leather briefcase on the floor. He said, "There was some kind of holdup on the trains. I had to get First Capital Connect to Beckenham."

"Oh," said Tess.

"But supper won't take long," he said. "The pork's been marinating since last night."

It might suit him better, she thought, if he had it cut. Although he's sensitive about his receding hairline. His father was almost entirely bald by the time he was forty.

"Oh good," called Dominic from the kitchen, "we've got some more house details. Anything we haven't seen before?"

No, thought Tess. There's nothing we haven't seen before.

"What do we think about a garage?" said Dominic, wandering back into the hall with the sheaf of estate agent particulars. "Essential? Or just desirable?"

"Dominic," said Tess.

"What?"

"Don't."

"Don't what?"

Tess took a deep breath. "I don't want to live in Beckenham."

Dominic looked up. "Oh come on. We can't go through this again. It's a good investment."

Tess shook her head.

"So where do you want to live?"

When she raised her eyes again, Dominic was still standing there, still holding on to all the house details.

She said, "I can't do this anymore."

"Can't do what?" said Dominic.

Tess couldn't speak.

"It's my fault," said Dominic. "I knew there was something wrong. Are you worried about the mortgage? Because I know we can afford it. Even with variables like redundancy. I've done a five-year projection. On a spreadsheet."

She said, in a very small voice, "It's not the mortgage."

"So it's the wedding."

She shook her head.

"We don't have to get married," said Dominic. "We haven't booked anything. It was only a future projection, and nothing has even been costed yet. Our mothers can put their hats back in the loft."

"Dominic—"

"I don't really want to get married either. It seems a lot of fuss for nothing. Just an excuse for a party. If you want to carry on as we are, that's fine by me." He smiled. "It'll save a lot of money."

"It's not the wedding."

"So what is it?"

She looked at him. He went very white.

"I'm sorry," she said.

"No," he said.

She couldn't think of anything to say.

"You're not serious," said Dominic.

In her mind she could see confetti falling—torn love letters, marriage certificates cut into very tiny pieces.

"Why?"

"I don't know," she said.

The house details dropped to the floor. He came forwards, holding out his hands. "Then, that's fine. If you don't know, there's nothing really wrong. It's just all the pressure. All the buildup. Which is completely understandable. It's been going on for weeks."

She shook her head.

"So what is it?" said Dominic.

"I don't know," she whispered.

"Come on. This isn't logical. If there isn't a reason."

"I need some time."

"It's just because we're taking some big steps," said Dominic.

"It's more than that."

They were standing close but apart, like magnets turned the wrong way round.

"If you need time, take time," said Dominic. "Take as much time as you need."

"I want to move out."

"You don't."

"I do," said Tess.

"But we've been together for years," said Dominic.

Tess stared at the beige carpet.

He said, in a voice so vulnerable that she wanted to cry, "Are you seeing someone else?"

She shook her head.

"Tess, I don't understand."

"I know," she said, looking up, "I'm sorry. I don't understand either. But I just know I can't do it anymore."

They stood, listening to the hopeless silence.

"So what will you do?" said Dominic.

"I don't know. Go and stay with someone."

"You don't have to do this."

"I do," said Tess.

"Now? You're going now?"

Before tonight, before she had opened her mouth to speak, Tess hadn't known what she was going to do, or when she was going to do it. But leaving, and leaving now, seemed the only sensible idea. She nodded.

"I'll go," said Dominic.

"No," said Tess. "This is my fault. I should go."

"I don't want you to go."

"I know," said Tess helplessly.

"Please, Tess," said Dominic.

She said, and she was crying now, "I have to."

"I'll wait for you."

She shook her head. She said, "Don't. It won't make any difference. I'm not going to change my mind."

It hurt to look at him. She felt as if she'd plunged a knife into his stomach and now, watching the agony on his face, was slowly twisting it round in his guts.

. . .

"It's shite," said Mo.

They were standing in George's well-appointed living room in Greenwich Village. Soft light glanced off the antique mirrors. There was a subtle smell of cinnamon and vanilla. George, astonished, had opened the door to Mo, who walked straight into the living room and now stood, all stocky aggression, surveying the whole sweep of the open-plan ground floor.

"Really?" said George.

"How did you end up here?"

"Stephanie. She's very successful."

"She must be," said Mo. "You landed on your feet, eh?"

"It's a partnership," said George.

"Bollocks," said Mo. "You're a kept man."

George tried very hard not to rise to the bait. He failed. He said defensively, "I'm looking after Mia."

"Who's Mia?"

"My daughter," said George.

"Your daughter?" said Mo.

"And Stephanie's, obviously," said George. "As well."

Mo looked at him, half smiling. "I didnae think it would last. I thought, What does she see in him? But I was wrong. You're two doves cooing in a loft."

"It's a partnership," said George.

"I know," said Mo. "You already said that."

George, flustered, said, "Would you like a drink?"

"What you got?"

"Anything."

"Tia Maria?"

"I'm not sure," said George, frowning.

"Lighten up, ya daft lummock," said Mo. "I want a beer." He wandered over to the mantelpiece. "So where are they, then?"

"Who?"

"Stephanie. And the wee girl."

"Mia's asleep," said George. "It's ten o'clock at night."

"And Stephanie?"

"She's probably at work still."

"You don't know?"

"I don't check on her every move."

"No," said Mo. "I can see that."

"Come and get a beer," said George.

Three, or possibly four, rooms had been knocked into one. In the middle of Manhattan, where most apartments were the size of a single bed, this amount of space was breathtaking.

"So what did this cost?" said Mo.

"You can't ask that," said George.

"Why not?"

"It's not public information."

Mo raised his eyebrows.

George opened the great silver fridge-freezer, took out two bottles of beer, and flipped off the caps. "So what are you doing here?"

Mo drank at least half a bottle in one gulp and wiped his mouth with his hand. He said, "I'm depping."

"Who for?"

"Standing in for a friend of mine. He said, We've got a gig in the States and I can't go. Do you want to do it? And I thought, Why not?"

"Aren't you a teacher now?"

"I am."

"So what did they say when you said you wanted to go to New York?"

"It's a private school. They have long holidays." Mo took another swig of his beer. "Anyway, I thought it was about time I checked on you."

George looked wary.

"It's true," said Mo. "No one knows where you are. Or what you're doing. So I thought, Well, if he won't come to us, I'll go to him."

"I saw Rhys," said George, "when I was in London."

"You did."

"So I kept in touch," said George.

"He said you hadn't been playing."

"That's all changed," said George. "And I'm asking round."

"For gigs?"

"Yes," said George, who wasn't. He wasn't sure who would want to hear the stuff he was playing now.

Mo finished his beer and offered George the empty bottle. George took it, opened the fridge, and found a new one.

"So why did you stop?" said Mo.

"Oh you know," said George, flipping off the cap and handing it over.

"No, I don't know."

"It's difficult when you have a child."

"Is it?"

George looked at him. "Yes."

Mo smiled as if George's taking a stand amused him. He pulled out a stool from the breakfast bar and hoisted himself up. "So are you coming to see me?"

George stared. "Of course I can't. Not tonight. Mia's asleep upstairs."

"So you'll come the morra. Bring the wife."

"It depends how busy she is," said George.

"Oh come on," said Mo. "Your old mate arrives from the UK and she's too busy to come and hear him play?"

"I didn't say she was," said George. "I said she might be."

"Well, that's settled then," said Mo.

"Are you really teaching physics?"

"Why?"

George couldn't think how to explain.

"You didnae think I had the brains?"

"I just can't imagine you doing it."

"You have to make things clear," said Mo. "You tell them from the beginning—step out of line and I'll kill ye. And then you all get along fine."

"Do you see Walter?"

Mo took another mouthful of beer. "I never really liked Walter. Too much up his own arse."

"But he was a good sax player. It was a good band."

Mo looked at him. "Pure dead brilliant."

George heard the front door. "That'll be Stephanie."

His heart sank when she walked in. She looked tired and tense, her face set in mean lines. When she was in this mood, she picked over his faults like a vulture ripping rotten meat.

"Who's this?"

"Do you not remember me, darlin'?" said Mo.

Stephanie peered at him. "Oh," she said faintly. "From England."

Mo laughed.

She turned her back on him. "How's Mia?" she said to George.

"She's fine."

"She had a slight cough when I left this morning."

George shook his head. "It was nothing."

"Well, I'm tired," said Stephanie. "I'm going to bed. What about you?"

"Mo's just arrived. I'm going to stay up for a bit."

"He's not staying, is he?"

George thought, You couldn't humiliate me more if you tried. He said, "I haven't asked him yet."

"I'd rather he didn't," said Stephanie. "I've got a lot on at the moment."

"I'll go and book in at the Plaza, shall I?" said Mo.

"I'm serious, George," she said. "There's a deal going through. I need everything at home to be completely quiet."

"That's fine," said George. "You go to bed."

They looked at each other. Then Stephanie turned on her heel and walked out of the room.

"Landed on your feet," said Mo.

"She's just tired," said George.

"Is she always that friendly?"

"I told you," said George. "She's tired. We were up at five with Mia, and she left for the office at six."

Mo held out his empty bottle.

"I think we ought to turn in," said George.

"You're forgetting," said Mo. "I've got a gig to play."

George looked at him in panic. "You're not planning to come back here afterwards, are you?"

"Where else would I go?"

"Didn't you hear what she said?"

"I'll come in quietly."

"I don't think," said George, "you have any idea how angry she'll be if you wake her up."

"I won't," said Mo. "I've had years of practice. Give us a key and she'll never know. I can sneak into any house in the middle of the night. It's my speciality."

George let out his breath in one long, hopeless sigh. "I know I'm going to regret this."

"No, you won't," said Mo.

George reached up to the shelf on top of the cooker and found the spare key.

"Better still," said Mo, "come with me. Come and see me play."

"I can't."

"Stephanie's here now. She can babysit."

"It's my job to look after Mia so that Stephanie can sleep."

Mo looked at him. "You're not even in the same room, are you?"

"Here's the key," said George, handing it to him.

"Are you?"

"It's none of your business."

Mo raised his eyebrows.

George said, desperately, "Mia wakes sometimes. I go through to see if she's OK. Stephanie gets disturbed when I get back into bed. So most of the time I sleep in the room next to Mia's. OK? No scandal. Perfectly normal. It's what a lot of working parents do."

"Do they?" said Mo.

"Yes. You'd know if you had kids."

"Sleep in separate rooms?" said Mo.

"It's no big deal," said George.

"Seems like a big deal to me." He frowned. "And how old is Mia?"

"She's nearly two and a half."

"Two years with no sex?"

"You know," said George, "I can see why Walter wanted to hit you. You don't let go. You're like a dog with your teeth in my leg."

"So am I right in thinking," said Mo, "that you're not gonnae give me another beer?"

"Yes."

"And when I come back tonight, where do I sleep?"

"Choose a sofa," said George.

"No featherbed? No pillows?"

"You don't deserve it."

"You can be very cruel," said Mo, "to your old mates."

When Mo had gone, George put the bottles in the recycling (Stephanie hated rubbish out of place) and checked the windows and doors were locked. Upstairs on the second floor, there was just one muted light. Everywhere else was in darkness. Stephanie—and George on the rare nights that she invited him in—slept in the large room at the back of the house. It had its own dressing room and a bathroom with both a walk-in shower and a freestanding bath on antique clawed feet. Tonight the bedroom door was firmly closed.

The piano was on this floor too, in the second reception room, overlooking the street. It was an arrangement that worked well at weekends. Stephanie played with a wary Mia downstairs (Mia saw so little of Stephanie that she wasn't really sure who she was) and George ("Could you shut the door, please, George? It's very noisy") played on the floor above. But on nights like this, it was an arrangement that didn't work at all.

After Mo's surprise appearance, George didn't feel the least bit tired. His mind was working overtime, full of memories of the band. He remembered the clubs all round London—in Smithfield and Peckham and Hammersmith and Shoreditch. He remembered their triumph in Paris. He remembered Walter at the bar mitzvah in Finchley and Mo at the wedding in Dorset. If, tonight, George could have sat at the piano and played, it might have calmed him. He could have disappeared into a Monk-like trance of rhythm and dissonance. But Stephanie must not be disturbed. So, wide awake, he headed for bed.

George climbed the second staircase to the top of the house, to what Stephanie called the nursery floor—Mia's bedroom overlooking the street, her bathroom next door, her bright, colorful playroom (big enough for several children to play hide-and-seek), and, at the very back, the spare room with two single beds where George, most nights, slept. He stepped quietly into Mia's room. A tiny red nightlight glowed by her bed.

George looked down at his sleeping daughter and felt, as he always did, a sudden rush of pride and protectiveness. He remembered that afternoon, sitting with Mia on his lap while she joyfully crashed the keys of the piano. I won't let you be like me, he told himself. I won't let you be full of self-doubt and self-questioning. I'll make sure you're happy and confident. Although, he thought sadly, your real education in assertiveness will come from your mother. She'll help you understand the world of money and law and business. Stephanie will make sure that you apply leverage, push the needle, shoot the puppy.

He looked down at Mia's flushed cheeks, the damp curl of her hair on her forehead. You'd never even met my daughter, he thought. But you put her first. You said, No guilty secrets. I don't want to do anything that either of us will regret. Because we're not the kind of people who can smash up other people's lives. He leant forwards and straightened the edge of Mia's blanket. At first, I wondered if it was just an excuse. I thought, Maybe she was looking for a way out, and that was the easiest and kindest rejection she could think of. Because why would she want to throw away the relationship she'd had for more than ten years for some kind of risky liaison with me? She'd only just met me. She didn't even know me. But then I thought about the way she looked that night, and I didn't believe it was an excuse. That night we both knew. If I'd been free, and she'd been free, we would have started a new life together. And that's why we sat in that noisy pub smelling of stale fat and old sweat and couldn't think of anything to say. It was all too trite, too trivial. You can't make small talk after a death sentence.

George looked at Mia as she breathed, her little mouth slightly open. You were right, thought George. Of course you were right. My small daughter comes first. And you knew that. You knew that nothing was worth tearing her life apart. But should I have fought harder? he wondered, running over the same miserable doubts that had obsessed him since getting back from London. People do smash up lives. It happens all the time. Marriages break up. Parents separate. He thought of his mother, her hands in her pockets, turning her face to the hot Cornish sun. When you have the chance to be happy, maybe it's your duty to grab it and hold on. Otherwise you're not really living. You're just marking time. And now he was a child again, sitting in the great wing chair, his bare legs on cold leather, listening to the tick of the clock in the hall.

George stayed in the darkness for a long time. He sat on the floor next to Mia's bed and let himself remember Tess and her dark eyes and the smile that lit up her face. You made me feel stronger. You made me see what was important. You made me feel myself again.

Much later, back in his room—the spare room—George pulled down the blind. But he wasn't tired. He picked up a book and put it down again. He turned on his laptop but decided not to bother after he saw all the waiting emails he didn't want to read. After a while he came to the conclusion that it would be a good idea to take down the duvet and pillows from the other bed and put them on the red sofa in the living room. Mo would have a more comfortable night.

So, moving as quietly as possible, careful not to bang into cupboards or door frames and wake Stephanie, George gathered everything up and tiptoed down the stairs. In the living room, he arranged the duvet on the sofa. It looks quite inviting, he thought. I don't think even Mo would have much to complain about.

He sat back and reached for the remote. Stephanie didn't approve of late-night TV-watching. It makes you dull in the morning, she said. She doesn't have to know, thought George. By the time she wakes up, I'll be down here giving Mia her breakfast.

It was Mia's crying that woke him. George, opening his eyes, found himself stretched out on the sofa, lying on his back, his mouth in Mo's red hair. Someone had turned on the overhead light. Stephanie, in her cream silk dressing gown, Mia struggling in her arms, was standing in the doorway looking at him with contempt. Mia, yelling, was trying so hard to get away from her mother's grip that she was in danger of falling headfirst to the floor. Desperate to get to Mia but pinned to the sofa cushions by Mo's whole body weight, George pushed himself out from underneath Mo's ribs and rolled sideways onto the rug. He staggered to his feet. "Mia!" he said. "It's OK! It's OK!"

"Here," said Stephanie, pushing her furious, sobbing daughter into his arms.

"What's the time?" said George.

"It's four thirty," said Stephanie, in a voice like ice. "I have had five hours' sleep. There's no point in going back to bed. So now, because of you, I will spend my whole day utterly exhausted."

"Stephanie—"

"I don't mind at all," said Stephanie, "if you want to indulge in homosexual affairs with strange ginger Scotsmen who turn up uninvited on a Tuesday night, but I would be very grateful if you could remember that I need a good night's sleep in order to function at work. Our arrangement is that you get up to Mia in the middle of the night. So perhaps in future you would take your one-night stands upstairs to the spare room so that you can hear your daughter if she cries."

"Stephanie—"

"I'm going to have a shower. If you could possibly make a pot of coffee, that would be very kind."

She swept out of the living room. Mia, who had stopped crying, looked at her father with huge eyes.

"Well, that's telling you," said Mo in a muffled voice from underneath the duvet.

"Oh great," said George.

"She's magnificent," said Mo, laughing.

"What were you doing, lying on me?"

"You said I had to sleep on the sofa."

"It's not funny," said George.

Mia, anxious, put her thumb in her mouth.

"It is," said Mo. "Just a wee bit."

"Oh for God's sake," said George. "Get upstairs. Very top floor. Room at the back. And take the duvet with you."

Mo stood up. He was wearing nothing but dark blue underpants, too tight and way too small. He did a mock salute; gathered up the duvet, the pillow, and most of his clothes; and trailed off towards the stairs, dropping socks as he went. "Any chance of a full English?" he said from the bottom stair.

George, gritting his teeth, went to put the kettle on. Mia looked up at him with questioning eyes.

"We woke her up," said George, "that's all. She was a bit surprised."

If only, thought George, Stephanie would treat Mia a little more gently. She was an equable child. She liked people, shared her toys, and was enchanted by all animals, including spiders. But if she thought that anyone—including her mother—was trying to separate her from her father, she lost control. She cried. She screamed. She yelled at the top of her lungs. The babysitter, she tolerated. It was somehow clear, to all concerned, that this was a business arrangement, and Mia had dignity. If this was important to her father, she would give in gracefully. But unexpected separations terrified her. Faced with the prospect of losing George, she drowned out all adult interaction with earsplitting wails.

George sometimes thought, rather sadly, that Mia saw the fault lines in his relationship with her mother and was keen to declare her allegiances. She pinned her colors to the mast. Every day, he explained to Mia that Mummy had to go out to work to help people. Of course she would rather stay at home with Mia. But she couldn't. She had to go to the office. Mia frowned and nodded. But she didn't seem to believe him. Stephanie, after all, got bored with Mia very quickly. At weekends, very soon after she called up the stairs to ask George to shut the door on his noisy playing, she would shout, "George! Come and look after Mia! I need to take this call!"

If George and Mia smiled at each other in mutual adoration, Stephanie, excluded, stared.

After Stephanie had left for work, George and Mia played and sang and looked at picture books until it got light, and then got ready to go out shopping. Mia was particularly fond of the Italian deli, where everyone made a huge fuss of her. They went to the swings and fed the birds, and by the time they got back home at noon, Mia's eyes were closing. It had, after all, been a very early start. George took her out of the buggy and sat with her on the red sofa to look at the paper—Mia liked pretending that she could read the paper—and when George next looked down, she was fast asleep.

George leant his head back against the sofa. The noise of prolonged coughing woke him.

"Sorry," said Mo, in a loud whisper. He was dressed in a T-shirt that looked suspiciously like one of George's.

George struggled to focus through a fog of sleep. "What's the time?"

"About two," said Mo.

Very gently, George eased his arm out from under Mia's sleeping body and rearranged her on the cushions. He put his finger to his lips. Mo nodded. Neither of them spoke until they had tiptoed the length of the house, past the great shining dining table, to the kitchen area at the back.

George stretched and yawned. "Do you want something to eat?"

"What are you offering?" said Mo, taking out a packet of cigarettes.

George looked horrified. "You can't do that here. Stephanie hates the smell of smoke."

"So what does she like?"

"What do you mean, what does she like?"

Mo shrugged. "I just wondered what made her smile."

George thought about this. He was slightly disconcerted to realize that he couldn't think of anything.

. . .

In the afternoon, when Mia had woken up again, the three of them wandered round Greenwich Village. The sun was shining, and George felt his spirits lift. He saw a couple of shops selling vintage clothes and thought of Tess. When Mia got tired and fractious, Mo entertained her by pulling ludicrous faces until she laughed. Then, back home again, George and Mia played the piano while Mo improvised a drum kit from empty cake tins and a couple of chopsticks. Mia was enchanted. She kept stopping to clap her hands.

George played Mo the beginnings of a piece he was working on. It was something that had been going round in his head ever since that last night with Tess. Mo listened, concentrating hard. At the end, he nodded. "It's good," he said.

"It's not finished."

Mo looked at him closely. "It's sad. What were you thinking about when you wrote it?"

But George wouldn't say.

Much later, after Mia's tea, Mo said, "So are you coming tonight?"

"I'd like to. But I can't leave Mia."

"It's a good place. I could introduce you."

George shook his head.

"Get a babysitter," said Mo.

"I don't think Stephanie would like it."

"Ask her. Ring her at work."

"I don't want to disturb her."

There was a pause. Mo said, "This isn't a life, is it?"

George felt a rush of irritation. "It's what happens when you have children."

"Don't blame this on Mia," said Mo. "It's got nothing to do with her. If you're not careful, you'll wake up one day and it will all be over."

"I know," said George miserably.

"You're like a dog on a lead," said Mo. "A skinny wee Pekinese in her handbag. Stephanie's pet. She's bought you, fed you, and cut off your balls."

George stood up.

"You know I'm right," said Mo.

"It's called compromise," said George wearily.

"This isn't compromise," said Mo. "This is surrender."

. . .

"I can't believe it," said Kirsty.

"Neither can I," said Tess.

"And you don't know what made you do it?"

Tess shook her head.

They were sitting in Kirsty's flat in Kennington. There were packing cases everywhere. Kirsty was moving out. Rafael was moving back.

"Can I stay here again tonight?"

"Of course you can," said Kirsty.

The previous night, Tess had turned up at ten o'clock, rivulets of black mascara running down her face, clutching an overnight bag and a red silk evening gown (Norman Hartnell, 1948). What's with the dress? Kirsty had said. I don't know, Tess said. But it was something that reminded her of who she was. A comfort blanket. Or perhaps a flag.

"Will Rafael mind?"

"You know what Rafael's like," said Kirsty. "Loves drama. If you've just split up with your boyfriend he'll be desperate to keep you here."

"I've no idea what I'm going to do," said Tess.

"Come to Paris."

Tess caught her breath. "Paris?"

"Why not?"

Tess saw the Eiffel Tower, the Louvre, the flea markets.

"Well, for a start," said Tess, "I shouldn't imagine Philippe wants me there."

"It's not up to Philippe," said Kirsty.

"Thank you. But I can't."

"Why?" said Kirsty. "Life is closing a door. Come and kick open a new one."

"Lots of reasons," said Tess. "My job, for a start."

"Oh bugger Daisy Greenleaf," said Kirsty.

Tess thought, She's right. After all, Daisy Greenleaf doesn't even exist.

But, right at that moment, Tess felt that handling complaints about violently purple notepaper was the only thing in the world that was completely secure.

• • •

Every year, Stephanie's boss held a summer party at his second home in the Hamptons. The house was magnificent, set in sweeping grounds that overlooked the sea. Every employee of the law firm was invited, along with partners and children. There was music and dancing in the great white tent and live bands on a central stage. By the pool, next to the reclining chairs, were piles of fluffy pink towels. For the children, there were red-nosed clowns and magicians in starry wizard cloaks, a treasure hunt and a junior tennis challenge. Hors d'oeuvres were handed round by respectful waiters with white gloves, and trestle tables were laden with an astonishing buffet—shellfish, cascades of tropical fruit, and desserts topped with spun sugar. All drinks were there for the asking—champagne, white wine, and retro cocktails including Manhattans, mint juleps, and Long Island iced teas.

It was luxurious, ostentatious, slightly camp, and torture for all concerned. No one could drink because they were nervous of what they might say if alcohol loosened their tongues. No one could eat because they had cut out protein, wheat, and dairy and were trying to subsist on a diet of boiled quinoa. No one could relax in case they missed a barbed comment or failed to thrust themselves forward into the limelight—or, worse, in case one of their children whined or misbehaved or ate too much chocolate ice cream and vomited into the bushes.

George said, "Do we have to go?"

Stephanie said, "Don't be stupid."

Mia had the worst time of the three of them because Stephanie tried to show how maternal she was by smothering her small daughter in unwelcome attention. George would position himself just behind Stephanie's shoulder so that he could give Mia reassuring smiles.

"She's a very serious little thing, isn't she?" a senior partner's wife had said the previous year, with a look of alarm, when Mia fixed her with a baleful stare.

"Analytical," said Stephanie.

This year, because Mia was nearly three and quite capable of complaining about anything she didn't like (especially if it involved her mother), Stephanie recognized that her usual act of selfless devotion was unlikely to work.

"There's a day care for the little ones," she said as they arrived at the wrought-iron entry gates.

"I'm not sure Mia will like that," said George.

Stephanie shot him an irritated glance. "I don't care whether she likes it or not," she said. "We both have work to do. I have to get round and talk to everyone. You have to find yourself some new pupils."

Oh, thought George, his heart sinking. So that's why I'm here.

George took Mia to the crèche. He squatted down so that their eyes were on the same level. He said, "Can you do this?"

She looked at him gravely and nodded. He smiled.

She's going to have a lot more fun in there, he thought as he walked back out to where Stephanie was impatiently waiting, than I will out here.

After the obligatory hand-shaking with Stephanie's boss

("You remember my husband, George, don't you, Larry? Classical pianist, teaching so many of our colleagues' children at the moment"), George and Stephanie parted company. Or rather, Stephanie waved him off with a furious expression, hissing, "For God's sake, circulate!" before turning round and bestowing a brilliant smile on a thin man in a Hawaiian shirt.

"Are you George?" said a blond woman in a yellow dress that seemed to have too many petticoats. She had very large, very straight teeth that flashed white in the sunshine.

"Yes."

"You teach *piano*?" she said, as if this was a startlingly novel idea, like whittling eggplants or training mosquitoes. "To *children*?"

George, transfixed by her dentistry, stared back.

She leant closer. He could feel her breath on his face. "*Small* children?" She dropped her voice. "With *anger issues*?"

At the bar, George asked for a glass of water. "Where are you from?" said a red-faced man in baggy shorts.

"England," said George.

"No, really? I was there last fall."

"Which part?" said George politely.

The man in baggy shorts frowned. "Edinburgh?"

George loitered by the crèche for a while, trying to get a glimpse of Mia through the window. Eventually he caught sight of her having her face painted. She had been transformed into a tiger with orange, white, and black stripes.

Out in the sunshine, a new band was coming onstage.

When George saw a saxophone and a double bass, he edged his way closer. The keyboard and drum kit had already been set up. George found a white wooden chair garlanded with pink paper flowers that made a loud crunching noise as he sat down. The musicians were getting ready to start. When he saw them communicating with their eyes, he felt a plunge of nostalgia. I don't have friends here in New York, he thought. I'm cut off, cast adrift. There's no one to talk to about anything that's important to me.

At a signal from the saxophonist, the band started to play. It was good. They played well. They looked cool, too—black, shades, sharp suits. They were performing straight jazz classics—Miles Davis's "Freddie Freeloader," Sonny Rollins's "St. Thomas," John Coltrane's "My Favorite Things." There was some Thelonious Monk—"Sweet and Lovely," "Crepuscule with Nellie," "Blue Monk."

And then the band started on Monk's "Ruby, My Dear"—a tune he had always loved—and as they played the first few bars, George suddenly went cold. It came out of the blue, running along his skin like freezing water. He knew, suddenly, where to take it. He knew, if he was sitting at the keyboard, how he'd change the rhythm and the keys. He could hear every note of it, finished, perfect. He found himself looking round for Stephanie. He wanted to rush up to her and say, "We've got to go. We've got to pick up Mia and go. I need to go home," because, more than anything, he wanted to be sitting in Greenwich Village at the piano in their second-floor living room, playing and experimenting until he could feel beneath his fingers everything he had just heard in his mind. And then, his heart beating faster, sweat on his forehead, he was finding it hard to breathe. Because he knew, as surely as if his hands were tied behind his back, his ankles to the legs of the chair, that he was going nowhere. This was the summer party of Stephanie's boss. For her to leave would be professional suicide. For him to leave before her would cause raised eyebrows and unwelcome gossip. He was stuck.

They finished "Ruby, My Dear." The keyboard player stood up. The crowd broke into lazy applause—a polite fluttering—because that's what you do when musicians stop. The bass player pushed the instrument away from his body, making the two of them separate again.

He didn't know he was going to do it. I swear, he said to Stephanie afterwards, I had no idea. I promise I had no idea. George stood up. He ran up the three steps to the stage. He said to the keyboard player, "Can I?"

The keyboard player looked amused. "Sure," he said. Why would you argue with one of the guests? These people were his bread and butter.

So George sat down at the piano stool. He looked up. The bass player, doubtful, looked back. Please, said George with his eyes, back me up. He bent over the keyboard. He did a four-octave run to a low B flat. Then he began to play.

It was a long time before George looked up again. His hands were still. It was over. But he was breathing in quick shallow gasps as if he'd been running. He had no idea how long they'd been playing. He had been aware, from time to time, of the other musicians shouting encouragement. Now he realized that the drummer was covered in sweat. At some point, the saxophonist had taken off his jacket and his shirt was sticking to his back. The bass player was grinning from ear to ear. We did it, thought George. We played it. They knew what I wanted and they ran with it. George felt dizzy, elated, exhausted. He thought, this was the sound I've been looking for. This was the sound I wanted.

It was only then, at that precise moment, that George took in the silence of the crowd. He looked to his right, and there they were, staring openmouthed in horror like a multiplication of Munch's scream. It almost looked as if one of the women was crying. George felt the first faint stirrings of unease. No one clapped. No one said a word. They couldn't have looked more shocked if he'd chopped off bits of his body with a meat cleaver and let the blood spurt out onstage.

And then he saw Stephanie. He'd always thought of her as pretty tough. But she looked as if someone had sucked all the life out of her. She stood there swaying like a zombie in a horror film.

"Did someone say he was *English*?" said a voice.

. . .

Tess and her mother sat at the kitchen table in Kent. All around them, as usual, was chaos—cupboard doors wide open, the washing machine half-emptied, newspapers spilling out of the recycling bag. But Tess's mother, for once, was completely still. She was sitting opposite Tess, her face white with shock.

"Over?" she said.

Tess nodded. "I'm staying with Rafael. He's a friend of Kirsty's."

"But what about the flat?"

"We're going to sell it. And split the money in half."

"Oh," said her mother.

"I'm sorry," said Tess. "I just thought you ought to know."

"Is there someone else?"

Tess shook her head. Because there wasn't. George had gone home to New York.

"Not for him either?"

"No," said Tess.

Her mother sat back in her chair, both hands in her lap. "So what happened?"

"I didn't want to move to Beckenham."

Her mother nodded, as if this was a perfectly sensible answer.

After a while, Tess said, "I mean, there was more to it than that, obviously. But it was something about the move that made me think, I don't really want this."

Her mother didn't seem to be listening. She said, "I've never really liked Beckenham." After a pause, she said, "I've never really liked Dominic, either."

Tess's eyes opened wide. "What?"

"He always seemed a bit dull."

"Dull?"

"I know you're not supposed to say things like this in case people get back together, but I could never quite understand what you saw in him."

Tess opened her mouth to defend him, but her mother said, "And I always worried that he was bringing out the worst in you. You can be very serious, you see. You like everything safe and organized. But there's always been another side of you that's joyful and happy. And I thought he was squashing that flat. I thought he was making you old before your time."

Tess said, hurt, "You never said anything."

"Of course I didn't," said her mother. "How could I? All you can do when your daughter brings home a boyfriend is welcome him with open arms."

Oh, thought Tess miserably, is that how it works?

"People never say this, but that's what a good relationship is all about, really," said her mother thoughtfully. "It's about making each other laugh. Even when life hits you on the chin. That's what I miss most about your father. We laughed every day."

But he didn't pay the bills. He left a financial mess that made you cry.

"He wasn't perfect," said her mother. "I'm not saying that. But he made the world a better place to live in. And I want that for you. I want to see you smile again."

"Haven't I been smiling?"

"Not for about ten years," said her mother.

• • •

"George," said Stephanie, "I haven't got long."

"No," said George, gripping his cell phone. He hated phone calls with Stephanie. It always felt like an inquisition.

"I understand you're not teaching William anymore."

"Yes," said George.

"Why?"

"I'm not sure."

"Didn't you ask?"

"The maid came out with a note. William wants to give up."

There was a pause.

"He's got another teacher," said Stephanie. "His father told me today."

There was a longer pause.

"It was quite embarrassing," said Stephanie.

George couldn't think of a suitable response.

"George," said Stephanie in a softer voice, "I'm worried about you."

This unusual concern for his welfare was so shocking that he felt a small stab of alarm.

"I think you should go and see Dr. Mishkin."

"I'm fine," said George.

"I think you're depressed."

"Because I'm not teaching William?"

"Because you're just drifting about the house not doing anything."

"I'm playing," said George, "all the time."

"That's not a career option."

It would be, thought George, if only you let me out at night.

"I think antidepressants might make a world of difference," said Stephanie. "Just to tide you over."

"Tide me over?" said George.

"I've made you an appointment for Wednesday afternoon at four PM."

"What about Mia?"

"I've arranged the sitter."

George was silenced.

"I've got to go now," said Stephanie. "I'm ringing between meetings."

"What time will you be home?" said George.

"Late," said Stephanie, and hung up.

. . .

"You seem very distracted this morning," said Oliver Bankes.

Tess looked up guiltily.

"Bad news?" said Oliver.

"No," said Tess, putting down her mobile, "just a few domestic concerns."

"Ah, yes," said Oliver. "Water bill, gas bill. Burst pipes. That kind of thing. Always amazing how much time it takes up, dealing with the basics." He put his finger into the air as if testing for wind direction. "Can you pop into my office?

Quite like your views on the new marketing strategy. Big drive for Daisy Greenleaf. Exciting stuff."

"Yes, of course," said Tess. "Give me two minutes."

When Oliver had disappeared back into his tiny glass cubicle, Tess peered round her screen.

"Helen?"

Her assistant looked up with big, terrified eyes.

"Have you got enough to be getting on with if I have a meeting with Mr. Bankes?"

Helen nodded.

"I tell you what," said Tess, "I think you've been doing so well with the moaners and shouters, it might be time to move on to the liars."

Helen trembled with the excitement of new honors.

Tess looked again at Dominic's text. It read, *Need to sort out contents of flat. Vintage clothes?*

Maybe the time has come, thought Tess, to sell them all. Draw a line under everything and move on.

. . .

The worst thing about sacrificing your happiness in order to honor your commitment to the person you married, thought George, is that you expect them to be grateful. Which is, of course, ridiculous. Firstly, Stephanie has never shown gratitude for anything except, perhaps, the time I ran all the way to the specialist dry cleaner's to pick up a black evening dress embroidered with crystals seconds before they were due to close. Secondly, Stephanie doesn't know that I would have left her if Mia didn't exist. Thirdly, I never see Stephanie anymore. She's either at work or in bed with the door shut. So showing me any kind of emotion—happiness, fear, misery, gratitude—is completely impossible.

George, who had been piling clothes into the washing machine, sat back on his heels. The whole situation was getting worse. He sometimes felt that Stephanie was actively trying to make it impossible for him to earn money. Recently, he'd raised again the idea of having a live-in nanny. Stephanie could afford it. They had the room. It was even possible, in the fullness of time, that the money George could scrape together from performing might just about cover her wages.

"Mia wouldn't like it," said Stephanie.

"If we interviewed carefully," said George, "and found someone she really liked, I think she'd be OK."

"I wouldn't like it either," said Stephanie. "I don't want to have to talk to some stranger in the mornings."

This was something George had worried about. Stephanie wasn't very good at keeping her temper at the best of times, but mornings were particularly bad. Her words fell like paint stripper onto open wounds. We'd have to find someone, thought George, who could ignore verbal abuse. Or maybe an experienced nanny with a poor grasp of English?

"It would make it easier if we went away," said George. "There'd be someone to look after the house."

"When do we go away?" said Stephanie.

"But that's the point," said George. "If we had live-in child care, we could. We could even go away for a weekend by ourselves."

Stephanie gave him a look of such incredulity that George felt ridiculous. "I think we're fine as we are," she said. "The ideal, after all, is to have a parent looking after a child."

"Stephanie—"

"George, I think we should park this one. We've exhausted all possible avenues of discussion."

When she turned round, George felt like sticking his tongue out at her bony back. But that, of course, would only prove what Stephanie always said—that he was essentially operating on the level of a child.

It was because he was so preoccupied with Mia and his music that George hadn't really noticed how rarely he saw Stephanie. Then one morning she came into the house just as he and Mia were having breakfast and he realized, with some surprise, that she hadn't been home all night.

"Are you OK?" said George, guiltily getting to his feet.

"Fine," said Stephanie. "Tired. I'm going to have a shower and get changed."

"You're not going back into work?" said George.

"I have to."

"But you've been there all night."

"Don't fuss, George," said Stephanie, and he heard her running up the stairs with surprising energy for someone who hadn't slept for twenty-four hours.

The deal Stephanie was working on seemed to drag on for weeks. She even went into the office on Saturdays.

"They can't expect you to carry on like this," said George.

"I've told you before," said Stephanie, "that it doesn't help if you make a fuss."

"I'm just concerned about you."

"Well, don't be." She peered at him more closely. "Are you taking your antidepressants?"

"Yes," said George, who wasn't.

It had seemed easier all round to go to the appointment she'd made with Dr. Mishkin. The doctor had asked him a few vague questions and had taken his blood pressure, and George found himself on the street a few minutes later clutching a prescription. He was sorry that Stephanie thought he was depressed, as he had been feeling better recently than he'd felt for a long time. He was alive again. The music was in his head when he woke up and stayed with him all day. Sometimes he found himself singing a key change or banging the wooden work surface with a metal spoon to try to work out the rhythm. Mia, delighted, joined in. George noticed, to his horror, that there were spoon-shaped dents all over the butcher's block.

George had a lot on his mind. So he didn't think it was particularly strange that Stephanie always ended calls when he appeared in the room and occasionally, when staring at her iPhone, even smiled.

"Good news?"

She looked up, unfocused. "It's nothing."

But then, one evening, George knocked on her bedroom

door to say that Mia was ready for bed and did she want to say good night (she usually didn't, but he always felt he should ask) and found Stephanie lying on her back in small triangles of lacy black lingerie, hair spilling out onto the red bedclothes, whispering into her phone.

"Oh, sorry."

"Can't you knock?" said Stephanie, furiously, swinging herself upright.

"I did," said George, staring with astonishment at a push-up bra that gave the impression of voluptuous excess.

"What do you want?"

"Mia," said George, "she's ready for bed."

"I'll come up in a *minute,*" said Stephanie, "when I've finished my *call.*"

Downstairs George sat in one of the leather armchairs and thought about the past few weeks. He felt ashamed it had taken him so long to work it out. He also felt tired and old, as if he'd been running a marathon and suddenly realized that everyone else had passed the finishing line a long time ago.

When Stephanie eventually appeared downstairs, fully dressed, he said, "Are you having an affair?"

"Don't be stupid."

George took a deep breath. "Are you seeing someone?"

"Are you?"

"What?"

"Are you seeing someone? One of the other moms? I hear about it all the time. Playdates. Flirting by the swings."

George said, "I'm not seeing anyone." Briefly, fleetingly, he thought of Tess. No guilty secrets, he thought.

Stephanie, frowning, looked almost disappointed.

"You didn't answer the question," said George.

"I don't think you have the right to ask."

George stared at her. "We're married. We have a child."

"Ah, yes," said Stephanie, her voice crisp with dislike. "The doting daddy. Do you realize, George, quite how boring you've become?"

There was a pause.

"I want a divorce," said Stephanie.

She said it so coolly that he wasn't sure he'd heard what she said. "What?"

"I have tried. I have tried very hard. My firm much prefers its senior staff to be in stable relationships. But I don't think it's possible to keep up the pretense any longer."

"What about Mia?"

"I want you to move out," she said.

"What about Mia?" he said again.

"I'll get a nanny."

"But you don't want a nanny."

"I don't think you quite understand," said Stephanie. "I want a divorce, I want you to move out, and I want sole custody of Mia."

"Don't do this," said George.

"Don't do what?" Her tone was mocking.

"Don't start a fight. We have to do what's best for Mia. She's three years old."

"I know how old she is, George. She's my daughter. In my view, it's not good for her to have parents at each other's throats. A clean break is better all round."

"No," said George. "I won't let you do this."

"I don't think you can stop me."

"If you want a divorce," said George, "that's fine. I'll even move out. But you can't cut me out of Mia's life."

"It might be better for her."

George shook his head in disbelief. "How do you work that out? I've been looking after her since she was born."

"During the week, George. And she has a sitter on three afternoons. At weekends I have sole charge. And I'm the one who gets up to her in the night."

He stared at her.

"In my opinion, an unemployed father with mental health problems isn't the ideal carer for a three-year-old."

George found his voice. "What are you talking about?"

"Clinical depression."

George shouted, "I don't have depression!"

"I don't think losing your temper will help."

Blind with rage, George took a deep breath and forced himself to calm down. "I'm not depressed."

"If I were you, George, I would sit down and think things through very carefully. Personally, I don't think you're in a very strong position. On any level. But by all means, take advice." She smiled sweetly. "If you can raise the money for an attorney."

• • •

"It's called *The Artist,*" said Ellie.

They were in an American diner in Soho. It was late. Ellie was talking and eating French toast at the same time. Tess was looking at her plate of salt beef with some anxiety. She didn't feel hungry at all.

"Everyone's talking about it," said Ellie. "It's going to be up for all the awards. Kirsty's seen it, and says it'll be one of the biggest French films ever. It's set in 1920s Hollywood, and it's got everything going for it—glamour, style, humor, music, lovely whimsical moments with the dog—"

"The dog?"

"A Jack Russell called Uggie."

Tess looked at her. "How do you know these things?"

Ellie frowned, surprised. "I don't know. I just do." She looked at Tess's untouched plate. "Can I have some of your fries?"

"Go ahead," said Tess.

Ellie leant forward and helped herself. "The funny thing is that Kirsty said the night she went, some of the audience walked out halfway through because there was no talking and no color. Which is really stupid, because that's the point of it. That's the point of the whole thing. It's silent. Black and white. I mean, it's not meant to be like real life."

No, thought Tess, thinking of her silent, empty flat in Brixton. She said, "So what's it about?"

Ellie took a sip of her beer. "It's a love story."

"Oh," said Tess, sadly.

. . .

George found a room in East Harlem. The door was paper-thin. A single kick would have demolished it. He didn't care. He didn't have anything worth taking. At night he lay awake listening to shouting and screaming. During the day, he went to the 125th Street Library, desperately researching everything he could about child custody. He abandoned all his pupils. Cut off from his piano, he couldn't play, but he didn't miss it. It seemed unimportant.

He missed Mia, on the other hand, with a physical longing that hurt. There was a hole in his heart. The thought of her crying made him close his eyes in pain. The thought of her not crying, of becoming silent, was worse. That's what children do when there's no hope. They stop protesting because they've learned that there's no point.

Two days after Stephanie kicked him out—she said she would claim he was physically abusing her if he didn't go—George went to get free legal advice. He filled out a form. He waited for three hours. Finally, a woman with black glasses and a thin white face called his name. He followed her into a tiny room smelling of paint.

"OK," she said. "I'll come straight to the point. As I see it, the crucial issue here is not custody but your immigration status. Your right to stay in the US. If you and your wife divorce, you'll have to leave."

He looked at her in horror. But she had her back to him, tugging at the cord of the blind so that the sunlight fell in white lines on her desk.

"But my daughter's here," he said.

She turned back to face him. “It makes no difference.”

“She was born here. She’s a US citizen.”

“Your wife has the right to stay. You don’t.”

“So what can I do?”

“Your best option is to talk to your wife. Counseling, mediation, a neutral third party.”

“She won’t talk to me.”

“Keep trying.” She sat down, picked up a pen, and pivoted it fast on the fulcrum of her fingers. It flickered to and fro like helicopter blades that wouldn’t spin. She seemed tired. She seemed distracted. She seemed very young.

George looked at her, pleading with his eyes. “Isn’t there anything else you can do?”

“I can explain all your options in a little more detail,” she said. “But I have to warn you. It doesn’t look good.”

. . .

Tess stood in M & S in Brixton. It was Saturday afternoon. So far in her basket she had a five-pack of knickers, some forty-denier black opaque tights, and a thermal undershirt. She wasn’t sure about the thermal undershirt. She’d never bought one before. But recently she’d become quite irritated by feeling cold. It seemed silly, really, to shiver your way through a British winter when you had the option of clothing yourself more sensibly.

“What color would you say this was?” said a large elderly lady in a blue felt hat.

Tess wondered, for a minute, who the woman was talking to. “Oh,” she said. “I think it’s beige, isn’t it?”

They both contemplated the garment hanging on a rail in front of them. Tess wasn’t really sure what it was. A sort of cardigan?

“I’ve been looking for something like this for a long time,” said the elderly lady.

“Have you?” said Tess. She desperately wanted to slide away and finish her shopping. But she didn’t want to be rude. This poor old dear probably hadn’t talked to anyone all day. Although neither have I, thought Tess, with a jolt of surprise.

The elderly lady put her head on one side, considering. “I’m not sure. They only do it in this color.”

“I think you should get it,” said Tess, thinking she needed a bit of encouragement. “Before they sell out,” she added helpfully.

“I don’t know. Would it suit me?”

My life may be rubbish, thought Tess, but at least I can try to make other people feel a bit happier. “You could always dye it,” she said.

The elderly lady looked up, offended. “They don’t recommend dieting at my age, you know.”

. . .

Sometimes, in the long weeks that followed, George thought about going home, back to London. I know London, he thought. I’d be on solid ground. I’d be able to fight. He lay in bed dreaming about old friends, imagining an army from *The Lord of the Rings,* everyone he had ever known armed to the teeth, coming to his defense. His dreams of battle were so vivid that he would wake shouting and punching the air, the cries strangled in his throat. Once he even called out to his father.

But if the nights were full of turmoil, the mornings, with their silence, were worse. With the first gray widening of light, he knew that nothing had changed, that no help was coming, that today was just another pile of sludge to push through. The trouble was, he had invested so little in New York. He had no friends to call on. Sometimes he sat in his cold room with his cell phone in his hand and wondered whether to ring Rhys. Sometimes he even wondered whether to ring Mo. But what could they do? Even if they came to New York, there was nothing practical they could offer. Fleetingly, he considered calling Walter. But he hadn't spoken to him for four or five years. And he was an English solicitor, not an American attorney. He wouldn't know anything about visas and immigration.

So George lay on his hard thin bed in his dirty rented room, and the thoughts buzzed about in his skull like flies banging against the window.

He tried to spend as little as possible. He knew his money was going to run out fast. So he didn't eat very often. Most of the time he wasn't hungry anyway. But he was always tired. If he went outside, he soon found himself sitting on a wall or a bench, staring at the ground. He wondered whether he was depressed. How ironic, he thought, that I was so outraged at the idea of taking antidepressants. They might help me function if I took them now.

Every few days, he left a voicemail for Stephanie. He always said the same thing. Please can we talk. All I want is what's best for Mia. Please can we talk. She never replied.

Then, one morning, his phone rang. For a moment, startled, he just stared. It had been so long since he'd spoken to anyone, he didn't even think to check who was calling.

"Hello?"

"George?"

He couldn't speak. It felt as if someone had a hand round his throat.

"I'll come straight to the point," said Stephanie. "I have been thinking things over."

"What do you mean?"

"My position has changed. I am prepared for you to see Mia."

"When?"

"Well, as it happens," said Stephanie, "I have a meeting to attend this afternoon and my sitter has let me down. I know it's short notice, but I wondered whether you might be free."

George said, in a cracked voice, "I might be free."

"Good. Can you come to the house at two PM? The housekeeper will let you in. Could you be prompt? She has to leave almost immediately."

"Yes," said George.

Stephanie hung up.

George sat there, staring at his phone. He questioned nothing. If you've been in solitary confinement for six weeks and the jailer unlocks the door, you don't ask why.

For the first time in days, he shaved properly. He was shocked to see how white and thin he looked. He washed as carefully as he could in the small, dirty sink. He cut his nails. He found his last clean shirt. He set out for Greenwich Village so early that he arrived outside the house at half past one. He waited a quarter of an hour. Then he couldn't wait any longer.

A middle-aged Hispanic woman in a white apron answered the door.

"I'm Mia's father."

She said nothing. She stood back and let him in.

Mia was sitting on the red sofa. She didn't move. Her eyes were huge. George sat down facing her. The space between them stretched out like a desert. He wanted to reach out to her but he didn't dare. He had let her down. He had abandoned her. He had no right to touch her.

"I'm sorry," he said. "I'm so sorry."

He bent his head, unable to carry on.

Then he felt her hand on his neck. He pulled her to him, blinded by tears, his face in her hair, breathing in the smell of her, crushing her tightly, bone to bone, flesh to flesh, and they rocked to and fro while George tried, with all his strength, to stanch the great bleeding wound of separation.

. . .

It was cold in the champagne bar at St. Pancras—beautiful, but cold. Under the vast domed glass ceiling, Tess, shivering, sat and waited for Kirsty, who was arriving on the Eurostar from Paris. Tess considered buying herself a glass of champagne while she waited, but was slightly worried about alcohol on an empty stomach. Her day at Daisy Greenleaf had been ridiculously busy. Oliver's grandiose and ambitious marketing plan could have used up the entire working day of at least twenty people. But most of it, as usual, had fallen on her desk. Tess was beginning to wonder if it was time to talk to Oliver about a promotion. She was definitely his number two these days. What would that make her? Managing director? Tess smiled. Only thirty-two, she thought, and already running a West End company.

And then she saw Kirsty. Everyone else saw Kirsty, too. Heads turned. The bar fell silent. Kirsty was wearing a midnight-blue dress with a high collar that plunged to a deep V and a tiny nipped-in waist with four vertical buttons. The fabric, very full, danced out to midcalf. She wore elbow-length gloves, and her hair was swept up from her face. As usual, her catlike eyes were emphasized with black eyeliner. Her lips were bright red. She sauntered over, smiling, and Tess stared openmouthed. It was as if the 1947 New Look had stepped out from a glass case in a museum.

"Do you like it?" said Kirsty, giving a quick catwalk turn so that the dress flared out before settling back against her hips.

"It's amazing," said Tess. "Where did you find it?"

"Oh, just one of the vintage clothes shops in Paris."

"It's not," said Tess, who was finding it hard to breathe, "Dior?"

Kirsty laughed. "No. It's a copy. But it's good."

"Very good," said Tess. She stroked the fabric. "Silk. And look at the ruching at the neck."

"So go on, then," said Kirsty. "When are you coming to Paris? You, too, can look like this."

"Hardly," said Tess. "I'm six inches shorter than you."

"Let's have a drink," said Kirsty, stepping up onto the bar stool and drawing every single male eye in her direction. She looked at Tess's face and laughed again. "You can't take your eyes off it, can you?"

"It's so beautiful," said Tess.

"I knew you were spending too much time at work. You've forgotten how to enjoy yourself."

"It's just that I was thinking recently," said Tess, "that I wasn't obsessed with vintage fashion anymore. But I am. Like the person who made this. They really cared. They wanted to copy every stitch."

"There's still time for that shop in Brixton."

Tess's air of excitement faded. "It was only a dream," she said.

"You could make it happen."

"I don't know." She looked down at her sensible work shoes. Splitting up from Dominic had used up every bit of courage she'd ever had. "Maybe I'm too old."

"Too old?" Kirsty laughed. "Life is just beginning."

They ordered champagne. Kirsty told Tess about the gallery, about their apartment, about Parisian shops, and about Philippe. She clearly adored him. Tess tried hard to listen to everything Kirsty was saying, but she kept feeling that she was watching a film. It was partly the architectural drama of their surroundings—the Victorian brilliance of St. Pancras. It was partly that Kirsty had dressed up in 1940s clothes that made her look like a Hollywood actress. But it was also that this was a story coming to an end. Kirsty would marry Philippe. She knew that. The gallery would be a resounding success, and they would have French babies, and Kirsty would live happily ever after. Sitting in the champagne bar, Tess felt like the spectator of someone else's much more interesting life. She didn't want to talk about Daisy Greenleaf Designs. She didn't want to talk about the small flat she'd rented in Brixton. There was nothing to say about vintage clothes except that her collection was all packed up in boxes in her mother's loft in Kent.

By the time she'd drunk her second glass of champagne, Tess was beginning to feel depressed. Kirsty had never let caution get the better of her. She had always lived for the moment, taken risks, and gone for what she wanted. That's the right way to live, thought Tess. Not the way I've lived. Curled up like a field mouse in a nest of tissue paper.

I even sent away the one man who could have made me happy.

She came back to the present to hear Kirsty saying, "And I've got a bit of gossip. Do you remember Gareth?"

Tess frowned. "Gareth?"

"Rhys's brother. The one who went off to South America to get over me."

Tess's face cleared. "Oh, Gareth. I remember him. I always liked him."

"Well, he bumped into a friend of mine on top of a mountain in Machu Picchu."

"Where?"

"The ancient Inca site in Peru."

"Oh," said Tess. Once again, she felt the extreme blandness of her life by comparison.

"And apparently George's wife, Stephanie, is talking on Facebook about her divorce."

Tess stared. "What?"

"George's wife, Stephanie."

Tess shook her head. "I don't understand."

"Gareth is a Facebook friend of Stephanie's. God knows why. I didn't think she liked any of George's old friends."

Tess felt as if she couldn't breathe. "Tell me again," she said, "what did George's wife say?"

"Something about a divorce. And being committed to working together in their daughter's best interests. Which usually means they're fighting over custody."

"Yes."

"Tess?"

"What?"

"You've gone very pale. Are you OK?"

"I just feel a bit dizzy," said Tess.

"Can I get you something?"

"Yes," said Tess. "Can you get me George's phone number?"

. . .

It's hard when you lock up the way you feel, cramming it away as if you're stuffing old clothes into a small dank cupboard in the cellar, because when you turn the rusty key and pull back the creaky bolts, everything flies out just the same as before but older, and dirtier, and tattier, and it's just as difficult to cope with, except now it's slippery with damp and mildew and indeterminate grime.

Tess was just as lost as when George first left. But now, after all this time, she felt she had even less reason to contact him. The whole situation had got matted and complicated like hair in a plughole. She hadn't seen him for nearly a year. Would he even remember her? If he did remember her, would he want to see her? After all, if the stories were true, he'd just been through a divorce. You don't feel like rekindling old romances if you've just been through a divorce.

Kirsty gave Tess a lot of flak to begin with. "You never told me you even liked him."

"There wasn't any point," said Tess. "It couldn't go anywhere."

"Like *Brief Encounter*. Very British. Repressed passion and shoulder pads."

"Kirsty," said Tess, "this isn't helping."

"Well, you shouldn't keep secrets from your friends."

But there was nothing to tell, thought Tess.

Once Kirsty had allowed herself to be mollified, she promised to ring Rhys—because Tess didn't really see Rhys anymore—and he gave Kirsty the last number he had for George. But Rhys also explained that he didn't normally ring George, because he always got in touch with him by email, but don't even think of trying that, because he hasn't answered an email for months. And he's never been one for the social network, has he? Doesn't even lurk round Facebook. Now I come to think about it, Mo was the last one to actually see him. But he didn't say anything about a divorce. Although it wouldn't surprise me, really, because after Mo stayed the night in New York, Stephanie got really angry and accused him and George of being gay lovers.

"He said what?"

"Gay lovers," said Kirsty, who was ringing from the gallery in Paris. Suddenly bored with her impersonation of Rhys in full flow, she added, in her normal voice, "But then Rhys always was a bit dramatic."

So Tess sat at her desk in Daisy Greenleaf Designs and looked at the number she'd copied into her phone and wondered whether George had come out and was living it up in gay nightclubs, or couldn't come out and was stuck indoors with no Internet connection and a broken laptop. Was it true that he was divorced? She couldn't bear to think of him fighting for custody of Mia—not after the way he'd talked about her. Several times she found his name and number, and her thumb hovered over the call button, but she couldn't do it. How can you ring someone after a year of not seeing them based on a rumor heard on a mountaintop in Peru?

Eventually—and she wasn't proud of this—she sat on the sofa in her tiny flat in Brixton and knocked back most of a bottle of red wine to give her courage. She could feel her heart hammering as she waited for him to answer. But then, as she opened her mouth to speak, there was a woman's recorded voice asking her to leave a message. Tess hesitated but didn't say anything. Was that Stephanie's voice? Was this the right number?

"It goes straight through to voicemail," she said to Kirsty on the phone. "And it's a woman and I keep thinking it might be Stephanie."

"Why don't you just leave a message?"

That was, of course, the obvious solution. But what would she say? Hello, George, this is Tess. Hello, George, voice from the past—do you remember, we met at Kirsty's party in Kennington?

Hello, George, this is your soul mate.

What am I doing? she whispered to herself, lying alone at night. I don't know you, George. I have no idea if you ever even think of me. And she would turn her pillow over and over, trying to find a cool spot, and get angry with herself for her lack of courage.

About a fortnight after Kirsty had given her George's phone number, Tess was sitting in her flat one Saturday afternoon, finalizing her latest marketing report for Daisy

Greenleaf, when she heard the doorbell. She pressed the little intercom button and said, "Hello?"

"Tess?"

She caught her breath.

"Can I come up?"

Tess glanced in the hall mirror and smoothed her hair. She waited a few seconds, took a deep breath, and opened the door. And there, coming up the stairs, flicking his long blond hair out of his eyes, was Dominic.

"Come in," she said.

But once they were both in the hallway together, neither knew what to do. They hadn't spoken for weeks. The flat had been sold. They had divided all their possessions. How do you talk to the person who shared your life for over ten years but now has even less involvement in your day-to-day activities than the postman?

"How are you?"

"I'm fine," said Dominic. "How are you?"

We'll be talking about the weather next, thought Tess. "Would you like a cup of tea?" she said, going for the easy option.

"Yes," said Dominic, looking pathetically grateful. "Yes, thank you."

So Tess led him through to the tiny kitchen, and he sat on one of the two chairs while she put the kettle on. It was strange seeing him again. She was able to be objective and see that he definitely was good-looking, despite his beaky nose. Very wholesome and blond and Californian. A catch for any girl. But when we were splitting up, I couldn't see it for a while. Because no man quite measured up to George.

She said, "No sugar, still?"

"No sugar."

She found two mugs. She said, "So how have you been?"

"Fine," said Dominic. "You?"

"Fine," she said.

The kettle performed its usual party trick of banging like a misfiring exhaust as its metal sides got hotter.

"I was just passing, really," said Dominic.

Tess poured boiling water into the cups. "How are your parents?"

"Fine," said Dominic.

"And your sister?"

"Fine, thanks," said Dominic.

Tess fished out the tea bags and dropped them in the bin. Was it always this bad? she thought. Did we never have anything to talk about?

"And your mum?" said Dominic.

Tess put both mugs on the table. "Why are you really here?"

Dominic looked away.

"It's lovely to see you," said Tess, "but you could have rung. I just wondered why you wanted to come over."

Dominic seemed unable to answer.

"Maybe you wanted to check I'd maximized my tax-free savings allowance."

Dominic shot her a quick look from his very blue eyes.

"That was a joke," said Tess.

"I still don't understand," said Dominic suddenly, "why we broke up. I keep thinking about it, and I don't get any closer. And it's worse now the flat's sold. I kept hoping for months that you'd change your mind. I know you said you wouldn't. But I thought you might. Because there was never any reason. And you don't stay with someone for years and years and then just break up. You don't do that. It doesn't make any sense."

Tess sat down as if her chair was made of glass.

"I kept thinking, Something must have happened. But I couldn't think what it was. Because nothing seemed to have changed. I looked at all the reasons, and I thought about them, and none of them stood up."

Tess sipped her tea. It burned her mouth.

"There was no logic to it," said Dominic.

It was this one word—Dominic's favorite word—that shamed her. She shouldn't have left it like this, without explanation or excuse. It was cruel—the coward's way out. He deserved better than that. She took a deep breath. Slowly and hesitantly, nervous of his reaction but desperate for him to understand, she told him about George—how they had met twice, and nothing had happened, but how meeting him had made her realize that she wasn't happy, because they had fitted so perfectly, as if destiny, or fate, had wanted them to be together. She told him they had agreed never to meet again, and he had gone back to New York, to his wife and child. She said that none of it made sense but was, at the same time, stronger than anything she had ever experienced. She told him she felt lonely and sad and didn't like being on her own, but felt it was more honest than sharing her life with anyone who wasn't George. And that she was very, very sorry. And that she hoped Dominic would find someone who would love him in the way he deserved to be loved, without reservations or regrets.

After she'd stopped speaking, there was a long silence. Dominic's face was very sad and still. Eventually, he said, "What happened to him?"

"I don't know." Then Tess said, in a rush, "There's a rumor that he's left his wife. But no one knows. And no one can get hold of him."

"Left his wife?"

Tess nodded.

"So he's free," said Dominic. "And you're free."

Awkwardly, because her freedom had been bought at his expense, Tess nodded again. "Although in New York," she said, trying to smile. "And not answering emails or calls."

Dominic said, "You've got to go and find him."

She looked at him in astonishment.

"If you feel like this," he said, "you've got to go."

"All the way to New York?"

"Yes."

She said, because she couldn't understand how he could say this after the way she'd treated him, after the way she'd abandoned him and hurt him, "Why?"

"Why?" said Dominic, puzzled. "Because it's the only logical thing to do."

. . .

"So I'm prepared to grant you limited access," said Stephanie.

George waited.

"Where are you living now?"

He shook his head.

"What?" said Stephanie.

"I can't take her there. It's a bad neighborhood."

Stephanie raised an eyebrow.

"It's all I can afford," said George.

"I see." She breathed in deeply as if he was trying her patience on purpose. "Then it had better be here. Of course some of the internal doors will be locked. I prefer to keep our lives completely separate. But I'm prepared to be generous. Access on a regular basis?"

"Yes," said George.

"How will this fit in with your work?"

"I'm not teaching anymore."

Again, Stephanie looked surprised.

"I couldn't," he said. "Not with all this uncertainty."

Stephanie looked at her watch. "I have to go. Every afternoon? Would that suit you? Until I get back from work?"

"Every day would suit me better."

She narrowed her eyes. "What are you saying?"

"Use me as child care. I'll fit in with whatever hours you like."

Stephanie looked at him for a long time. She said, "What do you want in return?"

"Food. And enough money to pay my rent."

She considered this. "Whatever hours I like? Every day?"

George nodded.

"I think that's probably an offer I can't refuse," Stephanie said. "Since you left, the agency's sent three nannies and they've all been completely hopeless." She picked up her coat. "On the understanding, of course, that it's entirely discretionary. If anything happens that I don't like, it stops straightaway. Do you understand?"

. . .

At Poole station, Tess got into a cab.

"Branksome," she said.

The journey to her grandmother's house brought back so many memories of being small and coming to the seaside—the big orange beach towel, buckets full of shells, fish-paste sandwiches, and strawberry ice cream. Her father always played the fool, one minute Long John Silver, the next a boiling lobster. On the beach, holding imaginary reins, they jumped over the wooden groynes. Sitting on the promenade, they conducted choirs of seagulls. Tess had followed his every lead, Robin to his Batman, Snow White to his seven dwarfs.

She smiled. For some reason, he had always called Tess's grandmother Ma. She can't have liked it, thought Tess. She was too dignified to be called Ma. And she cared about the social niceties—crusts off sandwiches, milk in a jug, jam in a bowl with a silver spoon.

As the car pulled up in front of her grandmother's house, Tess wondered for the first time whether her father's teasing had been unkind. Perhaps calling her Ma had been a way of trying to cut her down to size. They hadn't liked each other. Even as a child, she knew that her grandmother didn't really approve of him. She smiled politely when he clowned around, but the smile never quite reached her eyes. Most of the time, she looked at him with intense but detached curiosity, like a scientist observing the erratic behavior of a drugged mouse.

As Tess paid the cab driver, she saw her grandmother standing in the open doorway, tiny, like a daisy in a giant frame.

In the living room, the table was already set for tea—a white lacy tablecloth, cups and saucers painted with pink roses. On a plate with a doily were thin pink wafers and almond biscuits dusted with sugar.

Tess said, "I love coming here. You make me feel like a princess."

"And so you should," said her grandmother.

Tess's grandmother was nearly ninety. She had silver-white hair and faded blue eyes. These days, she moved very slowly. She always walked with a stick. But she was adamant that she didn't want to move into a nursing home. I'm fine, she would say firmly. I've lived here all my life. I've got very good friends in Branksome, and a doctor who calls whenever I need him.

As a young woman—you could see it in all the photographs round the room—she had looked very like Tess, petite with shiny dark hair. Those were the days, thought Tess, as she always did whenever she visited her grandmother, when wide hips and a tiny waist were in fashion. Nowadays we get upset about fat bottoms in jeans.

"I'll make the tea," said Tess.

In the kitchen, as she waited for the kettle to boil, Tess looked out onto the back garden. She used to help her grandfather with the vegetable patch when she was a child. He had been a maths teacher at the local secondary school. But he had also been an intensely practical man. He had turned his hand to everything—plumbing, carpentry, wiring, car maintenance. Even the scaffold for the runner beans had been a feat of engineering. He used to say, bending down so that she could see the seriousness in his eyes, "Pleasure in the job puts perfection in the work."

Which is true, thought Tess. I always used to find my best pieces of vintage fashion—the ones that used to make me catch my breath with excitement—when I was spending hours happily pottering in some dingy old charity shop. She remembered the way he carefully knotted string, how he cleaned his gardening tools before putting them away in the shed, how he labeled tins of leftover paint with the names of the colors and the rooms they had decorated. How strange, she thought, that my steady, conservative grandparents produced a daughter as scatty and impulsive as my mother. Perhaps that's what happens. You rebel against the way you were brought up. So it alternates every generation—sensible, mad, sensible, mad. Which makes me, she thought rather sadly, sensible.

In the living room, Tess set down the teapot on the little stand and covered it with a cozy. “So how are you?”

“I think the question,” said her grandmother, “is how are you?”

Tess, who had never been sure what her grandmother thought about her living with a man she hadn’t married, said, “I’m fine. Really. We’re much better apart.”

“And you’ve sold the flat?”

“Yes.” After a while, she said, “I do miss him sometimes. But it was the right thing to do. It was when we were thinking about moving to a bigger place. I just thought, I’m not sure this is what I want.”

“A wedding concentrates the mind,” said her grandmother.

Although it had never been the wedding, really, that had bothered her. That had just seemed like a performance demanded by Dominic’s mother. An excuse for high heels and a hat.

“Marry in haste, repent at leisure, as they used to say,” said her grandmother.

Tess smiled. But she wondered whether dithering for over a decade could really be described as haste.

“And was that the only reason?”

“Sorry?”

“General misgivings?”

“Yes,” said Tess. But then, suddenly, she didn’t want to lie anymore. “No.”

Her grandmother said, with evident satisfaction, "I thought not."

Tess looked at her, surprised.

"Does your mother know?"

Tess shook her head.

"So," said her grandmother, carefully putting her cup back in the saucer, "who is he?"

So Tess told her about George.

She wondered, when it had all been said, whether her grandmother was still listening, because she was looking over at a point in the room somewhere behind Tess's back, and her head was slightly to one side as if she was hearing a distant sound. Tess drained her tepid tea and put the cup and saucer down on the table.

Her grandmother said, "I remember my father telling me that some critics say the study of history is worthless, because there will never be exactly the same people in exactly the same circumstances, so you can learn nothing from the past."

Tess waited.

"But I think you can learn from the past. Or at least from the people who tell you their stories. So I'm going to tell you about something that happened to me a long time ago. I've never told your mother. I don't particularly want her to know." She looked at Tess for confirmation. Tess nodded.

"I loved your grandfather. You know that. He was a good man."

She said nothing for a moment, just sitting with her hands in her lap, looking at somewhere Tess couldn't see.

"I was twenty-two. The end of the war. We were tired. And hungry. And dirty. We did our best, but there was no hot water and no soap. My father was fighting in France. My mother was exhausted. So many nights disturbed by sirens and air raids. I caught her sleeping standing up once, still in her apron, leaning against the kitchen sink.

"England was so gray. You queued for hours. Sometimes you didn't even know what you were queuing for. The beach was cut off by barbed wire and there were signs everywhere telling you all the things you couldn't do. It felt sometimes as if you couldn't even smile. Some people enjoyed it. The people who liked rules and regulations. But the rest of us had had enough. Especially the young ones. All we wanted was a bit of life. We were tired of the cold and the dark and the fear and the bad food and everything you ever wanted cut down by the war.

"One afternoon, I rode my bicycle through the pinewoods. That's where they stored all the ammunition. You couldn't see it. I don't know how they managed it, but it was all completely hidden. And everywhere in the woods were the trucks with white stars. American trucks. We had thousands of GIs in Dorset at the end of the war. One big military camp. They were getting ready for D-day. The invasion of Europe.

"The front wheel caught on something. A stone or a rabbit hole. I went right over the handlebars. And I lay there on the pine needles, and I thought, What have I broken? I was too frightened to move. I remember looking up through the trees, and the sky was very blue. And then I heard his voice. He said, 'Are you all right?' It was straight out of the pictures. He squatted down next to me. He said, 'You take your time now.' The bicycle was all buckled but he pulled it back into shape. He straightened the front wheel so it was as good as new. And then he set it down and asked me if I could stand. And I had never seen a man like him before. He had such a beautiful smile. He took my breath away. He was so happy in his skin, so unlike any British man I had ever met—open, easygoing, relaxed. He said, 'My name is James,' and held out his hand, and I said, 'I'm Iris,' and he said, 'That's a very pretty name,' and I remember longing for that moment to go on forever. But then he helped me up, and there was nothing wrong at all, not even a twisted ankle. No excuse not to leave. So I got back on my bicycle and set off again. But I turned round and waved, and he waved back.

"A few days later, I came up with a reason to cycle the same way through the woods, and I saw some American soldiers, but not him. I couldn't stop thinking about him. It felt as though that moment when I'd fallen off my bicycle was the end of one life and the start of another. Nothing was the same. My life had been gray. But now I could see something different.

"I thought I would never see him again. But then my friend Jean said that the Methodist minister had invited some Yanks to tea in the church hall, and did I want to come? I didn't ask my mother. She would have said no. I thought, Ten minutes. I'll stay for ten minutes. What's the harm in that? And there he was. I saw him the moment I walked in. He stood up and gave me the biggest smile. It was like standing in the sun after months of rain. We talked all afternoon. He told me about living on a farm in Louisiana with his parents and two little sisters. We talked about the English words he didn't understand. I told him about my brother, Tommy, and how my father taught history at the grammar school and how the house was full of books about the English Civil War. And then I said to him, 'Would you like to come and meet my family? I know my mother would be pleased.' Which was a lie, of course, but he wasn't to know. And he said, 'I'd be honored.' And afterwards, Jean said, 'What did you say that for?' And I said, 'What do you mean?' And she said, 'You'll be for it now.'

"He came the following Sunday. I told my mother that all the local families had been asked to have an American to tea. He brought tinned peaches and chocolate for her, and gum and sweets for Tommy. He sat with Tommy in the garden looking at all his pictures of planes. He was so patient. He looked so big and strong next to this thin, scrawny little boy.

"My mother and I went out to the kitchen to make the tea. Of course she wasn't fooled at all. She said, 'What are you doing?' I said, 'They're on our side. We have to be friendly.' She said, 'It would be no life for you.' I felt very angry. I said, 'I just asked him to tea,' but she looked at me and I blushed. Because she was right. I didn't just want him to come to tea.

"And then he went and sat down in the drawing room

and played the piano for us. And he sang, too. He had a beautiful strong tenor voice. He said he'd played with Louis Armstrong once. I said, 'Did you?' And he laughed and said, 'Iris, you shouldn't believe everything a man says. Especially when he wants to impress you.'"

There was a pause. Tess said, "He was black?"

"Oh yes," said her grandmother.

They sat for a while, letting the ghosts from the past live again. Her grandmother seemed very tired. She said, "Back then, there were race riots in America. There was segregation in the South. My mother wanted to protect me. She said if I went back with him, I would have no kind of life. I said I didn't care. I loved him. He made me happier than anyone I'd ever met. But I didn't, in the end, go against her. When he asked me to marry him, I said no."

"What happened to him?"

"I don't know. He never wrote. But there was no reason why he should. Why would you write to the girl who turned you down?"

"And then he went back to the States," said Tess.

"A year later, I met your grandfather. My parents were happy. It seemed a good match. He was a teacher, like my father. He was steady and responsible and able to provide for me." She looked down at her hands in her lap. "But I will never know," she said, "if I made the right decision."

"It wasn't your decision to make," said Tess, angry on her behalf. "Your mother stopped you."

Her grandmother looked at her, her eyes very blue. She

said, "We say these things, don't we? But it's never really true. It's your life. No one else's. Most of the time, the only thing that stops us is ourselves."

Tess thought, Is that really what happens? She felt ashamed.

Her grandmother leant forwards. She had an air of urgency, as if she needed Tess to understand. "Don't make the same mistake. Whatever you do, don't make the same mistake I did. Go to New York. Find this young man and tell him you love him." She paused. "Because if you don't, you'll be wondering about him for the rest of your life."

• • •

"That's wonderful news."

"Isn't it?" said Ellie, her voice on the phone sounding rather hysterical. "I can't keep still. I want to run down the street screaming."

"Managing editor," said Tess. "That's amazing. Do you get your very own PA?"

"I do," said Ellie. "And more money. And expenses."

Tess, who was battling to hold on to her mobile and her umbrella in blinding rain, ducked into a doorway to shelter. "We need to get together and celebrate. Are you free this week?"

"No," said Ellie. "I've got stuff happening every night. Can it be after the weekend?"

"I won't be here after the weekend," said Tess.

There was a small, stunned pause.

"You're not."

"I am."

"You're going to New York?"

"Monday morning."

"I don't believe it."

"I don't, either," said Tess. "I'm terrified."

"What will you do when you get there?"

"I've got an address. His address, I hope."

"You know, I never thought you'd do something like this. It's so out of character."

"But the funny thing is," said Tess, "I feel more like me than I have ever felt in my entire life."

"What did Oliver say?"

"He wasn't very pleased."

"Did he make a fuss about giving you the time off?"

"You could say that. I said, I need to take two weeks off for urgent personal reasons. May I have unpaid leave? And he said, when? And I said, now. And he said, that's impossible, we're in the middle of a marketing campaign. And I said, so when I can I go? And he said, maybe in a couple of months' time."

"So what did you do?"

"I quit," said Tess.

"You didn't."

"I did."

"You left Daisy Greenleaf Designs?"

"Well, I never really liked the job much anyway," said Tess.

. . .

The cab drew up outside a tall terrace of brownstones. The street was quiet. Tess's hands were shaking so much that the $20 bills jumped out of her purse and scattered all over the shiny brown seat. Her heart was beating fast. All I want, she thought, cramming money back into her bag, is to turn round, go back to the airport, and go home. I don't want to knock on George's door. I don't want to stand there waiting to see if he recognizes me. Why am I here? Why have I flown halfway round the world to see someone I hardly know? What will I do if he's out? I can't leave a note. I can't leave a note saying, "Hi, George. This is Tess. Just happened to be passing." But it's worse if he's in. Because then I'll have to face him. And I don't know what to say. I can't explain.

Perhaps, she thought, as she scrambled out of the cab and stood on the sidewalk with her pathetically small suitcase (because what do you pack when you don't know where you're going or how long you're staying?), I should be completely direct. Perhaps I should just say, I have no idea why I'm here. Dominic told me to come. My grandmother told me to come. And leave him to work out whether I'm refreshingly honest or utterly insane.

She knew if she waited too long she wouldn't do it at all. So, even as the cab was pulling away, a bright spot of yellow disappearing down the street, she was looking for number 124. There were grand stone steps, decorated by black wrought-iron handrails, leading up to all the front doors.

And now there it was, the numbers picked out in brass on a door of polished brown wood.

I can't do this, thought Tess. I can't do this.

She picked up her case and ran up the steps. She paused at the top, out of breath. In the distance, far away, she heard the bass grunt of a fire engine. But this street, this exclusive, tree-lined street, was completely empty. Don't rich people ever go for a walk?

She rang the bell.

Nothing happened.

Nervously she retreated back down one step.

Then the door opened. And there he was, looking down at her. It was George, the same George, the man she'd been thinking about for months, the man she'd flown thousands of miles to see, but a more detailed version, because the George in her mind had become more of a feeling, a touch, the sound of a voice, and she'd forgotten that the real George was physical and substantial, that he could take up space outside a front door in Manhattan. He stood there, looking at her, both familiar and strange—older, perhaps, or more tired—and she felt a little joyful skip of recognition. She opened her mouth to say something (George! George! It's you!) but no words came. So they stood, quite still, staring at each other. Tess felt as if the world might stop forever at this precise moment, on a Monday afternoon at half past two.

George was holding a little girl who was looking at her with a very serious expression. She thought, He doesn't recognize me. He doesn't recognize me at all. And her heart sank in shame.

George's eyes widened. He said, "Tess?" and made a small movement as if he was going to come towards her. But then he stopped, shifting the little girl in his arms.

Tess couldn't move. She was frozen to the step.

He said, "But what are you doing here?"

Tess said, "I heard New York was good for vintage clothes."

George stared. The little girl stared. Time stretched thin like a long thread of chewing gum.

Then he said, "Come in."

Inside, the hall was dark and cool. He said, "Give it a good push," and the front door shut behind her with a heavy clunk, as if multiple locks were slotting back into place. There was a semicircular table against the wall, covered with scraps of paper and plastic bags, and beyond that a buggy with a purple seat. Tess followed him through a door to the left into a room that ran the length of the house. Cold gray light shone off the polished wooden floor. At the far end were French windows covered by a white security grille—metal strips crisscrossed into diamond shapes. The room was both empty and untidy, like a vast warehouse where someone had dumped the contents of a jumble sale. It smelt of something decaying—apple cores or chicken skin or wet black tea leaves rotting in a bin.

George gestured to a small red sofa. "Sit down," he said, "and I'll get some coffee." But he didn't move. The little girl had her head on his shoulder, her arms round his neck. She eyed Tess warily. He said, "Mia's not been well."

Tess looked at the cloud of Mia's hair.

"We were going to the park," he said.

"Is this a bad time?"

He looked shocked. "No," he said, "no, not at all."

They stood politely, each waiting for the other to speak.

Eventually Tess said, "I could make the coffee, if you like."

He shrank back as if she'd threatened him with a baseball bat. "No," hc said, "I'll do it." He swung round and tried to set Mia down on the seat of a leather armchair, but she started crying, clinging on with her arms and legs like a monkey, and Tess felt horribly guilty—the interloper, the intruder, making a small child wail in distress. She said, "Really—show me where it is and I'll do it," but George didn't hear because Mia's yells were increasing in volume, and he was still trying to set her down on the chair, and she was still clinging on to him, and her weight had bent him double, pulling his head down into the brown leather armrest, and they were wrestling, he and Mia, a many-limbed Hydra in a small noisy heap.

Tess stood there, uncertain what to do next. She put her bag on the floor by the sofa and took off her bright pink coat. Still George and Mia were wrapped round each other. Should she go? Did George want her to go? She had almost decided to leave when George, with a sudden ungainly lurch, pulled himself upright, and now he and Mia were staggering dangerously close to the glass coffee table. In a panic, Tess put up both her arms to stop them if they fell, shouting, over Mia's renewed howling, "I don't need coffee!" But he wasn't listening, because it was enough of a job to keep his balance, and all the while he was murmuring, over and over again, his voice low and insistent, "It's OK, Mia, it's OK, we'll do it together, we'll do it together."

After a long time, still clinging on to him but gradually reassured by the pressure of his arms and the repetition of his words, Mia stopped yelling. But she carried on crying in a lonely, defeated kind of way. Then she was quiet.

The silence, after all the noise, battered Tess's ears like the banging of a drum.

She said, "Show me where—" as he said, "She hasn't been well—" and they both stopped.

George's hair was sticking up. His shirt had come untucked from his trousers.

Tess said, "I could come back another time," although she had nowhere to stay in New York.

George looked at her with an exhausted expression, as if she'd just suggested going for a run.

The little girl took in a long shuddering breath and let it out again in a sigh. Her eyes, after all that terrible crying, were closing. He said, "As long as I hold her, I think she's OK."

Tess said, "I really don't mind about the coffee."

"We could have tea."

She nodded.

"If I had any," he said.

Quite suddenly, he smiled. Tess's heart turned over. They stood there, motionless, the little girl half-asleep on his shoulder.

Tess said, "So this is Mia."

George was still smiling. She wanted to kiss his mouth.

"Not a good introduction," he said.

"How old is she?"

"She's just three. I know people always say this, but she's never normally like this. She's normally very happy."

"I remember you telling me about her."

For one fleeting moment, time fell away and they were back in Kirsty's flat, at the birthday party. They looked at each other, remembering.

"She hasn't been well," he said again.

And you? Tess wanted to say. What about you? Everyone's worried about you. Rhys says you haven't answered emails or phone calls for months. But she couldn't think how to frame the question.

George turned awkwardly towards the end of the room, towards the French windows. "Are you sure I can't get you some coffee?"

"Maybe a glass of water," she said, because he so badly wanted to offer her something.

So they left the living area with its sofas and leather chairs, and walked through the dining area, with the great dark table piled high with newspapers and discarded clothes and yellow plastic toys, and now they were in the kitchen. There was a square butler sink and white cupboards with gray pewter handles, and a butcher's block with a wooden top misshapen and shiny with age. On the wall were orange and green tiles. A rustic, countryside kitchen, thought Tess, in one of the most expensive cities in the world.

"I'm sorry about the mess," said George. "The housekeeper walked out. There was a row . . ." He trailed off, awkwardly. He said, "There's filtered water in the jug."

"I'll do it. You've got your hands full."

Watching her, still holding his sleeping daughter, George leant back against the stub of a wall—where there had once been a door frame before everything was knocked through for easy family living—and he said, "So how long are you staying?"

Tess found a fluted glass on the wooden draining board and filled it with water. She said, "I'm not sure, really."

There was an empty silence, like a hole in the road.

"It's a holiday?" he said.

She could feel his eyes on her back. "Sort of."

"Not work?"

"No." She turned round. "I've left my job."

He looked surprised.

"It's a good thing. It wasn't right for me."

He nodded. "Are you looking for something else?"

"Yes."

He said, hesitantly, "You could come to New York. Try something different."

Her heart soared. She wanted to tell him that she'd left Dominic. But no one ever said it was a good idea to strip yourself naked and offer yourself like a present, all tied up with red ribbon. So she just stared at him, tongue-tied, and everything got more complicated, like somewhere full of cul-de-sacs with roadwork and barriers and broken streetlamps.

He said, "Hold on a minute." He walked away from her, back towards the living area at the front of the house. She watched as he stopped by the red sofa in the bay window and very gently started to lower Mia onto the fat feather cushions. Tess held her breath. Perhaps he was putting Mia down so that he could concentrate on what he was going to say next. She hoped so. She so wanted him to concentrate on what he was going to say next.

But it didn't work. Mia woke. Jolted from sleep, she felt this new betrayal keenly. She started to cry, great howls of despair. It seemed now as if the sound reverberating round the big empty room was louder than before. Tess felt it had become part of her, had rushed into her head like a flapping wind. She put down her glass of water. She walked towards the bay window. Outside the sky had darkened to lavender gray. She said, "I'll come back. When Mia's feeling better."

"Yes," he said, distracted.

And then she said—without knowing why, because she didn't plan to say it, she didn't want to say it, she wouldn't have dreamt of saying it like that, blurting it out with no preamble, no warning—"You left your wife."

"No," he said.

The wailing got louder.

He said, "She's never normally like this."

Tess picked up her bag and her bright pink coat. Mia's cries were inside her head, scrubbing at her like a green scouring pad. She said, "I think I should go."

His face was all crumpled with anxiety. "What?"

At the front door, she heard him calling her name. But she didn't stop.

Outside it had started to rain.

. . .

It happened so fast, thought George. I looked up to say, No, wait, she's tired, she'll fall asleep in a minute, and she'd gone. I shouted, "Tess!" over Mia's crying, but she didn't come back. The front door slammed shut. I stood there, holding Mia, my head against hers, and then, quite suddenly, Mia fell asleep. I shut my eyes. I couldn't believe it. Tess had been a few feet away from me, in Stephanie's house, in New York. Tess. And I'd let her go.

George felt a flood of anger towards Mia. Pointless, stupid crying. Then he felt angry towards himself because that was stupid, too, to blame a three-year-old. But now that the crying had stopped, he could think clearly. He tracked back the conversation in his mind. What did I say? All he could remember was Mia's loud wailing. But he knew, with overwhelming certainty, that he must have said the wrong thing. Why else had she left? He had skewered his hopes, sliced through the possibility of a fragile understanding. He felt sick with the realization of his own stupidity. He had to find Tess. He had to track her down, make her come back.

He looked round for his cell phone. It took five minutes to find it. There's something about looking after Mia, thought George, that makes me lose things all the time.

He couldn't risk putting Mia down, even though his left arm was aching with her weight.

The first person he rang was Rhys.

There was a sort of roar down the phone. "Where the hell are you?"

"Manhattan."

Rhys said, "Where have you been?"

But George didn't want to talk about that now. He said, "Listen, have you got Kirsty's number?"

"Kirsty?"

"Kirsty. Brixton Kirsty."

There was a pause. Then Rhys said, "I'll text it to you."

"Thanks."

"Are you going to tell me what's been going on?"

George said, "Another time. I'll ring you. But I've got to go now." He could almost hear the puzzlement down the phone.

A few minutes later, he got the text from Rhys with Kirsty's number. It said, "Call me, you bastard."

George took a deep breath. Kirsty answered almost immediately. He had a picture of her in his mind straightaway—the long black hair, the raised eyebrow, the slightly mocking expression.

"Kirsty, it's George."

"George?"

"In New York."

"I know where you live," she said. "I was just checking it's you. Where have you been?"

"Have you got a number for Tess?"

"Why? What's happened?"

"She was here just now. She turned up out of the blue. And now she's gone."

"Gone where?"

"I don't know."

"George," said Kirsty, "what have you done?"

"What do you mean, what have I done?"

"You must have said something. She wouldn't just go."

"I didn't say anything. It was just a misunderstanding."

"What kind of misunderstanding?"

George wanted to scream down the phone, Just give me the number, just give me the number. He said, "It's a bit complicated."

"You do realize why she came to New York, don't you?"

"She's looking for work."

"Oh for God's sake," said Kirsty, wearily.

"Please? Please give me her number?"

"She and Dominic split up. Did she tell you that?"

I didn't give her the chance, thought George. Despair yawned inside him.

Kirsty gave an exaggerated sigh. "OK," she said, "I'll give you the number. But if you hurt her, I'll kill you. OK?"

George said, "I don't want to hurt her."

"Then think," said Kirsty. "Think very hard before you ring her."

After he'd rung off, George stood there looking at the number he'd scribbled down. Nothing made any sense. Mia was hot and heavy against his shoulder.

Each time he rang, it went to voicemail. In the end, he left a message. But all he said was, "Tess, it's George."

Mia didn't protest when he put her in the purple buggy. It took a long time to find the rain hood. He put blankets round her. He didn't want to risk waking her by putting on her coat.

Outside, it was raining hard. The green of the trees was bright. He had no idea which way to go. For some reason, this made him walk faster. He stopped to check that Mia was OK, and she was fine, sleeping underneath the plastic hood, all steamed up. But after a while, wheeling her at speed through the streets of Greenwich Village, he started to panic. What if Tess had just called a cab and gone to the airport? Each time he got to a junction, he stood there, staring at the traffic. There were umbrellas everywhere. People were walking fast, their heads ducked down.

The rain got so heavy that it battered his skull as if someone was throwing gravel at his head. He couldn't see Tess anywhere. And now he knew, deep down, that it was pointless, because the chances of finding her were nil. And it made him feel heavy and dull inside, as if he'd been filled with stones. If he couldn't find her, she would never know. She would never know that he thought of her night and day, that he constantly replayed in his mind everything she'd ever said, every time she'd ever smiled, every moment she'd ever looked at him with that expression that said she understood, she knew who he was, she knew why he did what he did. It was too late. And it was all his fault. She had given him a chance. And he'd blown it.

And then he remembered. He remembered the vintage clothes. So he turned round and headed for Christopher Street. By now it was getting hard to see. The sky was gray and the rain was so heavy it was like walking through a waterfall. People barged into him, running from the deluge, and cars threw up great slews of water.

Please, please, please, thought George, stumbling through the rain.

Then he turned a corner and saw a bright pink coat. She was there, only twenty, thirty feet away. He stopped. She was standing outside a thrift shop, looking into the window, her dark hair in long straight strings.

He shouted, "Tess."

Water splattered down from the awning onto the sidewalk, like a gutter overflowing, obscuring his view.

It took him a while to realize the truth. The coat was red, not pink. Her hair was far too long. His yearning had pushed his memory of Tess onto a stranger's body—a woman who was taller and thinner, unlovely in every way.

It wasn't Tess. Tess had gone.

. . .

"I need to go back to London."

"Why?"

"You know why."

"Your father?"

"It's becoming critical."

"Your brother's there. He can look after him."

George looked at her. Stephanie had that air of acute impatience she always had these days whenever she talked to him. He said, "It may be my last chance. I have to go back before it's too late."

"So what am I supposed to do? I can't find child care at the drop of a hat. The agency's useless. The last time I used them they kept sending me girls who didn't even understand English."

Which, thought George, given the way you talk to them, was probably a good thing. He glanced across to the other side of the room, where Mia, still in her pajamas, was lining up her collection of soft animals in neat attentive rows.

"Let me take her with me."

Stephanie stared at him.

"I want her to see her grandfather," said George.

"A hospital is hardly a suitable environment for a three-year-old," said Stephanie.

"We won't be spending all day there."

"No," said Stephanie.

"Why not?" said George.

"I don't think it's a good idea. Illness is extremely depressing." She looked at her watch. "Now, if you'll excuse me, I have to get off to work. I'm already late."

"I'll be gone when you get back."

Stephanie, who had turned her neat tailored back on him to put her keys in her bag, whipped round to face him. "What?"

"I'm getting a flight back this afternoon."

"What about Mia?"

"I've told you. The best solution is for me to take her with me. If you won't allow that, you'll have to sort out child care. It's your choice."

She looked at him in astonishment. "What's got into you?"

Tess, thought George. I have to find Tess.

"You're never normally this confrontational."

He said nothing.

"This is blackmail," she said.

"No," said George. "This is an opportunity for you to concentrate on work while Mia has a short holiday with her English relatives."

"It's completely unreasonable," said Stephanie, "for you to bring up something as important as this when I have so much on my mind. I can't see why your brother can't manage on his own."

George waited.

Stephanie took a deep breath. "You've put me in an impossible situation. I do not appreciate having to choose between two unattractive alternatives. Mia can go. But I want her back in a week." She shot him a quick, suspicious glance. "Is there something going on, George? You're being very peculiar."

"You'd better go," he said.

"Yes," she said. Her phone bleeped. Stephanie looked down, made a face, and took the call. Without a backwards glance, she walked out of the house, already negotiating terms with some distant lawyer who was equally uninterested in breakfast.

Mia looked up, saw her mother's disappearing back, and returned to her toys. George, stunned, leant back against the wooden work surface like a boxer who's unexpectedly won a tough round.

. . .

When her mobile rang, Tess turned over and pulled the pillow over her head. It would be Oliver. It had been Oliver every day for the past week, ever since she'd got back to London. *I think we may both have been a little hasty. Daisy Greenleaf can't manage without you. Would you consider coming back? You're driving a hard bargain, here, Tess. What are your terms?*

Oliver, please, she thought. Leave me alone. She felt like someone who's swept out of the house in a ball gown and tiara only to find that it's raining, there are no taxis, and she's wearing Wellington boots. I made a grand gesture. It felt magnificent. I threw in my job and flew to New York to see the man I love. And now you're asking me to slot back into my old life like a piece of white bread in a toaster. I can't do it. Not yet. I have been humiliated. I gambled. I put everything on red and it came up black. I've lost everything. And I can't, at the moment, feel anything for ethical stationery.

I can't, thought Tess, her head under the pillow, feel much for anything at all.

Sometimes, despite herself, she remembered New York. She remembered the warm, soupy quality of the air after the rain, the shop doorways smelling of cumin and hot bread and vanilla, the roads—Walk, Don't Walk—full of yellow cabs and wide white buses.

Everything she remembered had the peculiar logic of a dream, making perfect sense and no sense at the same time. He had been so pleased to see her. She knew that. When he went to settle Mia on the red sofa, she had been sure he had been about to say something important. She felt they were on the brink of something new.

But he hadn't left his wife. So nothing had changed. He wasn't free. They were stuck in the same hopeless mess as before.

You can't, thought Tess miserably, have to work this hard to find your soul mate. I thought George and I were destined to be together. But maybe not. Maybe that's what this whole horrible confusion is trying to tell me. You tried to make it work. But it didn't. Now is the time to give up.

Kirsty, of course, had said she'd drop everything and come over. But she had just discovered she was ten weeks pregnant. Both she and Philippe were delighted. But Kirsty wasn't finding it easy. She was currently spending her days either throwing up or slumped in a chair feeling like death. Tess refused to let her come.

"George rang me," Kirsty said on the phone.

"Did he?" said Tess, politely.

"I said I wouldn't speak to him."

"Oh," said Tess.

"I think I might have been quite angry."

Tess flinched at the thought of Kirsty shouting at George down the phone.

"Tess?"

"Yes?"

"Are you all right? I'm worried about you."

"Don't be. I'm fine."

"Come to Paris."

"No," said Tess. "It's really kind, but I just need to be on my own for a while. I think I'll probably have to go back to Daisy Greenleaf. But not yet. I'm going to take a few days off."

"It's all my fault," said Kirsty. "I should never have told you what Gareth said."

"You weren't to know," said Tess.

Eventually, with a heavy heart, Tess rang Oliver and said she would come back to work the following Monday. Oliver sounded pathetically grateful. Then Tess put her bedclothes in the wash, cleaned and tidied the flat, and got dressed for the first time in a week. She was able to do up her belt a notch tighter. Misery, she thought, makes you thinner. She decided, for no particular reason, to go to Covent Garden. But at the last minute, buttoning her coat, she changed her mind. The South Bank, she thought. A wide expanse of dirty gray Thames will match the way I'm feeling.

Unfortunately, as Tess walked down the stone steps from Waterloo Bridge, the sun broke away from a black curtain of clouds and beamed benevolently. The pavement by the side of the river was crowded with laughing tourists taking pictures of each other, and the desolate expanse of gray concrete that Tess had remembered looked clean and white. You can't even rely on depressing surroundings anymore, she thought. She walked over to the trestle tables set out with secondhand books and read the titles on the spines. Happy endings, she thought, sadly. All these stories with happy endings.

The man next to her was far too close. How rude, she thought. Haven't people heard of personal space? She looked away and pretended to be interested in *101 Ways with Lentils*.

"Tess?"

She looked up. The man was staring at her.

"Yes?" she said, suspiciously.

"Don't you recognize me?"

Tess blinked. She tried hard. There were faint flutterings of memory at the back of her mind. "Can you remind me?"

"Cappuccino?" he said.

No, she thought. It can't be. "Colin?"

He smiled. Tess was so shocked she couldn't think what to say. It was as if the ghost of Shakespeare had popped up outside the Globe Theatre.

"You look so different," she said.

"Fatter, probably," he said.

No, she thought, not fatter. Alive. You look different because you look well. He was clean-shaven, his gray hair cut short. He was wearing a black shirt, open at the neck; black trousers; and a gray jacket with narrow lapels. If you looked very hard, you could see a lot of fine lines round his eyes, as if he had spent years squinting against the sun or wincing at sharp pain. But nothing would have connected this man to the bundle of bad-smelling rags that used to huddle in the doorway near Daisy Greenleaf Designs.

"You disappeared," she said.

"Have you got time for a cup of coffee?"

"Yes," she said. "I've got lots of time."

So they found a seat in one of the American chains, and Tess waited while Colin went off to the counter and she sat watching him, enjoying the sight of his transformation. I always wondered, she thought, what had happened to him. Sometimes I used to worry that he'd died, that he'd been buried without ceremony, no mourners at his funeral. And now here he is, walking towards me with a brown plastic tray, balancing it carefully so that nothing gets spilled.

"So," he said, setting everything down on the table, "how have you been?"

"No," she said, firmly. "You first."

Colin tried to duck out of talking to begin with. He said, "You don't want to know. You don't want to know about me." She managed to get out of him that he lived in a village near Cambridge and came up to London twice a year for medical checkups. But then he kept shaking his head when she asked him questions. Eventually she said, "Well, we're going to have to sit here in silence then. Because I'm not saying another word until you tell me what happened."

"Were you always this bossy?" he said.

"Always," she said cheerfully.

So he gave in.

He remembered her visiting him in hospital. "I can't tell you how much that meant to me. I felt more alone in there than I had ever felt in my entire life. And then, there you were. You asked me what I wanted, what you could bring. I didn't think you were real. I thought you were probably an angel."

Tess smiled.

"And then you asked me who you could contact. That hurt. Because that was the problem. I'd cut myself off. And I couldn't go back. You weren't to know. But I'd lost everything and there was no way of making it right."

Oh, thought Tess, distressed. I never meant to hurt you.

"And then one day the nurse came up and said, Your wife's here. And she was. Right there, in the hospital. She had never stopped looking for me from the day I went missing. She never gave up. It's not that easy to find people if they're determined to disappear. She was lucky. I was lucky. A friend of hers worked in the hospital and recognized me. So she came and arranged for me to be transferred. And then took me home."

"She never gave up," said Tess.

"No." Colin smiled. "I'm not sure what I did to deserve her."

"But why? Why did you walk out?" Almost immediately, she regretted the question. She was being too intrusive. She could see that from the slight tightening of the muscles round his mouth.

"They used to call it a breakdown. They have all sorts of fancy names for it now. But basically I cracked up. Couldn't make sense of anything." He looked at her. "If anyone else asked me I'd change the subject. Make a joke. But you deserve an explanation. For quite a long time, you were the only person in the world who showed any interest in me at all."

"I don't want you to tell me if it's painful," said Tess, awkwardly.

"It's not painful. I'm just ashamed. They say things happen sometimes that trigger memories from the past. I got kicked out of my job, and something snapped in my head. I walked out of the house and didn't come back. I don't remember anything about it. I just knew I couldn't go home. I put them all through hell. I don't know why she carried on looking for me. But she did. And so I'm here today."

"Have you got children?"

"Two. A boy and a girl. They grew up while I was away. It's hard to forgive myself for that."

"You were ill," said Tess.

"Yes." Colin nodded. "That's what my wife says. Like a fever. Something with a long convalescence."

"And are you OK now?"

"Pretty much." He smiled. "I had to have a lot of dental treatment."

"Are you working?"

"In a homeless shelter. It seemed the least I could do."

Tess's eyes filled with tears.

"What?" said Colin. "Have I made you cry?"

She shook her head. "I just remembered something you said to me once. You said there were no second chances. That people say there are, but there aren't."

"I said that?"

Tess nodded. "But it's not true, is it? Look at you."

"Of course it's not true," said Colin. "I can't believe I ever said it. Or that you believed it."

Tess looked down at the table.

"So come on, then," said Colin.

"What?"

"Your turn."

"There's nothing to tell," said Tess.

"There's something about second chances that's making you cry."

"I don't really want to talk about it," said Tess in a small voice.

"Well, I'm not leaving," said Colin, "until you do."

. . .

When Rhys peered round the front door of the house in Hackney, his mouth dropped open in astonishment.

"It's not you," he said.

"It is," said George. "And Mia."

"What are you doing here?"

"Can we come in?" said George.

Rhys hesitated. His black hair was sticking up in all directions as if it had been gelled with sugar syrup. "I'm not going to lie to you. This house has been a lot tidier. But in the past few weeks, housework hasn't been at the top of my list of priorities."

"That's OK," said George.

With evident reluctance, Rhys opened the door. George, holding Mia, frowned. Rhys was wearing a short, baby-pink dressing gown.

"I'm not dressed, you see," said Rhys. "Having an afternoon nap."

"Is it a bad time?" said George.

"Rhys," called a female voice from the floor above, "who is it?"

George raised his eyebrows.

"That's Natalie," said Rhys. "She's a friend of mine. From Swansea. Thought she'd have a bit of a holiday in London."

"In Hackney," said George.

"That's right."

"With you."

"Well, why not?" said Rhys. "Always good to get away."

"Who is it?" called the voice again.

Rhys pulled the dressing gown closer and tightened the sash. "The thing is, you see," he said in a whisper, "I thought it was all over. But she says she missed me. She's been here three weeks."

"Rhys?" shouted Natalie.

"I tell you what," said Rhys, "why don't you go through to the kitchen and have a cup of tea and I'll run upstairs and see what's happening."

"OK," said George, smiling.

"Although I'm not sure we've got any milk," said Rhys. He frowned. "To be honest with you, I'm not sure we've got any tea."

George and Mia were drumming the kitchen table with wooden spoons when Rhys reappeared dressed in black jeans and an acid-green T-shirt. "She'll be down in a minute," he said. "I think she wants to put on a bit of makeup. Although she doesn't need to, of course. Looks lovely as she is." He looked at Mia. "Like this one here." He frowned. "Where does she get it from, then? I've told you before—doesn't look a bit like you."

"Thank you," said George.

Mia, suddenly shy, climbed up onto George's lap.

Rhys ran water into the kettle. "So what are you doing in London?" He stopped, remembering. "Is it your dad?"

"We'll go and see him while we're here. But that's not the reason we came."

Rhys said, "You're not Kirsty's favorite person, you know."

George nodded. Kirsty was very protective of Tess.

"She's pregnant. Did you know?"

"Who?" said George, panicked.

"Kirsty." Rhys, his back to the table, reached up to the top shelf of the cupboard to get mugs. "I quite envy her, to tell you the truth. I always thought Paris was dead romantic. All the writers who've lived there—Samuel Beckett, James Joyce, Ezra Pound." He sighed. "The inspiration you'd get from that, from knowing you were walking in their footsteps."

George, taking a deep breath, said, "Do you know where she lives?"

"In one of the posh bits, I think," said Rhys, searching for the teapot. "Although I'm not sure I could pronounce it, even if I could remember where it was."

"It used to be Penge," said George.

"No, that wasn't it," said Rhys.

"Crystal Palace?"

Rhys swung round. "Are we talking about Kirsty?"

"No, Tess," said George, surprised.

"Why do you want to know about Tess?"

George looked back, confused. "I want to see her."

Rhys stopped, holding the bright blue teapot. Then he set it down carefully, shaking his head in a sorrowful fashion. He pulled out one of the wooden chairs and sat down heavily at the table, leaning forwards as if confiding a dreadful secret. "I may be old-fashioned," he said, "but I always think it's better to end one relationship before you start the next."

George opened his mouth to speak but Rhys held up his hand.

"You're obviously very keen. Which is lovely. And I'd like to help you. Of course I would. You're one of my oldest friends. But I can't. Because from what Kirsty tells me, she was heartbroken. In pieces. She's not the kind of girl to have an affair with a married man. And to be honest with you, I don't think you should put her through it. It's not fair. She's a lovely girl. She deserves better."

Mia, listening hard, had twisted round to look at George's face.

Oh, thought George, wondering how much she'd understood. "Mia," he said, "if I found your rabbit and your bear, do you think you'd like to play in the front room while I talk to Rhys?"

Mia shook her head.

George said, desperately, "Just for five minutes?"

Mia considered this. She shook her head again.

George said to Rhys, trying to communicate as much as possible with his eyes, "It's over. It's all over."

"Well, I know that," said Rhys. "That's what I'm telling you. She doesn't want to see you. And if you ask my opinion, I think she's absolutely right. I think you should leave her alone."

. . .

"Tess? Just checking you're OK."

"Oliver, it's Sunday afternoon."

"Is it?"

Tess, frowning, held the phone a little tighter. "Yes," she said carefully. "Not a working day."

"No. Right. Yes." There was a pause. "I just wanted to be sure, really, that you were planning to come in tomorrow."

"Yes," said Tess.

"Good," said Oliver. There was a pause. "I mean, I know you said you would. But I just wanted to be sure, you know, that your domestic emergency was under control. The personal reasons. Nothing to stop you coming back to Daisy Greenleaf."

"No," said Tess, sadly, "there's nothing to stop me coming back to Daisy Greenleaf."

"Everything all sorted, then?"

"Yes," said Tess.

"Good," said Oliver. "Splendid."

"See you tomorrow, then."

"Just one more thing."

"Yes?" said Tess, her heart sinking.

"That chap was asking after you."

"What chap?"

"You know the—" Tess heard the deep sigh at the other end of the phone. "No, it's no good. It's gone. Friend of—ah—a school friend of yours?"

"Which one?" said Tess.

"That's the problem, you see. The name escapes me. Come Fly with Me. That kind of thing."

"Frank Sinatra?" said Tess.

"That's it!" shouted Oliver down the phone. "That's it!"

"Frank Sinatra came to see you?" said Tess. "I thought he was dead."

"No," said Oliver. "At my mother's."

"Oh," said Tess, totally lost.

"Obviously I couldn't give out your address," said Oliver. "Data protection."

"Right," said Tess, wondering if she should turn the

sound back up on the DVD and let Oliver carry on until he ran out of steam.

"Are you lonesome tonight?" said Oliver.

"What?" said Tess, horrified.

"That was Frank, I think," said Oliver. "Wasn't it?"

. . .

"Because he was found at Paddington station," said George, "wearing a black hat, with a label round his neck asking people to look after him."

Mia looked up at him with big eyes.

"He had traveled all the way from darkest Peru," said George. "And a family in London found him and took him back home and gave him marmalade sandwiches, because that was his favorite food. And cocoa, I think. He used to give people hard stares, like this"—George frowned—"when he thought they were being naughty."

Mia laughed.

"And Rhys has a brother called Gareth, and Gareth is in Peru. Which is where Paddington Bear comes from. And any minute now, Gareth is going to ring me. All the way from South America."

As if on cue, the phone rang.

"Hello?" said George in a voice that came out as more of a shout.

"I've told more lies today," said Gareth, thousands of miles away on the other side of the world, "than I've told in my entire life."

"But did you get it?" said George.

"I got it," said Gareth. "But I want to know what you're going to give me to pay me back. Because whatever it is, it won't be enough."

"Did you speak to Kirsty?"

"I spoke to Kirsty. It wasn't pleasant. She broke my heart years ago. And it was hard for me, hearing her voice after all this time. But I did everything you asked. And she believed every word. A long string of lies, and she swallowed every one."

"Handmade paper," said George. "Created by indigenous tribes in the rain forests of Peru."

"She said that Tess would be very interested."

"All the colors of the rainbow," said George.

"She said it sounded exactly the kind of thing that Tess would like."

"And gave you her address?" said George.

"After a bit of a struggle. She said, Wouldn't it be better to send all the samples to her office in the West End? But I said no, I wanted it to be a surprise. Which doesn't make a lot of sense, really. But she seemed quite happy. And I told her she had to keep it a secret." There was a pause. "I'm not sure you'll be lucky with that one. She was never that good at keeping secrets. I remember she told Rhys once that I'd taken a tenner out of his piggy bank."

"Gareth?"

"Yes?"

"Are you going to give it to me?"

"Give you what?"

"The address," said George.

"What's it worth?"

There was a pause.

"Not in the mood for jokes, then," said Gareth.

"You could say that," said George.

. . .

"And he just turned up at the gallery," said Kirsty, "and stood there looking at my stomach and said, 'When were you going to tell me?' I could have died with embarrassment. The cream of French society wondering why this man in white platform shoes and a gold lamé jacket was claiming to be the father of my child."

"He hasn't changed, then," said Tess. She was beginning to wish she hadn't rung Kirsty to complain about Oliver. Sunday afternoon was fading fast and she hadn't even begun to work out what to wear for her first day back.

"Was it you? Did you tell him?"

"Maybe it was Ellie," said Tess. "She probably rang him to tell him about getting civilly partnered."

"So I said, 'Akash! How lovely to see you! You must come and meet Philippe!' And then, guess what?"

"What?"

"He wasn't alone."

Well, I suppose he wouldn't be, thought Tess. You don't go to the most romantic city in the world all on your own.

"Go on, then," said Kirsty, "guess. Guess who he was with."

The doorbell rang.

"There's someone at the door," said Tess. "Can I ring you back?"

"Five minutes," said Kirsty. "I've got something else to tell you. Something really weird but quite exciting."

Tess pressed the little button on the intercom. "Hello?"

"Tess?"

She stood there motionless, her finger on the button.

"Tess?" said George again. "Can I come in?"

Tess thought about this. She said, "Up the stairs," and pressed the entry buzzer.

She looked up at the hall mirror. Her eyes looked back at her, black, terrified.

When she opened the front door, there he was, climbing the last section of the stairs. He stopped. They stared at each other.

George, thought Tess.

"I tried to find you," he said. "When you left."

She thought, I wish you hadn't come. Each time I get myself sorted out, and make compromises, and try to be realistic, and realize that life isn't some romantic rerun of *Cinderella*, you appear again and I lose all logic, and I'm back to square one.

"I looked everywhere. For hours."

"I had to get back," she said.

He changes everything, she thought, just by standing there. Her flat had been safe. Her home had been a no-George area. Now he was here, and it was just four walls in

Brixton, no defense against anything—no defense against the way she felt, or the pain of going through it all again, or the wild hope that this time something might be different.

"Can I come in?" He looked anxious, hesitant.

She wanted to be strong. She wanted to say, No, George, you can't come in. Enough is enough. Time to move on. But she couldn't. It might have been the politeness to visitors that had been drummed into her since childhood. Or it might have been because he looked so vulnerable and she couldn't bear to see him that way.

She stood back to let him in. When she turned round after shutting the door, he was still standing there uncertainly.

"Go through," she said, looking towards the open door of the living room.

She had a sensation of pressure in her ears as if she was swimming underwater. She felt it was important to keep moving but her legs were too unsteady to support her. So she stopped as soon as she could, standing still in the living room, opposite George, cold and rigid like a block of ice. She tried to think of welcoming things to say, as you do when someone visits from a country far away, but her mind was blank. Stiffly, she bent down and picked the Sunday paper from the sofa next to her. George looked at the empty seat. But she didn't invite him to sit down. So he didn't.

After a long time, she said, "How's your father?"

"He's OK," said George. And then, after a while, he said, "As well as can be expected." Outside a police car turned on its siren. They listened as the sound filled the air, faded into the distance, and died.

Tess swallowed. "How's Mia?"

"She's fine," said George. "She's in the car. Outside. With my brother."

She said, flustered, "Would they like to come in?"

"No, it's OK," said George, but didn't offer an explanation. So it must be a flying visit, she thought. Or perhaps, she realized rather sadly, I'm not important enough to be introduced to his family.

He said, "I thought you lived in Penge."

"I did."

"But not anymore."

"No," she said. "I moved."

When she didn't elaborate, he said, "What about Dominic?"

"He lives in Croydon."

"Oh."

She tried to work out from his expression what "Oh" meant, but he was looking down at the carpet.

She said, "This is just temporary, really. Until I buy somewhere. Although I like Brixton. I'll look for somewhere round here."

Tess stared at her feet. So this is it, she thought. Whatever we had died somewhere along the way. Like a plant in dry earth in the dark. Now we talk to each other like people at a party hoping someone more interesting is about to come along. She curled her fingers into her palms so that the nails dug into her skin and the pain stopped her from crying.

"When you came to New York—" said George.

"It was a bad time," said Tess.

"You asked me if I'd left my wife. And I said no."

"It doesn't matter," said Tess quickly, like a hostess trying to make a guest feel better about spilling red wine on the carpet. "Really. It's fine." Then she had to look away quickly in case he could see from her eyes how little she believed in what she was saying.

He said, "I didn't leave her. She left me."

Tess looked up. He was a bit blurry, because of the tears.

"I wanted to explain, but when I turned round you'd gone."

Tess blinked hard.

"She just employs me to look after Mia. She pays my rent. On a room uptown. Full of cockroaches. I come back to the house every day when she's at work." He had that same panicked look she remembered from the first time she met him, as if he felt someone else should be doing the talking. "Otherwise there's no one else. She's fallen out with every nanny she's ever employed. That's what she does. Has arguments with people who don't agree with her. The housekeeper had walked out the week you came."

Tess tried to understand what he was saying, but it was so different from the version she had built up in her mind that the words just floated past, like they do when the radio's on and the commentators get too technical.

"I can't leave Mia," he said. "I'm all she's got. Stephanie doesn't really care about her. Most of the time she wishes Mia didn't exist. She's an inconvenience. She gets in the way."

A lone tear trickled down Tess's face.

"She stopped me seeing her for six weeks. I had to fight to get her to change her mind. You don't do that to a child. It's cruel. I sometimes wonder whether Stephanie's even got a heart. I think she's more of a robot, really. Very logical. But not very human."

Still Tess said nothing.

George said, desperately, "I've got nothing to offer you. I know that. But I had to come and tell you that I think about you every day. All the time. I would give anything to make you change your mind and give me another chance. I can't see why you would. I'm broke, I'm unemployed, I've got a child to support. I'm going to have to fight Stephanie for custody, which is going to take time and money and energy for months. For years. But I had to come and tell you the truth. I should have told you in New York. I should have stopped you leaving. Everything I said came out wrong. But this is the truth. I can't live without you. I've tried, and I can't do it. I love you. We should be together. We have to be together. You said before that we couldn't smash up other people's lives. But Stephanie's doing it anyway. She wants a divorce." He stopped, pleading with his eyes. "Until I met you, I'd forgotten who I was. I'd given up on everything that was important to me. I'd stopped fighting for what I believed in. But you changed all that. Please, Tess. Please. Give me another chance."

Her legs were trembling so badly she could hardly believe she was still standing.

Tess said, "You've got it all wrong."

George's shoulders slumped.

She said, "You do fight for what you believe in."

He shook his head.

"You fought for Mia."

He looked away. He said, "That's different. Mia needs me."

There was a long silence.

When George looked up again, Tess was crying.

"I need you," she said.

And finally . . .

"How lovely," said Glenda. "I wasn't sure you ever would, to be honest. I know you said you would, but that's what happens, isn't it? People say, 'Oh, I'll come down and see you.' And then the years go by and they never do."

Tess, fascinated, watched the wet pink lips open and shut. It was like watching a talking strawberry. She said, "Well, it seemed a shame not to, really. We were just the other side of Poole Harbour. Visiting my grandmother."

"Oh, that's nice," said Glenda. "Is she getting on a bit now, then?"

"She's ninety," said Tess.

"No," breathed Glenda.

Tess looked out of the conservatory windows at the blue, blue sea stretching out into the distance. The sun was shining. Little triangular sails, so tiny they looked like cabbage whites with folded wings, floated on the water. Somewhere, she thought, somewhere over there is France. She said, genuinely admiring, "This is such a beautiful view."

"It is, isn't it?" said Glenda, with a social smile, drawing her lips together in a sort of baby-pink kiss. "I never get tired of it. Some mornings, I stand here with my first cup of tea, and I look out to the sea, and I just drift off into my own thoughts. I don't know what I think about, really. Life, you know. People. And then I look down, and my tea's gone stone cold. I've just stood there daydreaming. But the thing is, I never feel lonely. I used to feel lonely all the time in London. Crowds everywhere, but no one who really cared. Not really. But here, people nod and give a little wave. They go right past this window up to those cliffs over there. Walkers in their brown shorts and sandals with those great long sticks. Sometimes they sit over there on the wooden bench and eat their sandwiches. Cheese and tomato, I always imagine. Or egg. With a bit of Battenberg for afters. And I smile and think how lovely Swanage is. There's the pier and the cinema and the shops if you want a bit of action. Fudge, mohair, a garden rake. Or you can just get away from it all and walk along the cliff path to Old Harry. So peaceful. Big empty sky. Except for the seagulls, of course. They can be very aggressive if you're holding an ice-cream cone. Now, George, how do you like your tea?"

George blinked. I'd forgotten, thought Tess, quite how overwhelming Glenda can be. All those words rushing out like floodwater.

"I remember you, of course," said Glenda. "I remember you coming in to see Oliver. I thought at the time you'd be a lovely catch for a young lady. But, of course, Tess wasn't available, was she?" Her voice dropped to such a low whisper that both Tess and George leant forwards in their wicker basket chairs. She mouthed with exaggerated facial expressions, like a singer doing warm-up exercises, "She was with someone else."

"But it all worked out well in the end," said Tess hastily, sitting back as if discovering that Glenda was an angry wasp buzzing about in a teaspoon of jam.

"Oh yes," said Glenda. "It was obviously meant to be. You just had to wait for all the extras onstage to disappear. Now am I hearing wedding bells?"

Tess, taken by surprise, shot a glance at George, whose expression of panic increased.

"Not at the moment," said Tess, wondering how to explain that George was already married and had a three-year-old daughter.

"That's a shame. I love a good wedding."

"But we'll let you know," said George, "the minute it's arranged."

Tess looked at him. He smiled, his eyes crinkling at the corners. Her heart turned over.

Oh, thought Tess, faint with love. Oh.

. . .

"I thought I ought to tell you," said Stephanie, her voice on the phone sounding so clear that it felt, alarmingly, as if she was in the next room, "that I've been offered a new position."

"Really?" said George, politely. He was always very polite to Stephanie these days. So far this policy seemed to have worked. Mia's one-week holiday had already been extended twice, although Stephanie had made it very clear that she didn't approve of a three-year-old going to her grandfather's funeral. Even if it was in Guildford.

"I have been asked whether I'd like to head up the operation in Hong Kong."

George's heart sank. "In Hong Kong?"

Tess, curled up on the sofa, looked up. She waited, very still, her eyes on George's face.

"From the beginning of next month. Very short notice, of course, but they're absolutely desperate to have me. And it's a huge promotion. Everything I've ever wanted."

"Right," said George. "Congratulations," he added hastily, after a pause, remembering his resolution to be polite at all times.

"It's not going to be possible for me to take Mia straightaway," said Stephanie. "Not until I find my feet. A small child really isn't compatible with the kind of responsibilities I'll be expected to take on."

"You don't want to take Mia," said George slowly, looking at Tess in disbelief.

"Not straightaway. It simply isn't possible. That's what I'm trying to explain to you."

"Of course," said George, hardly able to speak.

"So do you think you'll be able to look after her full-time for a month or two?"

"Yes," said George. "I think I can manage that."

"The other thing I need to talk to you about is packing up the house. I'm going to let it out while I'm away. So it would make sense for me to send Mia's belongings on to you. So that she's got all her toys and clothes."

"Yes," said George.

"I don't have your address."

"I'm in south London. In Brixton."

"Brixton?" said Stephanie. "Why?"

"I like it," said George. "Good restaurants. Great second-hand bookshop. And a new vintage clothes shop. Just opened. Getting brilliant reviews."

"Secondhand clothes?" said Stephanie.

"Vintage," said George, looking at Tess. "Nineteen forties, mostly."

There was a small, baffled silence.

"I'm selling the piano," said Stephanie.

"OK."

"George, are you all right?"

"Why?"

"I thought you'd be upset."

"No, that's fine," said George. "It belongs to you. And I've got Dad's piano now. He left it to me. In his will."

"You really are sounding very peculiar, George."

"Am I?"

"Quite different."

"I'm just happy," said George. "That's all."

"What?"

"Glad to be back in London. Would you like to speak to Mia?"

"I haven't got time. I'm between meetings. Just give me

the address in Brixton. I need to get everything organized." She paused. "And I'll come over before I go to Hong Kong. Just to check Mia's OK."

"She's fine," said George quickly.

"I'm her mother," said Stephanie. "It's my responsibility to make sure she's all right."

"Yes," said George, miserably.

When the call was over, George stood there motionless. Tess got up from the sofa and went to stand next to him. "What?" she said, looking up at his face. "What is it?"

"She's got a new job in Hong Kong."

"That's good," said Tess.

"And she's happy for Mia to be with me while she gets settled in."

"And that's good, too," said Tess. "She might find she wants Mia to stay in England full-time."

"And she wants to come to London to check Mia's OK."

"Oh," said Tess.

They looked at each other.

"I could go out for the day," said Tess. "Or you could meet somewhere neutral?"

"Mia will tell her," said George. "I'm amazed she hasn't already. It's only because Stephanie's always so rushed on the phone."

Tess bit her lip. "She won't like it, will she?"

George leant back heavily against the wall. "She never likes anything that makes me happy."

"But it wouldn't make her change her mind, would it? She

wouldn't take one look at me and decide to take Mia to Hong Kong?"

"Who knows?"

"How long have we got?"

"Less than a month."

No, thought Tess. This can't be happening. We've only been happy for five minutes.

"It's going to be all right," she said.

"Is it?"

"Yes," said Tess, because she loved him. "Trust me."

• • •

"Who's that with Akash?"

Kirsty frowned. "You know who that is."

"No, I don't," said Tess. The lighting in the club wasn't really meant to help you see. It was all about creating an atmosphere. "It's not that ballet dancer, is it?"

"The very same," said Kirsty.

"Tom," said Tess. "That was his name. Broken foot. He had supper in our flat. Years ago. I didn't know he was gay."

"Neither did I," said Kirsty. "And I was the one sleeping with him."

"You're not checking your phone again."

"What if she wakes up?"

"I know for certain that she's fast asleep in her little travel cot," said Tess. "With Mia tucked up next to her. And Cora's watching *Mad Men* with the sound turned down so that she can hear the slightest sniffle from either of them."

"She's so small," said Kirsty. "And she's in a strange country."

"She's in England."

"You forget," said Kirsty. "I live in France now."

"Don't remind me."

"I come over for all the important stuff. Flat warmings. Shop openings. Supporting friends who are newly pregnant."

Tess looked at her, shocked.

"I knew it," said Kirsty.

"No," said Tess. "Kirsty—"

"I knew it. I said to Philippe, 'There's something she's not telling me.'"

"It's too early to tell anyone."

"Even me?"

"We only found out last week," said Tess, anguished.

"What does Mia think?"

"We haven't told her yet."

"I promise I won't tell a soul," said Kirsty.

"You can't keep a secret to save your life."

"That's a horrible thing to say."

"It's true, though."

Kirsty laughed. "So how do you feel? Sick? Bursting into tears every five minutes?"

"I feel wonderful," said Tess, beaming.

"How come?" said Kirsty. "I thought I was going to die when I was pregnant. I was in such a bad mood that Philippe had to put me in the back office in case I put off the customers. Oh look, there's Ellie."

"Lovely Ellie," said Tess. "A whole feature. And pictures of the shop."

"That's what friends are for."

Tess looked at her. "Are you saying my vintage clothes shop wasn't good enough to go in Britain's leading fashion magazine?"

"Of course not," said Kirsty. "I'm just saying it helps to know people in high places. When does George start?"

"Eight thirty."

"Is he nervous?"

"Yes. He's been quiet for days. I've had to explain to Mia that Daddy's got so much music in his head he can't hear anything else."

Kirsty looked at her. "I may have forgotten to tell you this. But I am so happy for you. There was a time when I was really worried it was going to be Dominic and Penge."

Tess blushed. "So was I."

"And it was really OK when George's wife came over?"

Tess took a deep breath. "Yes," she said.

Sometimes you lie even to your best friend. Tess still woke from nightmares in which Stephanie had morphed into a cross between Cruella de Vil and the yellow-eyed devil from *Rosemary's Baby*. It was hard to forget the afternoon when they'd finally met. George and Mia had gone to meet Stephanie at the airport, where George had explained, with wise economy, that he and Tess were very old friends who had only recently realized they wanted to be together.

"How convenient," said Stephanie.

"I promise," said George, "that it all happened after I came back from New York."

"You seem to be very good," said Stephanie, "at getting women to pay your rent."

In the living room of the flat in Brixton, Stephanie had let her eyes travel very slowly from Tess's head to her recently polished shoes. The tension was so tight that even Mia was silenced.

"How extraordinary," Stephanie said rudely.

"It's lovely to meet you, too," said Tess.

"You work in a shop," said Stephanie.

"Well—" Tess was about to explain about vintage clothes but realized, just in time, that this was a game of one-upmanship and her job was to lie down and let Stephanie walk all over her. "Yes," she said. "That's right."

Out of the corner of her eye, she saw George wince.

"People are so different, aren't they?" said Stephanie. "Personally I need something that challenges me intellectually."

"I think Mia will probably be the same," said Tess. "She's very bright. She obviously takes after you."

Stephanie allowed herself a satisfied smile. "I intend to keep a close eye on her education while I'm away. I will expect regular reports."

"Of course," said Tess, wondering what Stephanie meant, as Mia hadn't even started nursery school. Had Stephanie already decided that Mia should stay in England with George? She took a deep breath. "A good education is very important if she's to follow in your footsteps. George has told me so much about your success. There was an article about you in the *New York Times*, wasn't there?"

Later, George said, "Was that deeply humiliating?"

"No," said Tess.

"I love you," said George, taking her face in his hands. "Especially when you tell lies to make me feel better."

Tess smiled at the memory.

"Are you sure," said Kirsty, scrutinizing her closely, "that you've told me everything about Stephanie?"

"Absolutely everything," said Tess, waving at Ellie.

"I thought she'd fight you to the bitter end."

But there was no need, thought Tess. Stephanie got what she wanted. And it wasn't Mia. Or George.

Ellie, who was wearing a black dinner jacket, ruffled white shirt, and bow tie, was slightly breathless. "I haven't missed anything, have I?"

"The support act," said Kirsty. "They were good."

"But not George."

"No," said Tess. "He's on in ten minutes."

"Can I get you a drink?" said Ellie.

"She's having a Coke," said Kirsty.

"Really? Why?"

"I don't drink all the time."

"But you don't like Coke." Ellie stopped. "Oh."

"For goodness' sake," said Tess.

Ellie hugged her. "That's such good news. I can't wait to tell Rhys."

"It's a secret," said Kirsty. "Much too early to tell anyone."

"Oh," said Ellie. "Mum's the word."

Tess glared at them both.

"Tess," said Kirsty, nodding behind her. "Someone you know."

"Oliver!" said Tess.

"Absolutely incredible," said Oliver. "I mean I knew he was good. At my mother's. All the old classics. The Way You Look Tonight. That sort of thing. But really. Legendary jazz club. West End. Saturday night. Can't do better than that, can you?"

"It was just a wonderful coincidence," said Tess. "He'd heard him in Paris years ago. When the band was together. Said he'd never forgotten it. Sitting in an empty club listening to George play. He couldn't wait to book him."

"Well, that's marvelous," said Oliver. He hesitated. "And how's Helen?"

Tess screwed up her eyes in embarrassment. "Oh, she's doing really well. She's a bit of a natural, really."

"Not sure I've quite forgiven you yet," said Oliver. "My whole marketing department moving en masse. Blink of an eye."

"Did you know she loved vintage clothes?"

"No," said Oliver gloomily. "But then I never really talked to her. She looked as if she might die of shock if I tried."

"She's much more confident these days," said Tess.

"I don't suppose," said Oliver, "that the shop's doing really badly and you need to sell up in a hurry and find jobs for you and your staff?"

Tess shook her head happily.

"Oh well," said Oliver. "Worth a try."

Kirsty was waving.

"Who is it?" said Tess, too small to see over all the heads.

"Walter. With Sonya. And Rhys behind him. And Colin's just arriving with his wife."

"Rhys told George," said Tess, "that they're moving back to Swansea. Natalie isn't that keen on London."

"What does she do as a job?"

Tess frowned. "I'm not sure. I asked her once and she said she had to manage grief."

"Like a counselor?" said Kirsty. "Or working in a hospice?"

"I think she's a traffic warden," said Tess.

Kirsty, who had been gesturing frantically to get Rhys's attention, looked round the table. "Have we got enough room for everyone? Ellie, can you get some more chairs? Tess shouldn't be lifting anything."

"Oh," said Oliver, "bad back?"

And now here was Rhys, beaming, his hair and beard wild like an Old Testament prophet's. "All my favorite people," he said. "I knew this day would come. I knew one day we'd all gather to celebrate George."

"He hasn't played yet," said Tess nervously.

"And I always knew," he said, looking at Tess, "that you two should be together. That was obvious."

"It was, wasn't it?" said Kirsty. "I can't believe it took them so long."

"Brilliant turnout," said Rhys, looking round. "Absolutely packed."

"You don't feel faint, do you?" said Kirsty to Tess. "I always used to feel faint in crowds."

"Low blood sugar," said Rhys.

"No, when I was pregnant," said Kirsty.

"Look," said Tess. "Over there by the door. Isn't that Mo?"

"It makes me feel quite emotional, really," said Rhys. "George's friends coming from all corners of the globe."

"Where does Mo live?" said Kirsty.

"Kentish Town," said Rhys.

"I haven't seen Mo for years," said Tess. "What's he up to these days?"

"Still teaching," said Rhys. "I think he's head of the department now."

"Is he with anyone?" said Tess.

"What, now?" said Rhys, turning round.

"No, I meant generally. Has he got a partner?"

"I don't think so," said Rhys. "He said to me once that it's much easier to travel alone."

"Travel where?"

"Through life, I think," said Rhys.

"Not half as much fun, though," said Kirsty.

Mo fought his way over to their table. He looked just the same—muscular and pugnacious with flaming red hair and an expression of extreme fury. He stood for a moment, hands in his pockets, staring at the piano on the empty stage. "He made it, then," he said to Tess.

"Eventually," said Tess, smiling.

Mo nodded. All around them, people were beginning to

take their seats. There was an air of expectant excitement, as if everyone knew this was the start of something big, that this night would be talked about for years to come.

"I didnae think he would," said Mo. "I mean he can play. I know he can play. But I thought, No way will George make it. Hasn't got the confidence. Hasn't got the balls."

Tess's smile faded.

"But I was wrong," said Mo. "I'm glad to be wrong. Couldn't have happened to a nicer bloke."

He leant back in his chair.

"It didn't just happen," said Tess.

"No?"

Tess was on the point of saying, No, it happened because we found each other. Once we were together, all the things we couldn't do before became possible. We gave each other courage. We gave each other hope. Because that's the truth of it. Some people make it alone. But they're the rare ones. They're the ones made of steel. The rest of us need to find someone to love us and encourage us and keep us safe. She looked at Mo, who was still waiting for her answer with that slightly mocking raised eyebrow. No, she thought. You wouldn't understand. There's no point in trying to explain.

"It took a lot of hard work as well," said Tess.

Mo smiled. "For a minute there, you had me worried."

"Why?"

"I just remembered. You were the one who believed in soul mates."

"Did I?"

"You were full of it," said Mo. "Souls split in two searching the earth. Limping along, the walking wounded. Unfulfilled. Confused. Weak. Unable to function until they found their other halves." He laughed. "The biggest romantic crap you've heard in your life. I remember I told you where it came from. Just a story. A big joke that people made up years ago to make each other laugh. And I remember your face. You couldnae believe it. You looked so shocked."

"I remember that," said Tess.

"Do you?"

"Yes," said Tess. She said, thoughtfully, "Are you sure it's a load of crap?"

Mo looked at her incredulously. "You're not saying you still believe it?"

Just at that moment, the house lights dimmed. The spotlights focused on the piano. The crowd fell silent. All faces turned to the stage, waiting for George to appear.

Tess, her hands on her stomach, smiled.

Acknowledgments

Thanks and love to the friends who read the first draft—Yvonne Wilcox, Alexandra Fabian, Sally Eden, and Simon Pinkerton. Thanks to my agent Annette Green, and her co-agent Adrian Weston, and to all at Text Publishing and Emily Bestler Books. I'm also grateful to Tim Minchin whose song "If I Didn't Have You" set me thinking about soul mates, and to everyone who answered queries or offered support, especially Ruth Evans, Jane Doyle, Tamsin Kelly, Kevin Jackson, Jill Hunter, Tony Williams, Sarah Wise, Eve Zeese, Daniel Loup, and Monty Taylor. Finally, thanks to the Morgan-Thomas and Kavanagh families, especially Joe, Ben, and Alice. But the biggest thank-you of all to my husband, Matt.